EZEKIOLA
AND THE
EMERALD
BELT

THE FOUNTAIN OF FIRE

1

LUCY KYAN

ISBN(eBook): 979-8-9855985-0-6
ISBN (Paperback): 979-8-9855985-1-3
Library of Congress Control Number: 2022900961

This is a work of fiction. The characters, names, incidents, places, and dialogue are products of the author's imagination, and are not to be construed as real.

Digital distribution | 2022
Paperback | 2022

2nd Edition 2023

Leone Potere Press—Pompano Beach, FL

Title Production by The Book Whisperer

Cover design by Jane Dixon-Smith

*For Diana, who loves imaginary stories,
and for Jesse, who questions them all.*

Chapter 1

Written in the Stars

The pencil in Ezekiola's hand had completed a few dozen flips before it finally catapulted in the air. He lunged forward to catch it, but too late. It struck the student sitting in front of him on the back of the head.

"Hey!" An angry face turned around. "What's your problem?"

Ezekiola mouthed sorry and quickly disappeared under his desk to pick up his pencil.

The new fall semester had barely begun at Cypress School, and Ezekiola wondered, as he sat back up, what on Circa's seven moons had possessed him to take another language class. He had a natural knack for languages and already knew a dozen of the most popular ones. Did he really need to learn another? He pondered. Then again, it's always good to learn something new, he convinced himself, and Neptunian dialects were supposed to be really fun. But by the looks of the teacher who had just waltzed into class, he was starting to doubt his own words of wisdom. Indeed, Professor Almon Vers didn't quite make Cypress School's top five list of fun teachers. Quite the opposite.

"Good morning, everyone," the professor blurted joyfully. "You're one lucky bunch this morning!" he said before writing his name on the board. For some reason, there were a few extra letters in the teacher's name. Almon Vers had become *Almonte Versutus*.

"You will please address me as Professor Versutus in this class," he said with great satisfaction in his voice, "and you'll soon see why," he added with a smile, leaving everyone agape.

Ezekiola wondered what this was all about. He'd already taken a class with this teacher before, and what he remembered most was his style. Professor Almon Vers was fond of anything old or ancient, borderline archaic, as long as it had substance. He held onto things, hoping to give them one last breath of life, from obscure notions to obsolete words. It even went as far as his own clothes. The outfits he wore dated back to his youthful years, and with the signs of time, they had gradually turned into compression garments. Yet he held on to them like a dog would a bone. And if the tightness of his clothes wasn't enough of an eyesore, the patches holding the different fabrics together definitely were. The professor clearly sewed them on himself. A skill he did not possess with the level of refinement he did the language he was about to teach. Ezekiola had learned quickly not to judge him by his appearances, though. What Professor *Vers...utus* lacked in style, he compensated greatly for in knowledge.

"I have fantastic news for you! The curriculum for this class has much changed," he said, grabbing everyone's attention, "for the better," he added with a smirk. "We won't be learning some boring Neptunian dialect this fall, but something much greater and entirely new, never taught before at Cypress School! And you should know," he paused for effect, "I fought tooth and nail to convince your headmaster," he said, gleaming with pride and a hint of conspiracy. The sound of shuffling papers came to a stop as the students looked up at him, perplexed.

Everyone stared at the board as Professor Versutus turned to the board once more and wrote, in large uppercase letters, an L, followed by A, T, I, and N.

"We... are going to learn Latin from Planet Blue!" he said with a voice that contained far too much excitement for a morning class.

"What?" A rumbling murmur erupted from the students, some of it audible enough for the professor to hear.

"But we're supposed to learn a Neptunian language!"

"Latin's not on the agenda!"

"Is that why you changed your name?"

All of these fell on the professor's deaf ears as he continued to write on the board.

Finally, one gutsy student's voice rose above the others: "Excuse me, professor, but isn't Latin a dead language?" he asked, bringing everyone back into silence. The professor turned around and looked hard at him. "And who told you that?" he challenged.

"Well, um, nobody really, but I thought—"

"Well then, you shouldn't say that, should you? It's not dead. In fact, Latin has words that never die. Not only that, but the language has infiltrated itself throughout the cosmos, influencing our very own vocabulary. You should pay attention to the words around you, and you'll see," he stated matter-of-factly. Without giving a chance for anyone else to speak, he jumped right in.

"We'll start with attendance. You there, go first!" the professor said, catching Ezekiola completely off guard. Ezekiola froze. Going first was never his plan. He had barely registered the day's unexpected twist, and, at that moment, all he could do was blurt out a lamblike bleat: "Bah… me?"

"Bah-yes, you, stand up, say your name."

"Sure," he said as nonchalantly as he could, although his heart was hammering in his chest. Why does it always do that? He wondered, looking as if he was about to have a fit while every pair of eyes in the room was set on him.

"Ezekiola Astrid," he said and moved quickly to sit back down, but his teacher wasn't done.

"What? Spell your name, please?" His teacher asked as he looked for the name on his list.

"Ezekiola Astrid," he spelled out his name, "but you can call me Zek."

"Oh, I think you were in one of my classes before," he said thoughtfully, crushing Ezekiola's hope of just sitting back down and passing incognito. "Your name meant something, didn't it?"

"Um, no. I don't think so…" Ezekiola ventured, hoping his teacher's memory would fail him.

"Oh yes, there was something to it. I think there was even a Latin connection. Where's that name from?" the teacher probed. "Some old family name, wasn't it?"

Ezekiola shook his head, making his teacher look like he was the confused one.

"Oh, but you told me before, I'm quite certain. Wait a minute, Ezekiola, Ezekiola," he spoke, closing his eyes, and searching, while everyone was watching. "Oh, I remember! You're named after a star, could it be?" he asked. Ezekiola had no choice but to give a faint nod.

"You ARE a star! A *stella* everyone!" he almost shouted in Latin, as if the word needed to be resuscitated right this moment. Ezekiola's cheeks turned red. Maybe he should just quit this class.

"You even told me where the star was located… Where was

it again?" the professor's memory was sharpening way too fast for Ezekiola's liking. There was now no way out of this conversation. It also helped that Ezekiola could read his teacher's mind, a skill very few students possessed at his school. Just give him what he wants, he told himself.

"In the constellation of Gemini, between Castor and Pollux," he said, letting out those names reluctantly.

"AHA! And there's some Latin for you! I knew it! You may sit down, Ezekiola of the stars," the professor finally released him, provoking a collective snort from his classmates. The professor turned and wrote Gemini, Castor, and Pollux on the board, adding them to his list of Latin words.

Ezekiola sat back down and exhaled. It was a strange breath mixed with relief and dread. Would he be able to make it through this class? Latin, from Planet Blue? Despite their planets being close, Ezekiola couldn't remember the last time he'd studied something from Planet Blue. And Professor Almon Vers', or rather *Almonte Versutus*', teaching methods weren't going to help. His questions were sometimes as confusing as his answers. Ezekiola listened half-heartedly to what came next. "Now, class, I almost forgot Ezekiola's name here and where it came from. So, you can't always trust your memory. Latin, as you'll learn, has some of the best truisms, and when it comes to memory, here's one of my favorites: *Verba volant, scripta manent.* Spoken words fly away, written words remain," the professor wrote on the board. "Now, can words actually fly away?" he then asked the class.

"Nooo." The entire class answered in unison.

"But of course they can!" he corrected everyone. "You just don't see them!"

What? Thought Ezekiola. *What does he mean? Is he speaking figuratively or literally?* He knew extraordinary things happened on Circa that never happened elsewhere, but for words to actually fly away? It was completely ludicrous. That man was not in his right mind.

"And not only that, but words disappear as fast as they are pronounced!" the professor continued, "Which is why I want you to write, write, write, everything I say in class!"

Ezekiola sighed as he opened his notebook to take notes. He grabbed hold of his pencil and wrote—*verba volant, scripta manent.* That would be the only thing he'd write that morning as his mind wandered to more important matters and, more specifically, the Ceremony of the Belts, which was only a few hours away. Ezekiola was finally going to graduate and get his Blue Belt. This very important ceremony came only once a year at Cypress School. It took place during summertime in the school's outdoor amphitheater. But the weather had been so bad this year that graduation kept getting canceled, so much so that it was finally pushed back to the beginning of the following school year. Ezekiola looked around the classroom, noting the familiar Grey Belt, the beginner's one, wrapped at waist level around every student's white tunic. It had been their standard uniform from their first day of school. As a consequence of what they wore, they were famously dubbed 'White Tunics.' And now that they were seventeen, they'd finally say goodbye to their Grey Belt and be bestowed a new colored one in line with their skills and interests. His school was renowned for its method of attributing belts and robes to prepare its students for adult life on Circa, each color representing a different field of study. After wearing their new belts for several years, they would eventually graduate to the robe level and take part in the Ceremony of the Robes, slowly transitioning into their mission in life. As the saying goes, they would finally be wearing their fate.

The assignment of the belts was no random decision. The graduating students had undergone extensive interviews with their Headmaster Nomi Antares, as well as their school council. Each student's inclinations had already been properly identified, which completely took away the element of surprise from the ceremony. Ezekiola already knew the brotherhood he was destined to join—the Blue Belts. For natural-born mind readers such as himself, there was no mystery as to where their fates resided. Matters of the mind and the art of thinking were what he liked best. His ultimate goal was to become a Sage of Circa and don the Blue Robe one day. A noble position indeed, where he would partake in the most important decisions concerning Circa.

As far as Ezekiola knew, there were barely a handful of students graduating to a Blue Belt this year. And although it came with a few downsides, thankfully, he thought, getting the Blue Belt was not the worst outcome. The Emerald Belt, which was given to those who pursued the warrior's path, was ranked worse. It was even considered to be the abandoned belt. Cypress School had stopped training Emerald Belt students years ago since no one wanted to venture down that risky path and become an Emerald, a warrior of Circa. It didn't help that rumors currently circulated about missing Emeralds. No one knew what had happened to them, and they were nowhere to be seen. Ezekiola was surprised his school continued to keep that option open. They should have closed it by now, he thought.

The chiming of the bells pulled Ezekiola right out of his reverie about belts and ceremonies. He forgot all about Professor Almonte's flying words. Clearly, time was the one that flew. With ceremony rehearsal next on his agenda, he stashed his papers into his bag and stepped out of the classroom. The amphitheater was located at the northwest end of the school grounds, in the most picturesque area, having as its backdrop the Limestone Mountains floating above the ocean. It was a deadly drop, but the temptation to climb the mountains just for the view was difficult to resist, especially when students had such easy access to them during graduation ceremonies.

It took Ezekiola longer than normal to arrive at the site. Most of the beaten paths in the Black Forest, located behind his school, were closed for landscaping. When he finally arrived, mayhem had taken over. Some White Tunics were hopping the stairs of the amphitheater two, even three at a time, while others had decided to take the adventurous route and risk their necks climbing the mountains. Meanwhile, the Brown Robes, who were the White Tunics' supervising body and in charge of discipline, were yelling like mad dogs, running after students as if they were trying to catch flies on walls. "Come down those stairs!" "Climb off those mountains!" "Get down here!" "Now!"

Among the Brown Robes trying to assert their authority on the group of teenagers was Borghis, his friend Nohlan's older brother. Ezekiola noticed he had attendance papers in one hand and a wooden staff in the other. He bore the expression of someone who was about to do something unnatural to some of the wayward boys.

"Graduating White Tunics backstage, NOW!" His thunderous voice resonated throughout the amphitheater. "If you don't listen, you can say goodbye to your new belt! And if you don't believe me, try me." Borghis had already earned himself quite a reputation for delaying a student's graduation the year before. Ezekiola quickly made his way backstage. The Brown Robe was quick to spot him and stopped him in his tracks.

"Where's my brother?" he asked, sweat streaming down his forehead. Ezekiola had never seen him so out of sorts.

"I don't know. We said we'd meet here," Ezekiola answered, throwing a hopeful glance at the crowd. He saw neither of his friends, though.

"He should've been here by now. Atlas too!" Borghis said, "You three are always late; you know that!" he scolded him.

"Well, all the shortcuts in the Black Forest are closed off." Ezekiola opened his mouth to say something else, then stopped when Borghis's eyebrows shot up at the sight of something. He turned to look in the same direction.

Nohlan was stomping hurriedly towards them. His tunic and pants, which had been white and crisp that very morning for graduation, were now splattered with mud from the neck down. He had every student's head turned to look at him. Some even chuckled.

"What happened to you?" Borghis asked, his hands in the air, his staff almost knocking down a student who was passing by.

"Nothing. I just need to change clothes," Nohlan answered candidly.

"Nothing? It's graduation day, Nohlan! Did you decide to mop the forest with your outfit?" Borghis asked, circling his brother to get an all-around view. His face turned scarlet red.

"I fell in a ditch on my way."

"You fell in a ditch?" Borghis asked, bewildered. Both Ezekiola and Borghis looked at Nohlan suspiciously. Ezekiola sensed that his friend was not being completely honest, but he did not dare probe his mind. It would only make matters worse in the current situation.

"Yes! What do you expect? You Brown Robes blocked off so many roads in the Black Forest to do your landscaping. I got lost and had to go off the path. And now, I have to go change before rehearsal," Nohlan answered, "except that I need to borrow a spare first," he added, looking both at his brother and his friend, expecting one of them to help him.

"Wish I could give you mine, but you won't fit in it. Nor in Atlas's," Ezekiola said ruefully. Nohlan was twice the size of

Ezekiola and three times that of Atlas, who was the thinnest of the three.

"What about yours, Nohlan? You're supposed to have two spares," Borghis asked him.

"Yes, but they're all dirty."

"What? But wash isn't for another week. How did you manage to dirty all three?!" Borghis replied, his voice suddenly one octave higher than before, his face ascending to a deeper hue of red.

"Well, that's why I need to *borrow* one," Nohlan repeated calmly, keeping his voice low, hoping to cool his brother down.

Borghis ran his fingers through his hair, trying to think his way through this one. Solving another of his brother's mishaps was not on his already full agenda. The commotion in the background didn't help.

The rowdy boys were growing increasingly agitated, like waves rising at sea before a hurricane, and all Borghis felt like doing was knocking each one out with his staff.

His eyes suddenly lit up. "Do you know how to get to the Brown Robes' lodge from here?" Borghis asked Nohlan, his blood pressure rising.

"Yes, of course!" his brother answered confidently. He had enthusiastically visited his brother's lodge several times in the past, especially when Borghis had first graduated to the Brown Robe level the year before. It hadn't taken long for Borghis to warn his brother to cut back on his visits a bit when his presence became more of a nuisance than a joy.

"Go over there and find my old uniform. It's folded in my souvenir chest in the back-end corner of the lodge. Look for my name on the chest. And don't start opening other boxes! I know how you can get. This is not the time for your curiosity to get the best of you. You change into my clean uniform, and you run back here on time for your graduation. And while you're at it, bring me back all the spare brown robes you find in the room. There should be a few. We need them for the Ceremony of the Robes, right after yours. Am I making myself clear?"

Nohlan had been moving his head up and down in exaggerated nods from the moment Borghis had started speaking, making Ezekiola wonder if he was even listening to his brother's instructions. Borghis, however, was not that naïve.

"Ezekiola!" he suddenly said, startling him. Ezekiola looked up at him and saw danger looming in his eyes.

"Go with Nohlan. He'll have less chances of getting lost and showing up even dirtier. I hold you just as responsible for getting him back here, *clean*, before the start of your graduation. And leave the spare robes backstage." Ezekiola nodded his understanding. There was no arguing with Borghis on this. "And if you see that tardy friend of yours on the way," he continued, "tell him to run if he wants to leave here with his red belt today. Now hurry!" he ordered.

With no time to spare, the boys cut through the Black Forest towards the Ye Ole' Brown Lodge, a rustic structure nestled in the middle of lush trees located further east. Coincidentally, as Borghis predicted, they saw Atlas on their way. He was just standing there, looking completely disoriented, staring at a forest map.

"Where are you two going?" Atlas asked with a sense of relief when he saw them. He then spotted Nohlan's outfit. "What happened to you?!"

"Nothing. Just got a little dirty. We have to stop at the Brown Robes' lodge. My brother needs a favor, and I need to change," Nohlan answered, short of breath, accentuating the favor part more than the other.

"What, we're doing the Brown Robes favors now?" Atlas asked. Things had not been going so well for him since school had started. The Brown Robes, Borghis among them, had already given Atlas two red notes in his first week of school for 'tardiness,' a concept, Atlas said, that desperately needed to be rethought.

"They're missing robes for their ceremony," Ezekiola explained, "and they want us to bring their spares."

"And that's why they let you come along?" Atlas asked Ezekiola.

"Actually, Borghis sort of insisted I tag along," Ezekiola said with a half-smile in Nohlan's direction. "Oh, and funny enough, he said if we saw you on the way, to tell you to run if you want to see your red belt today."

"Really? He thinks he's going to pressure me into showing up faster? No, I'm already late, and I'm coming with you. Besides, tardiness is always easier to pass when you're not alone," he said matter-of-factly as he started walking in the same direction as his friends.

"Run then! Don't stroll," Nohlan pressed him on.

"So, how come you're all muddy, Nohlan?" Atlas asked, catching up to him.

"I fell in a ditch."

"You fell in a ditch?" he repeated, sounding almost like Borghis. "Nohlan, there isn't a ditch anywhere close to here. Unless, of course, you dug one up today and threw yourself in."

"Yes, a ditch. Now stop asking questions and hurry!" Nohlan quickened his pace, leaving no choice for his friends but to run faster. Atlas stole a glance at Ezekiola and met the same look of disbelief. They both decided to remain quiet and not probe their friend any further.

When they arrived at the lodge, Nohlan was the first to dash onto its terrace like he was coming home. But for Atlas and Ezekiola, this was a first. Every inch of the Brown Robes' domain spurred their curiosity. They lingered outside, flooding Nohlan with questions.

"What are those cabins?"

"Study rooms and dorms."

"What are those things on tree trunks?"

"Bird carvings."

"What are those round symbols?"

"They're eyes."

"Why so many?"

"Can we please save the tour for another time?" Nohlan blurted. "I'm going inside to find my brother's chest!"

With no time to waste, Nohlan darted for the storage located at the rear end of the lodge. While he scavenged the place for Borghis' chest, both Ezekiola and Atlas walked into the lodge slowly as if they had just stepped into a museum. The silence of the place and the absence of people somehow increased their sense of awe. Atlas headed straight for the library section while Ezekiola stared at the artwork adorning the walls inside the lodge. Everywhere he looked, from the stair railings to the ceiling, were images of falcons. He knew falcons were the emblematic symbol of the Brown Robes, quiet yet powerful, which was the feeling they liked to impress on others. The drawings on the walls were quite fantastic too. There were all sorts of trees, leaves, plants, animals, and even some strange creatures Ezekiola had never seen before.

Ezekiola was slowly making his way to see Nohlan when he came across a circular room with a dome ceiling. He entered it and was at once mesmerized. The half-moon walls were adorned with charts, words, and shapes of all sorts. Coming nearer, he realized it was a layout of stars, constellations, and planets with names he had never seen or heard of before. If it hadn't been for the order and geometric shapes, the chart would have looked like a jumble of colors painted by a five-year-old. There was a large eye at the very top of the chart that almost felt as if it was staring back at him. Ezekiola approached the eye and read the inscription underneath: *Worlds and Mansions hold no veil over the Falcon's eye.* He read it again. The statement sparked his curiosity. Did the Brown Robes have detailed knowledge of *every* world out there? He had not studied much of the macrocosm in the past and only recognized a few of these worlds. He searched for his planet but couldn't find it at first glance. He looked for Planet Blue instead since it was the best way to locate Circa, both being in close proximity to each other. He spotted it, then naturally found Circa, and noticed its misty appearance, as if it were shrouded in clouds. He'd forgotten about that. His mother had vaguely explained that Circa was what you called a veiled planet. But when he had prodded her more about it, his mother's answers had been as unclear as the shroud surrounding their planet. She said it had something to do with its guardianship of Planet Blue but that somewhere down the line, things had gone wrong, and the link between the two planets had been broken. For some reason, Circa had then veiled itself, hiding in virtual obscurity, leaving Planet Blue on its own. This left him wondering why one planet would abandon another. He examined some of the other planets in proximity to his and noticed that several had the same misty appearance. Were there other veiled planets? He was suddenly struck by the magnitude of the things he didn't know. As he pondered this, the lower corner of the chart drew his attention, for it stood darker than the rest. He crouched lower to get a better view and dusted the surface to see it better. But he didn't. It was actually painted dark. There were various odd shapes bunched together, not spherical in form but more akin to irregular triangles. Their edges were uneven, and their points didn't meet. In their midst was inscribed the word SONS. He had heard the name before. It was an abbreviation that stood for *Sons of the Night Sky*. They were the fallen Emeralds, the warriors of Circa who had steered off the path of righteousness. Why would their name appear on a cosmic chart? He wondered. Ezekiola was brushing his fingers over their name when he suddenly heard Nohlan call out, "Tour's over, boys! Let's go!" He quickly got up and headed to the front door. Nohlan had already changed into clean clothes and had a load of spare robes in his arms. He was beaming at having accomplished his mission.

"Did you take all the spares?" Ezekiola asked Nohlan.

"Yes, we're good to go! Come on, we have to hurry!" he said and darted out.

Atlas followed him out quickly. Ezekiola noticed that the latter's bag seemed heavier than before.

"Did you grab some robes, too?" he asked, curious.

"Yes, to help our falcon brothers," Atlas answered him with a somewhat suspicious smile. Ezekiola stared at the shape of the bag. It didn't look like it was filled with robes. He didn't bother asking any more questions or probing his friend's mind. He just wanted to get to the ceremony on time. But as they made their way there, something kept gnawing at the back of Ezekiola's mind. He walked closer to his friend and asked: "Nohlan, what do you know about the veiling of Circa?"

"So that's what you were doing at the lodge!" Nohlan said, "Not much, really, I remember being told that we had to protect ourselves, and so we disappeared from view for safety reasons," he summed up plainly.

"That's it?"

"That's all."

"What about the SONS? How come they're on the chart?"

"Now that you ask, I don't know," Nohlan admitted. "Circa's veiled anyway. Nobody can find us. Regardless, it's nothing we'll ever need to worry about, and especially not you, Ezekiola the SAGE!" he added pompously, clapping his friend on the back. This got the three of them laughing as they neared the amphitheater. Ezekiola nodded at his friend's words, which rang true, the thought never crossing his mind about how wrong he could be.

The boys reached the amphitheater's stone walls without a minute to spare. When they walked backstage, the hundred-plus students attending the ceremony were all duly seated in silence, a rare feat that surely rested on the rugged shoulders of Borghis and his fellow Brown Robes. In fact, what could have ended badly for the trio went completely unnoticed, and luckily for them, they weren't the only ones running late. Indeed, the ceremony's most important attendee, Headmaster Nomi Antares, was nowhere to be seen.

Chapter 2

Fate in a Box

Nomi's sky-blue robe flapped wildly as he crossed the last bridge leading to the Black Mountains of Circa. The wind had picked up speed, and so had his heartbeat. This sudden call was unprecedented. Nomi had been woken early in the morning for an urgent meeting. And on this of all days—ceremony day—his most important day of the year. He tried to remember the last time he'd entered these mountains. Of all the natural splendors of the planet, they remained a bleak zone no one ever visited. What on Circa's seven moons could be so pressing as to call him to a meeting on such short notice?

As headmaster of the Boys' Division at Cypress School, Nomi had only an inkling of why his presence was being requested and none at all as to why he was being asked to bring the scroll he was now clutching to his chest. But he couldn't refuse a request made by the Count, one of the oldest members of the High Council of Circa. Whispers had come to Nomi's ears about the Count's increased involvement in recent High Council meetings, an unusual activity for someone who'd recently retired, but Nomi couldn't afford the time to keep up with the affairs of Circa. His task as headmaster of his school kept him busy enough. But today's special request worried him. Why would the Count send a messenger to him in the early hours of the morning, and why make the request that he did? When Nomi finally arrived, the Count was waiting for him at their rendezvous point. Older than Nomi, or so he figured, the Count looked neither young nor old in his royal blue robe. In fact, he looked almost ageless. Nomi took note of the shade of the man's robe since robes changed hues organically to reflect the emotional state of their bearers. Hints of black had seeped in, making the robe more somber and almost out of focus. Clearly, the Count showed signs of weariness. Even his usually serene blue eyes appeared dark and sunken under his hood. He looked like he hadn't seen any light for days.

The Count unrolled the scroll Nomi had handed to him and quickly scanned it to make sure he was in possession of what he had asked for. With a nod, he veered around and pushed through a pair of massive doors that Nomi thought were a rock formation. He was even more surprised when he followed the Count into a dark chamber inside the mountain. The instant they walked into the room, they were both hit by a wave of heat so thick it was almost palpable. There were a few dozen members present—some seated, some standing—and judging by the intense colors of their robes, a lot of tension in the air. Nomi quickly glanced at his indoor surroundings. The chamber was circular and slightly lit. By what light, Nomi could not tell. It looked like it came from beneath, for shadows were cast on the ceiling as if mountain ghosts were amongst them. There was a wide center area surrounded by flat rocks mounted on different layers, which served as seats. They seemed to be all taken. It was a full house. The Count guided Nomi to an empty seat next to him, making him wonder if seats were pre-assigned. The headmaster looked around again, this time in an attempt to identify colleagues he might know. But he recognized only a few faces. It was rare for him to attend meetings such as this, and never before in this chamber. It wasn't too hard, however, to guess which clans were in the room. The leaders of the Red Robes were present, along with those of the Purple Robes, Brown Robes, and Blue Robes. Each color represented a different field of expertise: The Red Robes were versed in logic; the Purple in ceremonial order; the Brown steeped in nature and the macrocosm; and the Blue, like Nomi and the Count, were natural-born mind readers known as Sages. There were other shades of robes attending the meeting as well, amongst them the White and the Silver, but none as plentiful as the Emerald Robes, present in far greater numbers than any of the others. Emeralds were Circa's famed warriors, they who tread the dangerous paths where no others dared venture. They stood out from the rest not only by the shade of their robes but by their strong build, accent, and mixed background. Some had darker complexions than the headmaster himself. Nomi was not accustomed to seeing so many Emeralds in one place. At his school, very few students chose that path. So few, in fact, that although Cypress still offered the prerequisite training, not a single teacher was officially assigned to it.

There was an Emerald in the center of the room, and from his stance, he looked to be their leader. He was speaking with emotion, pleading with the attentive crowd: "We need to halt this madness! We cannot send another one of our Emeralds to their deaths!"

"No," called out a second Emerald, "I disagree. This is not the moment to let our guard down. There is too much at stake!"

"But it would only be temporary," the leader said.

"Stopping temporarily is a luxury we cannot afford. We are at a critical juncture! There is word that the SONS have gained momentum and are about to complete their planetary links ahead of us! Circa must succeed in this task before them, else we will be vanquished!"

The leader's face flinched at hearing those words.

"How close are the SONS to linking?" asked a Red Robe in the crowd.

The Emerald leader motioned his arm sideways, and the ground beneath him dissolved, making it seem as if he was floating in the air. An image of the macrocosm suddenly appeared in the center of the room—planets in motion, stars exploding, others forming, and a geometric configuration slowly came into focus, then gradually magnified, capturing everyone's attention. Several of the planets displayed were linked together by a thin magnetic line. A shining blue marble stood intact in their midst, untouched by the line that seemed to be holding all the others together.

"You see this?" the leader said, pointing his finger at the linking pattern. "From what our sources tell us, the SONS are close to linking but not yet able. It takes the magnetic force created by the bonding of twelve planets to complete the link. And the last bond to be made for a planetary link to be complete is with Planet Blue, the very one our Emeralds have unsuccessfully been trying to link with. In its core rests the Fountain of Fire, the jewel everyone seeks, the elixir of life that can destroy us all if the SONS access it first."

"Our Emeralds must prevent them from succeeding then, or we'll lose for good!" someone from the crowd shouted in panic, "and the loss will be one that multitudes will lament for many lifetimes to come." Several members in the crowd nodded in agreement.

"Yet that's exactly what we've been doing, and we are still losing," the leader of the Emeralds replied, bringing everyone back to his foremost point. With a motion of his hand, he closed the cosmic image below, and the ground regained its original appearance. "The highly skilled SONS have defeated our Emeralds every single time we've tried to re-link with Planet Blue. We haven't made any progress. I ask you, how many of our warriors need to perish before we realize that our methods are not working?"

Many in the crowd muttered in agreement, opening the door for comments to pour through.

"Abandonment is the easy path, and if we choose it, we'll have blood on our hands!"

"We already have blood on our hands. It takes decades to train an Emerald, and they're being swatted and squashed like flies!"

"But there is no other way. We must continue to fight!"

"How many dead brothers and sisters would we consider to be a noble number in this conflict? How many more deaths until we stop this madness?"

"But we don't have the privilege of taking any pauses."

"We've already lost thousands of Emeralds! Can't you all see that the well is running dry?"

"This is no longer the right course of action; we must reassess our position!"

"Are we stuck at an impasse, or does someone have a proposal to make?" asked a woman in a Blue Robe. The crowd fell silent, and all gazes turned to her. Sages rarely spoke. They observed for the most part, and when they spoke, it was crucial to answer them concisely, for Circa's most important decisions rested on their shoulders. As they had the ability to change the course of destiny, answers given to them had to be precisely thought out.

"May I propose something to the High Council? A solution of sorts?" the Count said as he rose from his seat. His was an unexpected intervention, judging from some of the surprised faces in the council. For some reason, Nomi's heart was suddenly beating faster, as if he were the one addressing the council.

"If you please," the Sage signaled, nodding to the Count.

"Our opponents, the Sons of the Night Sky, or SONS, as you call them, know our methods well. Remember that they were once Emeralds before they broke away to follow a different path after tasting the power of linking with the fountain. Clearly, our opinions differed on how to rightfully use that power. Convinced of their superiority, they seek only to subdue others so that all living things become their servants. The SONS know our skills, our knowledge, and our purpose. They know how to link, and there are great minds among those who serve their cause as advanced as ours. They've also become quite innovative, successfully recruiting all sorts of followers in ways we could never have imagined. Perhaps it is time we employed new methods, something unforeseeable by them, something which I'm certain would come as a surprise to many but is worthy of exploration."

A few faces lit up at this bold statement.

"And what is it that you propose, Count?" asked the Sage.

"To make an attempt at linking in an unconventional manner, taking our chance on a candidate who would attract less attention, who wouldn't stand out as a warrior like a golden eagle soaring upward, but who would instead be quite the opposite, inconspicuous and unnoticeable."

The Count had everyone's attention by now; some faces looked eager to hear more. He paused to look at the scroll Nomi had brought him. "I hold in my hands information on the one who at first glance would appear as the most unlikely candidate for this task but whom I believe nonetheless has the potential to succeed."

He handed the scroll to the leader of the Emeralds standing

in the center of the room, who unfurled and studied the document briefly. He then looked at the Count in disbelief.

"You know very well what the rules are. Only warriors who've graduated with great skills may endeavor such arduous tasks as the one to link. This one is only a child!"

"Yet disturbances in old rules forge new ones and come as blessings in disguise. Even as masters, we must remain open to this possibility."

It was hard to counter this statement. The Count, indeed, was a unique being, always putting into practice what he preached. He had risen to the status of both an Emerald and a Blue Robe simultaneously because of his achievements, something that diverged drastically from Circa's longstanding rules. Even his robe attested to that. Indeed, although he donned a Blue Robe, remnants of his warrior life still reflected on his attire, which shimmered with shades of emerald green every now and then.

"Why him? And how will he link?" the leader of the Emeralds asked him.

"This I cannot reveal. Not to you, nor to our fellow members here in this room. This must and will remain confidential, and it is essential that I keep it that way because of what is at stake. Should our candidate be successful in accomplishing this task, everything will be disclosed to the members afterward."

The Sage rose and asked: "Are there any other proposals?" She paused and waited for an answer. No one spoke. She scanned the room to gather everyone's thoughts on the matter and sensed no resistance to the Count's proposal. They each communicated their agreement telepathically.

She looked back at the Count. "As long as your candidate wills it, you have everyone's general accord to proceed. But I must impose some restrictions: you must not infringe on this caterpillar's progress in order to hastily turn him into the butterfly you wish him to be. Present to him the Emerald Belt, then keep yourself at bay. If he chooses to wear it, let him take each step on his own and let the belt guide the way."

The Count nodded his agreement. "Consider this request to be done," he said. Nomi detected the hint of a smile forming on the edge of his mouth. Only he understood what that meant. Nomi's heart sank deep into his stomach. As surprised as he had been to be asked to bring that scroll, he never thought he would leave with a box whose content was about to introduce a world of chaos to a boy of no more than seventeen. For the moment, all Nomi could think about was making it back before the bells chimed at the school, signaling the beginning of the Ceremony of the Belts.

Chapter 3

The Ceremony of the Belts

The Ceremony of the Belts was running behind schedule. With the Brown Robes gone to look for the headmaster for over an hour and the ceremony stewards, who were Purple Robes, now in charge of discipline, all order had miraculously disappeared. As they waited for their headmaster, the graduating boys were like caged puppies that should have been let loose long ago. Nohlan had even taken to entertaining the crowd in his own special way, parading in an oversized brown robe and screeching like an eagle, something for which he had already been severely scolded by one of the stewards. Atlas met with the same reaction on their part when he voiced his opinion on the stewards' poor planning of the ceremony.

Ezekiola listened to the irritated questions of his restless friends. He, too, wondered why the headmaster had not arrived yet. And waiting didn't help his mind one bit. His initial nervousness of not making it on time to the ceremony had given way to a new form of anxiety. It was the mere thought of walking in front of a large crowd, with everyone's gaze and thoughts on him, which he could hear so well. It was the equivalent of mayhem. He wanted the ceremony over with. Now. And with each passing moment, it became harder to control his mind. It kept wandering off like a prancing pony, entertaining strange thoughts of what could happen, planning his reactions to all sorts of embarrassing incidents, tripping while on the stage being the one he feared the most.

Half an hour later, the headmaster finally showed up, clutching something to his side. From the corner of his eye, Ezekiola noticed the strange-looking box changing hands. It was different than the square boxes that held individual student belts. This one had more of a triangular shape. The bells finally rang, giving the cue to start the ceremony. The students' attention became suddenly focused, all of them instantly forgetting whatever had driven their anxiety to the point of frenzy. The curtains lifted to a picturesque scene of order up on the stage. Dozens of students in white tunic garments, their standard uniform, stood on one side, each with their grey beginner's belts wrapped around their waist.

The first round of applause came like a supernova, a star bursting as if to celebrate the end of its life. Even when the crowd had stopped, the sound of clapping never seemed to end, reverberating up into the mountains as if the mountains themselves were clapping along with them. The ceremony stewards then came forward, motioning the crowd to sit down. Dressed in their customary purple robes and plumed hats that bobbed with each shake of their heads, they made their introductory speeches. Behind them, a table with individual boxes supported the sacred belts that were to be handed out to the students. Ezekiola never understood the order in which the belts were given out. There was no order of color or name, but it was reassuring to see that the belt always matched the student it was given to. Perhaps the apparently random order was meant to keep the students alert throughout the ceremony since they never knew when their names might be called.

Like most of the students, Ezekiola had replayed this moment countless times in his mind. When a student's name was called, they would meet with the first steward, then be greeted by the second, who would call out the color of their belt, and then the third, who would complete the rite of passage by removing their old grey belt and wrapping the new one around their waist, and in this manner, bound each student forever to their new belt's brotherhood. The wait was long, and Ezekiola paid minimal attention until he heard his friends' names being called.

"Atlas Pleione... of the Red Belt... bound here, now and forever, to the Brotherhood of the Red Belts."

"Nohlan Eridanus... of the Brown Belt... bound here, now and forever to the Brotherhood of the Brown Belts."

With a handful of students left, Ezekiola's name was finally called.

"Ezekiola Astrid..."

Ezekiola got up, trying hard to hide a faint smile.

"... of the Emerald Belt."

He stopped midway on the stage as the entire crowd went suddenly quiet. Emerald? Had he heard correctly, or had the steward made a mistake? He was supposed to receive the Blue Belt. He looked at the stewards but saw no confusion on their faces. Yet his mind was unable to compute how his name could be followed by that word. He looked behind him to see if someone else had stood up but was met only by surprised faces urging him instead to move forward. Unable to process the scene before him, Ezekiola's mind came to a standstill while his body marched rigidly forward. How on Circa's seven moons could this be happening?

No one in their right mind wanted the Emerald Belt.

Lately, many of Circa's warriors had started to go missing, never to be seen again. Their numbers had decreased so much, in fact, that it was rumored Circa had to seek aid from other worlds. It was never a safe thing to have a shortage of warriors on a planet, they'd say, even in times of peace. Chaos could be at your doorstep when you least expected it. In a daze, Ezekiola saw the ceremony stewards take the green belt out of its box. This belt could not be mistaken for any other, not only because of its vibrant color but for its ornamented silk triangular markings all along the length of the delicate material and its lavishly plaited ends. He was sure this was the first time the ceremony stewards had erred. *There's a first for everything,* he thought ruefully. Stuck on stage as in a web and not wanting to make a scene in front of the crowd out of courtesy to the stewards, he went through with the ceremony and left with his new Emerald Belt around his waist, albeit with a look of surprise on his face. As he walked to his designated place, he didn't dare look up at the faces staring at him. It was a colossal enough feat to handle everyone's thoughts on the green attire adorning his waist. His own thoughts started rushing through his head, making it harder for him to control the emotional build-up within. Then it dawned on him: he was the only student of his promotion graduating to the Emerald level. In fact, he was the only one in over ten years.

Chapter 4

Revolving Doors

It had grown dark outside when he realized that he was still standing on the stage. There were no other students left there except for him. He could hear the sound of tempestuous sea waves crashing against the rocks down below. The audience, however, was still present in the amphitheater, but the expression appearing on most faces had changed. No longer were they clapping. Some had drawn closer to see better. And now, a few were even coming up on the stage, circling him, yet keeping a cautionary distance. The happiness usually marking such a joyous occasion had completely vanished. Everyone who had gathered around him had the same look of horror on their faces as they stared at his waist. That's when he felt the first movement. *What was that?* He looked down and noticed a bright green thing wrapped around his waist. He went to touch it, but it was burning hot, and he immediately pulled his hands away. His vision blurred for a moment as the sensation grew. It was alive, a living thing encircling him. When his vision had finally cleared, his eyes grew wide as he stared down at what was no longer his belt but rather a bright green snake wrapping its coils around him. To his horror, it grew in size each time it rotated around his waist, emitting a strange heat that burned his insides. Paralysis overcame him. He stood still, petrified. What was it about to do? Snap at him? Take a bite? Burn him? The more he thought about it, the more the snake's grip grew tighter and the hotter he got. His stomach was on fire, and his lungs compressed as it grew larger. His breath shortened; his vision blurred once more, and just when he couldn't take another gasp of air, he was blinded by a sharp light forcing his eyes shut.

Ezekiola opened his eyes. Sunlight crept through a small crack between the curtains of his dorm room, bathing his face in the morning light. There were six beds in his dimly lit room, the others being occupied by five of his schoolmates, who currently slept soundlessly. As light settled in, the carved leaves on each of their bed frames representing the Cypress School crest slowly came into view. There were white tunic uniforms placed neatly by each bedside, a colorful belt now replacing the old grey one laid on top of each garment. A picturesque serenity and order permeated the room. Ezekiola took a moment to wake his senses, then took note of his immediate surroundings: drenched bed sheets, sprained neck, as if he'd been pinned into a corner for hours by an invisible force, and his Emerald Belt, laying comfortably on his nightstand, next to a book on Blue Belts he had borrowed from the library. It was one hell of a dream to wake up from and a real nightmare to wake up to in the morning after the ceremony. The Emerald Belt. That hadn't been just a dream. He closed his eyes, hoping to escape this predicament, then came back to his senses once more. What little serenity the morning offered quickly evaporated as his thoughts went rampaging through his head, first about how he had been given the wrong belt, then quickly shifting to his friends, Atlas and Nohlan, whose belts were in perfect alignment with their interests as his should have been. Atlas had been bestowed with the Red Belt, for he had a mind sharp as a knife and enjoyed the logical side of things, while Nohlan had received the Brown Belt, finally embarking on his journey to study nature and the macrocosm. That thing lying on his nightstand had to be a mistake.

He remembered reading what had been on everyone's mind right after the ceremony. They all shared the same thought: genuine surprise at seeing Ezekiola with the Emerald Belt as if all along he had harbored some secret desire of becoming an Emerald, a warrior of Circa. Nothing could have been further from his true and desired path. The situation definitely had to be sorted out, and there was only one way to resolve it. Ezekiola quickly got out of bed and put his uniform on. He was going to see the headmaster after his first morning class. And in the meantime, he decided he was going to avoid everyone, even his friends. At least he had time on his side, he reassured himself. Transitioning into a new belt was a gradual process. Students still enjoyed a few classes together before integrating their respective fields. There was surely a way out, and he was going to find it.

After a morning class during which he had barely listened to what the teacher was saying, Ezekiola was walking resolutely through the school's West Wing, heading straight for the headmaster's quarters, when a movement in the corner of his eye caught his attention. He turned to look in that direction and noticed something new: a set of revolving doors turning on their own. They were erected exactly where the pivot doors leading to the East Wing of the school used to be. Ezekiola knew these doors well, as they were used mainly as a shortcut by students who were late for class.

It was strange, he thought, that they'd replace the pivot doors with a set of revolving ones, and right in the middle of the day, to boot. He also wondered why they were spinning when no one had gone through them. In fact, the hallways were already empty by the time he had stepped out of class. As anxious as he was to get to the headmaster's office, his curiosity got the better of him. He decided to have a look. He slowly approached the novel doors, and as he did so, they began turning rapidly, as if they'd been triggered by his approach. It made him wonder if there was a repairman running tests on the other side.

Perplexed, Ezekiola had barely approached the doors when he was suddenly drawn in violently as if he'd been caught by a giant suction cup. He couldn't tell at first if he'd unconsciously accelerated his pace or if some unseen force had pushed him in. Regardless, the sensation was so powerful it reminded him of a magnetic field his class had once visited during an outing to learn about the power of magnetic forces, which had been quickly followed by a warning against their wrongful manipulation. But he was clearly not manipulating this door. It was quite the reverse, in fact. No sooner was he sucked in than he was thrust out into what seemed to be another classroom.

Leanne was the last to pack up her things after class and was about to take leave when she was startled by a loud bang. She turned around in time to see several desks being tossed about and a body crashing down onto the floor. It had given her such a fright that she dropped everything she was holding in her hands. Her books crashed to the floor with a loud bang, followed a moment later by the sound of her apple rolling into the opposite corner until it hit the wall with a thud.

"Are you alright?" she asked. Ezekiola turned crimson red

and bolted to his feet, fixing his white tunic and crooked Emerald Belt, and brushing the dust off his uniform.

"Yes, I'm fine, thank you," he answered quickly, wondering what had just happened. This was quite the flashy entrance and very contrary to his usually low-key style.

Leanne felt bad for the boy and wondered if he had been shoved into her class by some bully. She had no clue as to who he was. She'd never seen him at Chester High, but noticing his white outfit and bright green belt, she figured he was some mid-level karate student heading to class. She studied him for a brief moment. His ocean-blue eyes contrasted heavily with his dark locks. She had definitely not seen the likes of him before, or she would have remembered him. Maybe he'd been trying to perfect one of his karate moves when he crashed into her class-room? She decided to make conversation to divert the attention away from the embarrassing incident. It must be terrible for a poor karate boy to fall down in front of a girl.

"Are you going to a martial arts class?" she asked, her eyes crinkling around the corners. Ezekiola kept his gaze downcast longer than necessary as he continued rearranging his outfit. He, too, was working hard at concealing a smile, it seemed.

"No. I didn't take that this cycle," he answered and looked at her for the first time. He was immediately struck by her hazel eyes and surprised himself for gazing at them longer than he should have.

"What's with the green belt then?" she asked.

"Oh, this? I just received it yesterday at my graduation."

"Really? I wasn't aware we had that at this time of the year. So, you just graduated?" she asked. As she slowly picked her books off the floor, she mulled over this curious statement.

"Partially, yes." He hesitated before speaking again, but somehow, he wanted to share more. There was something about her. "I graduated to ... um ... the emerald level," he said and helped her pick up the last of her books. He wished he could have said blue level, but the color on him was unmistakably green.

Leanne stared back at him, visibly confused.

"The emerald level," she repeated as if it would help her better understand. Worried she might offend him, she opted to be courteous about this weird graduation of his.

"Congratulations, that sounds like an interesting, um, degree," she replied. It was strange. She had definitely never heard of such a thing before. He was probably visiting Chester High from another school, she reasoned, and wondered what year he was in, having trouble guessing his age.

"How old are you?" she asked.

"I'm seventeen," he replied, a number that made Leanne's face drop. Surely, he couldn't be seventeen with a face as young as his.

"I know, I look younger. But really, I'm older," he added, sensing her reaction. She was more confused than ever. He sounded so innocent but mature at the same time. Some sort of strange boy-man. Yet he was finishing high school, she thought.

Ezekiola heard all of her thoughts but did not reply nor correct them. Suddenly, it dawned on him why she didn't know anything about his graduation. He may be seventeen, but what she thought of as high school was kindergarten compared to the level of studies he'd actually completed at his own school. He was beginning to figure out who she was just by analyzing the nature of her thoughts, which he could hear so well.

"That's amazing because you really don't look like it. You're seventeen, huh?" she asked again. Although it surprised her, part of her was glad to hear that.

"Yes, and how old are you?" he quickly asked to deflect all suspicion she may have about his mind-reading abilities. He noticed that she was already starting to have doubts about him.

He had studied somewhere that females, in general, had a strong intuition and could figure things out without any concrete details. Best be careful, he thought.

"Oh, I'm sixteen. A year short of you, actually!" she said, giggling. "I'm Leanne, by the way. What's your name?" she said finally.

The air started shifting around them. Ezekiola sensed that time was running out. This was both strange and new to him. She was definitely not a resident of Circa, he thought. He immediately froze at this thought, realizing his doubts about who this person was were fully justified.

Exhilarated about his discovery, he was about to say his name when the only Latin dictum he'd learned the day before came rushing into his mind: *verba volant, scripta manent*—spoken words fly away, written words remain. Instinctively, he reached into his bag for a pen and some paper and wrote down his name, thinking it increased his chances of her remembering. Being named after a star came with its disadvantages, one of which was that most people forgot it the minute they heard it. He was glad to have listened to at least that bit of Almonte Versutus's lessons. He never thought that it would serve a purpose, especially not in such a peculiar setting.

Leanne found it odd that he would write down his name instead of just saying it. She grabbed the piece of paper and read it: Ezekiola. But before anyone had time to say another word, a strangely disturbing melody suddenly resounded. Ezekiola was watching her eyes as she read his name, hoping she would look up one last time, but their time was up.

Just as fast as he had arrived, Ezekiola found himself back in the halls of his own school, as the classroom he had been standing in with Leanne suddenly dissipated as if it had never existed. Just like that, she was gone, leaving him with a burning desire to see her again. Ezekiola turned around and noticed with sadness the familiar surroundings that were his school. He stared at the old pivot doors, which now replaced the revolving doors he had apparently gone through. Was he dreaming? He shut his eyes tightly and reopened them a few times, to no avail. He then looked at his Emerald Belt and knew deep down that his imagination could never have run this wild.

Chapter 5

Riddles Away

"Where is everyone?"

Atlas burst into his classroom for his *Simulations* class, only to find a lone student sitting all by himself in the middle of the room, waiting. As chance would have it, it happened to be his friend Nohlan, crunching away on his favorite pastry, a Mr. Vulcan's biscuit.

"Finally, somebody shows up!" Nohlan said with a mouthful, happy to see a familiar face. Atlas, however, was not happy. He was breathing heavily as he had power-walked nervously through the long stretch of corridors to get to his class. He didn't like to be caught running, and after already receiving two red notes, he was mindful of raising suspicion again about his mismanagement of time. Hard as he tried, his unruly blond hair always gave him away, a perfect match for his usual disoriented air.

"Nohlan, where is everyone?" He was late and didn't see an empty classroom as a very good omen.

"I don't know," Nohlan answered, completely oblivious to the empty chairs around him.

"Well, did anybody else show up beside me? How long have you been waiting here?"

"Hmm ... maybe five minutes." It sounded more like a guess than anything else. There was also a certain nonchalance to Nohlan that did not fit. But having no time to waste, Atlas let it go and simply looked up at the clock hanging clearly above the classroom door. It read a quarter past three.

"Nohlan, class should have started fifteen minutes ago. Something's not right."

"What?" he said, suddenly agitated. "Really? You think so?"

"Yes, I think so. Something is definitely not right. Either it's been canceled or ..." But before he said another word, a treacherous thought crossed his mind.

"Oh no, he didn't!" Atlas looked like he finally understood why their classroom was empty. He hurried out of the classroom with a puzzled Nohlan scurrying after him.

"Professor Balthazar has gone completely mad! He's done it again! I'm sure of it. Otherwise, everyone would have been here by now."

"Done what?" Nohlan asked.

"He's posted a riddle again! That's WHAT!" he exclaimed, then took a deep breath to try to keep his cool. "That teacher has clearly crossed the line of normalcy."

This particular semester, the boys had had several unpleasant surprises such as this one. Every now and then, they were given riddles to solve in order to locate the classroom where their class had spontaneously been moved. And each time, they had a hard time deciphering it. It was their professor's brilliant idea to wake his sleepy students up before class, changing their destination on a random basis. Since school had started, he'd planted riddles in the main school hall an hour before class for his students to solve so they could find out where their next class would be held. Every classroom had a name, and since there were well over a hundred spread out mainly in the East and West wings of the school, and some in the North, this challenge was not an easy one. Students who failed to figure it out, or weren't lucky enough to bump into other students willing to share their answers, would be marked as absent. All this because Professor Balthazar wanted to give his students what they had asked to have more of—simulation classes. And in the professor's book, if you wanted more of something, you had to earn it. There were no handouts with him. "It's like fasting," he would say, "only for the mind—purifying the brain by depriving it of its propensity for lethargy." In the professor's view, his students were lazy, and 'activating' them was his sole mission. Nohlan hated this strategy, which he equated to taking away his lunch or snack time. Indeed, running around finding other students to get the answers plunged him each time into a state of havoc, so he was forced to eat fast to scurry off in search of clues. His stomach was always upset on days like these.

Atlas' mind was suddenly working overtime. He had already begun power walking towards the main hall of the school on the small chance that they could solve the riddle and make it to class, albeit very late. Nohlan, on the other hand, trailed behind and didn't seem all that concerned. He had his hands in his pockets and was fiddling with their contents, making rustling sounds as he walked. His passivity was beginning to annoy Atlas seriously.

"You look like a squirrel searching for nuts!" Atlas snapped at him. "By now, you should have already figured out that the classroom had been changed, Nohlan. I mean, how long were you going to wait like that, eating your biscuits all on your own?" Atlas walked faster and faster, making it hard for his pudgy friend to keep up.

Atlas continued ranting to himself: "I doubt if he'll even let us in class now, on the slim chance we make it, especially since we are NOT his favorites!"

"Wait a minute!" Nohlan was huffing, unable to keep up the pace that Atlas was setting. Nor could he keep silent any longer.

"I already went and took a look at the riddle," he said, now breathing heavily and looking down at his feet.

Atlas stopped and looked at him incredulously, now seeing the foe who had been hiding within his friend.

"Did you, now?" he said, marking his words.

The fact was that Nohlan had known all along that he was in the wrong classroom. He had initially showed up at a room called *Seven Moons*, thinking it was the right one. He had been wrong, of course, and after trying a few more classrooms, he had hopped back to the regular room, hoping one of his friends would forget to check for a riddle in the main hall and inadvertently show up. They would then go back, and he could depend on another to solve the riddle. He lucked out when that person happened to be his good friend Atlas, who was better at solving riddles than he was. He was so bad at it, in fact, that he had started coming up with weird stratagems to get the answers. And he despised his teacher with a passion for making him go through this every time.

"Here, take a look. I wrote it down." Nohlan finally replied, fiddling once more with the contents of his pocket. Several scribbled notes came out, some even falling to the ground. Nohlan finally found the right one and handed it over to his friend.

Atlas snatched the note out of his hand.

"You know, Nohlan, sometimes I really wonder if being your friend isn't more of a curse than a blessing. You lie to my face by hiding vital information, yet ironically, your presence might save us both from a possible absence by avoiding the long marathon to the main hall. Provided we can solve the riddle on time."

He glanced at Nohlan one last time, then got down to the business of solving the riddle. That was one of Atlas' many qualities: he never lingered long on any of his friends' short-comings. Once he had spoken his mind, which he never failed to do, he would quickly forget about it and move on.

He had barely glanced at it when Nohlan blurted out.

"It's completely absurd, as usual. I've read it ten times, and I just can't figure it out."

"Give me a minute here, Nohlan," Atlas said, then he read out loud:

"Grazing at night, blue kingdoms of high,
Luminous you are than the stable one bright,
Stranger no longer to carrier of tides,
An endurance plight has long come about.
See to your matrons, once a good seven,
Lest they dissolve into your neighboring patron."

He started going over the different classrooms in his mind and finally concluded. "The matrons have the number seven associated with them. It's got to be the *Seven Moons*," Atlas concluded.

"No, it's not. I already went there, and no one else showed up," Nohlan replied, suddenly collaborating. "I also went to *Jupiter's Triangle* and *Clouds of Venus*. They're the only ones that I thought made sense, but they, too, were empty."

"Clouds of Venus? What do clouds have to do with this?"

"Well, I thought there could be a relation between them and grazing animals. My brother studied life on other planets and told me that there are animals in those clouds."

Atlas started panting furiously. He could not for the life of him figure out something like this under pressure, although usually, he wasn't too bad at it. Unfortunately, his friend was no help, and the two together were like the blind leading the blind. They swerved through a corridor, turning left. They sighed with relief when they saw the third member of their trio looking utterly bewildered in the middle of the hallway, staring intensely at absolutely nothing.

"Zek!" Atlas yelled across the hallway, clapping his hands loudly near Nohlan's ears.

"What are you doing there, standing like a statue?"

Having barely had time to process what had just happened, Ezekiola's chain of thoughts about Leanne was broken by the clamor of anxious, demanding voices.

"We're late for our Simulations class, and we haven't figured out his riddle. Do you know the answer?"

"What? We're already late?" Ezekiola was shocked. His notion of time had never felt so distorted. For him, only a few moments had passed since his last class.

"Yes, we're late! And not only that, we haven't solved Balthazar's riddle!" Atlas exclaimed, thrusting the scribbled note he was holding in his friend's face.

"He posted one again? What does it say?"

Before Ezekiola could take it, Nohlan snatched his note back and, waving it in midair, reiterated his complaint: "It's completely absurd as usual," he said, making sure Ezekiola had also heard his opinion, and then in a theatrical manner raised his voice and read the riddle:

"Grazing at night, blue kingdoms of high,
Luminous you are than the stable one bright,
Stranger no longer to carrier of tides,
An endurance plight has long come about.

See to your matrons, once a..."

"Can I see your note?" Ezekiola interrupted him. He always had an easier time solving these things if the words stared him in the face. Nohlan handed him his note.

Ezekiola pondered it quietly, then looked back at Nohlan with a knowing smile: "How can *you*, Nohlan Eridanus, a fervent student of the macrocosm, not know the answer to this?"

"Don't you pull that one on me!" Nohlan replied, snatching his note back to look at it. He creased his brow as if the same visual riddle-solving charm would operate on him. That piece of paper was about to fall to pieces from switching hands over and over.

"I figured the grazing cow part out and went through the kingdom of numbers, stars, and planets... but then... the rest doesn't make any sense!" he responded defensively. Something about his friend calling him by his full name was nagging at him. A faint little voice in his head was telling him that perhaps his last name had something to do with the answer, but he was just too lazy to think about it.

"Well, do you want the answer, or do you want to wither away trying to figure it out?" asked Ezekiola.

"We have no time left," Atlas intervened. "Just say it."

"Pleiades," Ezekiola let drop with a smirk.

"Well, strike me twice!" Nohlan blurted, dumbfounded. His last name was indeed a clue, for Eridanus was one of the neighboring constellations of the Pleiades star cluster.

"Well, how did you figure that one out?" Atlas asked as they rushed through the corridors. He, too, felt a personal need for more than just the right answer. Like Nohlan, he should have known better. His parents had actually named him after one of the stars of the Pleiades. Out of all the ones they had to work out, this riddle should not have been so difficult to solve for either of them.

"It's not very complicated, really. The grazing is the cow, yes, but what else is in the same family?"

"A bull," they both answered.

"Right, and what does the bull have in common with something bright and blue that is related to the number seven, or at least used to, and is female?"

The two looked dazed. Ezekiola explained with a hint of mockery in his tone. "The constellation of Taurus, my dear friends, in which can be found seven sisters, the sisters being the matrons, in itself a cluster dominated by blue stars in the night sky; these stars, that shall one day disperse within its home galaxy, being of course the patron. It's called the Pleiades, which is the name of one of our classrooms, located further, and outdoors, in the North Wing."

Nohlan made that face he always did when being handed his corrected exam papers and realizing, to his astonishment, that he had missed an easy answer.

"Let's make a run for it and hope he'll let us in," Ezekiola blurted at them as he upped the pace.

Chapter 6

Just One Word

Leanne couldn't understand how a boy could fly right into her classroom like a shooting star, only to disappear a few moments later. She had merely taken her eyes off of him for one second to read his name when that treacherous Chester school bell rang, and he was gone. She stepped outside to see if he was in the hallway, but there were only a few students hanging around their lockers.

She went back into her classroom and assessed the damage. Desks sprawled, papers adrift, and books scattered here and there, all due to the whirlwind entrance of a single boy. How strange. He must have been up to something. Why else would someone burst into a classroom like that, karate-kicking his way through the furniture? She started quickly putting things back in order before anyone walked into the room and mistakenly thought she was the culprit. But she wasn't fast enough.

"Goodness! What happened here?!" Leanne jumped around to see her friend Andy walk in, wearing a deep frown.

"Oh, it's you!" Leanne said, relieved.

"Did you get into a brawl or something?" Andy asked as she eyed the mess.

"Well..."

Leanne wasn't sure how to explain what had happened or if she should even say anything at all. But then she opted to tell it as it was.

"No. No brawl. I just met this guy. He came in, more like crash landed here, and this is what happened," she said.

"A guy just came and did this! What was his problem? Was he raving mad?" Andy asked.

"Not at all. He was actually very calm. Maybe a bit nervous."

"I don't get it. Was it someone from our class?" she asked.

"No. I've never seen him here. He had a white outfit on with a green belt, karate style," she answered, a deep crease forming between her eyebrows. "Did you see anyone like that walking in the hallway?"

"No, they don't even give karate classes here."

"That's what I thought, too."

"What a show-off, really, trying to impress you like that. Was he cute, at least?"

Leanne laughed and gave Andy a barely perceptible nod.

"Well, did he tell you his name?" her friend pressed her further.

"Of course! Well... No, actually. He didn't say it, but he wrote it down. It's... um... an unusual name." She unfolded her paper and showed it to her friend.

"Ezekiola," Andy read it out loud, then frowned. "What kind of name is that?"

"I know, it's weird. It almost sounds like a girl's name, doesn't it?" Leanne said, looking at the name again. But he was definitely a boy.

The girls stepped out of the classroom and into the hallway

with their eyes glued to the note with the strange name written on it.

"You're right. And how odd that his name ends with an 'a.' Isn't that usually for girl names?" Andy replied.

"Then again, there's Luca and Noah in our ecology class. Their names finish with an 'a' sound," Leanne noted.

"True. What did he tell you? And what did he look like? Tell me everything!"

The girls set out to walk home instead of taking the bus, which was what they did when they had some juicy topics to discuss. After parting from Andy, Leanne replayed the scene with Ezekiola several times in her mind, like a movie she couldn't get over, with him writing down his name and disappearing. Why had he left so quickly? Was it the comment she had made about his age? Maybe she had offended him, and he wanted to have nothing to do with her. But then the whole thing didn't make sense. Why even write his name instead of just saying it? As if he wanted to leave her a souvenir.

On her way home, she decided to make a quick stop at Madame Camille's pawn shop, *Books for Less*. This second-hand store sold just about anything you could think of, including rare books, and the lady who owned it, Madame Camille, the French lady, always made her visits there memorable.

"Bonjour, Leanne! How are you today?" she asked.

"Hi, Madame Camille! Good enough, thanks. Having a busy day, I see."

Leanne noticed a larger-than-usual number of people in the store. Yet even so, Madame Camille never missed greeting her like she was one of her best customers. She would offer advice each time she spoke to her, as well as discounts and a few freebies here and there.

"Any new stuff come in?"

"Oh yes, in the box right there," Madame Camille said, pointing to the rear of the store. "You go ahead and take a peek, dear," she whispered. "My apologies. I did not have time to tidy up and properly display them."

Leanne headed to the back of the shop and looked at the latest shipment. As always, the oddest bits of trinkets one could imagine were all randomly mixed together. Cutlery and fancy knives, knitting wool, some books, belts, handbags, and odd little ornaments. The box in itself was like a one-stop pawn shop. A navy-blue bag caught Leanne's interest. As she seized it, a gardening book fell out of the box. She picked it up and read the title: *Trees, Gnomes and Healthy Greens*. Uninterested, she put it back into the box, but as she did, a bookmark slipped out. It was brown with something round in the middle. She took a closer look and saw it was a locket neatly attached to the center of the bookmark as if it were glued there. An image of a leaf was carved on the outside of the locket. It was a rather pretty ornament for a bookmark in a gardening book, Leanne thought, almost like a cheaper way to buy jewelry. Leanne wanted the locket very much but couldn't get it without buying the book, and she clearly was not interested in some gardening book with pictures of gnomes and trees on the cover. She checked the price. It was only a dollar. Maybe her father would make some use of it. He just loved to plant those little gnome figurines in their backyard. Without any further thought, she grabbed the book and headed toward the cash register.

"I will be with you in a minute, dear!" Madame Camille told her, tending to a client with a lamp in one hand who was looking for a matching set.

That extra minute of waiting got Leanne flipping through the most unlikely book she had ever decided to buy. She turned the book over and read the back cover: *How to turn your yard into a gnome haven! Get your plants and greens to be at their healthiest by attracting gnomes!* It was written by a certain Bona Paden, a lady in her later years whose untidy white hair filled most of the space in her picture. *I'm buying a gardening book written by someone who probably lost her marbles at the end of her life*, thought Leanne.

Madame Camille returned to the cash register and greeted her again. She had a magnificent grin, which made her annoyance from waiting immediately disappear. It was a gift that so few possessed.

"What have we got here today?" she asked, pointing towards the book.

"Trees, Gnomes and Healthy Greens by Bona Paden," Leanne answered.

"I have read a gardening book from this author before. A bit quirky but surprisingly effective. Is it for you?" she asked.

"It's for my dad, actually. He likes gnomes," Leanne said with a shy smile.

"Oh, and nice selection, I see. I thought you would like this since it's blue," she then pointed at the bag.

"Yes, I'm splurging a little since I don't really need one," Leanne said.

"Do not go feeling guilty about it. Truth be told, a lady never has enough bags and can always make room for more. Same goes for shoes!" she said.

"How about a gift for you today, then? Hmm?" Madame Camille winked at her. She punched in zero on the cash register for the bag and continued the transaction by adding the amount for the book.

"You don't have to do that. Please let me pay for the bag."

"It's nothing, just a little treat here and there."

"That's very nice of you. Thank you," she managed to reply.

Right when Leanne was about to pay, she noticed the jewel

hanging around Madame Camille's neck and froze. Her reaction was enough for Madame Camille to pause and take notice.

"You like my locket, dear?" she asked.

"Well, I just never noticed it," Leanne replied, staring intensely, unable to take her eyes away from Madame Camille's locket. What an odd coincidence!

"I have worn it for over fifty years since the day I laid eyes upon the one who would become my husband. We had this tradition in the old days of wearing the names of our loved ones around our necks. Sometimes, people would even wear them to help heal a sick sibling, for instance, whatever their wish might be. Most of the time, though, it was for a boy we liked." She smiled mischievously. "So, if you secretly admired someone, the myth was that you secretly wore his name. Be mindful about it and see if things... developed."

"So, it was like your own little secret?" Leanne asked.

"Exactly. And I never told a soul about it until it materialized. When things are revealed too soon, somehow, they fail to materialize. That is why it is best to keep secrets to yourself as long as you can before you share them with others."

"Does it work?" asked Leanne.

"Sure enough, things had a most unusual way of happening. So much so that if I were to recount these events to you the way they actually happened, they would sound even more far-fetched than any work of fiction in this store," she said, whispering as if she were confiding something remarkably important. "Has something ever happened to you like that, Leanne? So wildly incredible that you could not have made it up even if you had tried your hardest?"

"Maybe... but I can't think of one right now," she quickly added, inexplicably not wanting to reveal too much. She waited for Madame Camille to continue with her revelations, but she just smiled at her.

"How does it work exactly?" she then asked.

"A name is a word really that can be made powerful, for it can give life to the intentions you put into it. When you infuse a word with power, it comes alive the way you wish it to be. Creating my life with my husband was the greatest act of power for me, so I still continue to wear his name as a reminder of all the things I wish to attract into my life."

"It sounds so simple," Leanne said.

"Yes, we often overlook things that sound so simple we do not even try them. The key is to persist and not give up, especially when you do not see immediate results."

"I think I might try it," Leanne said eagerly.

Ideas flooded her mind as she left the store. *What if I wanted to see Ezekiola again?* she wondered. Although he was a stranger to her, as much as she tried, she couldn't get him out of her head. The sight of him remained with her, the way you still see the sun when you close your eyes after having stared at it. It was very convenient that he had written his name for her, for all she had to do was open her locket, insert it, and wear it. She decided to do just that and added the locket with Ezekiola's name inside onto her necklace, hoping something would come out of it.

Little did she know that wearing his name this way would awaken her presence in his mind and cause quite a remarkable stir.

Chapter 7

The Hydra Simulation

Cypress School had four wings: North, South, East, and West. The East and West wings were where classes for the White Tunics were held; the South Wing housed the learning halls, the library, and the cafeteria. Further South still were the student dorms, the headmaster's quarters, which were located outside of the school building. The northern section, however, was special, for it was composed of classrooms actually located within the Black Forest. Some were even in the open air, with connecting paths leading students directly into the simulation zones where they would have to overcome various challenges, including, among them—the labors of Hercules. The Pleiades classroom was outdoors and was easily recognizable by its angular-shaped rooftop held by seven wooden pillars. There were no walls to this classroom except for a single black slate stone wall that served as a writing board.

Students actually liked these outdoor classes, for they were allowed to sit on ground mats wherever they wished. Latecomers, though, had to sit on wooden benches located on the outer perimeter of the classroom so as not to disturb those already seated, and that's if they were granted entry in the first place, which was not always the case.

Today's simulation class was on the Hydra, Professor Balthazar's favorite Herculean trial, and thus he could not have been more in his element. This nine-headed beast that lived in a swamp was the much-feared mythological figure Hercules had had to conquer during one of his twelve labors. Whenever the subject of the Hydra came up in class, Professor Balthazar's head would jerk involuntarily, just like the creature's heads did. Often, his movements and expressions would make him seem as if he had completely lost control over his emotions. Nonetheless, he managed to remain calm and focused. This made following his class tricky since his students were never sure if he was angry or simply having another of his emotional overloads, and they had to do everything they could not to laugh whenever he'd go all herky-jerky on them. A man in his later years, it was rumored he was well over the venerable age of one hundred, although no one really knew how old Balthazar truly was. Some even ventured that he had passed the two-hundred mark. Whatever the number, the fact was that he didn't look his age at all, and his general appearance made it very hard for his students to keep a straight face. His slanted eyes were completely asymmetric, being different in both shape and size. When he looked at you, his eyes would never be entirely focused, as if one eye was always fighting with the other, making you wonder if he was looking at you at all. The barren patch of skin surrounded by white hair that stood up on the top of his head made it look as if he had an eagle nest on his head. When he spoke, weird humming sounds from his throat kept interrupting his speech pattern at odd intervals, so the students could not tell if he was agreeing to something, asking a question, or if it was just a tic he could not control. And finally,

Professor Balthazar had no sense of humor whatsoever and a reputation for being as hard as steel. He despised being laughed at, and his outbursts of anger could literally leave the class in a cloud of smoke. Most students remained docile throughout, swallowing their giggles as quietly as they could. But alas, there were always a few who couldn't keep it in.

"Now that we have reviewed yesterday's material, you can open your book to today's lesson: the Lernaean Hydra, the nine-headed beast the demigod Hercules had to conquer in the sign of Scorpio."

He turned and picked up a piece of light gray chalk from a nearby basket to write on the stone board when a knocking sound was heard on a wooden pillar. It was soft, almost timid, yet in the context, it felt as if it reverberated through the entire area that formed the classroom. As Professor Balthazar was very sensitive to noise, anything besides birds chirping away and the rustling of leaves was enough to break his concentration. He shut his eyes and exhaled sharply through his nose.

"Yes! Come in."

Atlas, Ezekiola, and Nohlan slipped in like cats. Keeping to the outer rim of the classroom, they tiptoed to the rear to sit on the uncomfortable benches reserved for latecomers. If they thought they could enter quietly without drawing attention, their professor made sure their tardiness did not go unnoticed.

"Ah, here comes our lagging trio, always freshly on time!" The professor glared at each one of them. Or so everyone assumed, given his wandering eyes.

"Perhaps if the motor of the brain worked faster, it would help solve the riddle in a more efficient manner. I wonder which one of you actually solved the riddle."

He eyed Ezekiola suspiciously. "Take your seats. And don't think I will let you off easy today." The three quietly headed to their seats. With a vengeance percolating in his heart, Nohlan, however, was fuming over his teacher's comments.

"Conquering the Lernaean Hydra," continued the professor, "was one of the hardest tasks Hercules had to overcome. So much so that he actually needed help on this one. Like you students would likely do!" he stated, writing the words 'Lernaean Hydra' on the board in his usual chalk-crushing style, with bits and pieces of chalk flaking down to the ground. Luckily for the professor, the Limestone Mountains provided chalk in abundance since he never failed to go through most of what was in the basket at the beginning of the class.

Sounds like a group assignment, Ezekiola thought. For once, a simulation that wasn't going to be solo. He was already running his choices in his head of which friend would be best suited to accompany him on this exercise.

"Each of the nine heads of the Hydra represents a challenge in life. Can anyone name a few?" the professor asked.

A bunch of students answered simultaneously, cutting each other off: "Fear... hate... cruelty... desire... power—"

"I expect you to raise your hands when you wish to speak! Hmmm!" Balthazar stopped them in their tracks, his head bopping sideways. The class went quiet again.

"Now, why does each of the nine heads grow back twice when Hercules slices it off? Hmmm? Hmmm? Anyone? Hmmm. Hmmm."

The class remained quiet, with the students holding their breath. Watching the professor's current mannerisms, the few who knew the answer to this Herculean question refrained from answering for fear of exploding into laughter. But Nohlan, he of the big mouth, could not handle remaining quietly seated anymore. Still angry about his professor's comments when he and his friends arrived, he finally let it out:

"Professor, what makes you so sure that it's the serpent's heads that double?" he asked.

His professor looked at him for an instant, unsure whether this was a legitimate question or an attempt at humor. Regardless, having arrived so late, Nohlan should not have been asking questions and acting smart, as if he had arrived in class in a timely fashion.

"What kind of question is that?" asked the professor.

Nohlan was now balancing himself on the two hind legs of his bench, giving off an air of complete control when he challenged his teacher once again: "Well don't you think for once that maybe your little Hercules is the problem?"

"Excuse me?" The professor's gaze became cross-eyed, with one eye on the verge of popping.

"Could it be that he can't see straight and sees double instead, especially after ingesting so many funny mushrooms for dinner?"

A giggle snort and a few chuckles flew out of some throats, despite the futile attempts by those responsible to keep it together.

The professor realized he was being mocked, and his facial expression changed rapidly.

"Hercules must surely have a need for food, doesn't he?" Nohlan, who wasn't done yet, asked innocently. After the few seconds of utter silence brought on by his last question, he let out a powerful harrumph, beating his teacher to it. He tried to make it sound like he simply needed to clear his throat, but everyone in the classroom knew he was imitating one of their professor's many tics, the professor included.

A violent burst of laughter came from those who couldn't contain themselves any longer. It was exaggerated, given the context, and sufficient to make Professor Balthazar's cauldron of emotions tip over.

"How funny you are, Mister Eridanus!" The chalk in his hand went flying into an innocent student.

"We will see who shall have the last laugh since you will be the lucky first to face the Hydra!"

Nohlan's expression went from cockiness to fury. Every student had to go through the simulation process for each Herculean quest. Even if it was a fun exercise, in hindsight, no one wanted to go first because the entire class watched how you performed. Those going first always made the worst mistakes, which made the ones going in afterward systematically perform better than the front liners.

"Why me?" Nohlan fired back, instantly bringing his bench back into its proper position. "I went first the last time, and it was a disaster! I'm your worst pick, and you know it. Plus, I abort too fast, according to *you,* so why should I go first?"

"Precisely! This way, your colleagues here may have a chance to learn off your back. This will bring you much-needed good karma, given your answers in class!" he concluded.

Many of the students were thankful not to go first. Ironically, simulation classes were the first thing students wanted more of in their school's curriculum, only to realize in retrospect that they were not fully ready for them. One student was courageous enough to address the fear that almost all of his colleagues felt, questioning the entire process altogether: "Professor, do you think maybe we should keep this particular simulation last since you said it was one of the tougher ones?" The professor's face went as white as if he had just seen a ghost. The class went quiet.

Thinking he was successfully shifting the mood, the student continued: "Could it be that the increase in the level of difficulty of these exercises was too hasty and should be revised?"

"I. Better. Not. Hear. One. Complaint. From any of you!"

Balthazar thundered, pointing a shaky finger at the whole class. The student had obviously hit a nerve. "Especially after we teachers gracefully delivered on your boyish requests to increase the number of simulation classes. I take it all of you are well aware of the adage: *Be careful what you wish for, for you just might get it?*" He paused for dramatic effect, looking at all the pairs of eyes staring at him uncertainly. "You wanted it? Hmmm... Well, here it is, Mister Eridanus and company. We professors have honored our end of the bargain, and thus, we will be holding simulation classes several times a week. And I shall decide which ones and in what order, and I can assure you it won't be the ones you wish for! Hmmm!" He took a moment to let his words sink in while his students gazed back at him glumly.

"Everyone, line up now, and as dictated, Nohlan shall lead this one so you can all breathe easy a little longer. There will be no pity for deserters!" Balthazar hammered these last words into his students' ears with a smug smirk, knowing full well how nervous they were, especially Nohlan.

The boys stepped out of the classroom with a sense of gloom hovering above them. They walked almost in a single file towards the Herculean area located in the Black Forest, one of the several domains built by Cypress School, for simulation purposes. Nohlan followed the others, brooding over his predicament, when Ezekiola finally caught up with him. His mind had been buzzing painfully since his mysterious incident with Leanne, and he was still wondering if his new Emerald Belt had anything to do with it.

"Nohlan, remember when your brother studied magnetic cross-world portals in Circa, and he claimed that there were hidden ones? Did you ever find out where they were?" he asked discreetly. Being a notch higher, Brown Robes like Borghis knew far more about these things than simple Brown Belts.

"What?" Nohlan's eyes widened as he stopped dead. "What kind of question is that? What does it have to do with the death trap I'm about to go into? The professor is about to smoke me alive–AGAIN–while everyone watches me like spectators at a freak show!"

Nohlan's mind was running wild. He was furious about once again being the class guinea pig for a new simulation. He got even more flustered just thinking about it.

"I'm just curious, that's all. I came across a book on the subject, and it made me wonder about those hidden paths, or Sporadic Doors, as the Brown Robes call them."

He pointed towards the Brown Belt around his friend's waist. Nohlan took a doubtful glance at his waist and remained quiet. There was something suspicious about his friend's odd question. Nohlan was only a Brown Belt and hadn't acquired that knowledge yet. Brown Robes were not only knowledgeable about nature and worlds outside of Circa, but they had the ability to access these worlds, often through Sporadic Doors. This enabled them to keep track of evolution outside of Circa and stimulate the growth process in various mineral, animal, and vegetable kingdoms in such worlds.

They continued walking in silence, past thorn bushes and branches that lashed Nohlan's various body parts, adding to his growing frustration. Just then, the student ahead of him released a particularly leafy branch he had passed, one that, in Nohlan's opinion, should have been properly trimmed. It whipped violently back in its original position and slapped Nohlan hard in the face. He exploded.

"THOSE LAZY HALF PINT BROWNIES!" he screamed. "These good for nothing Gemins should have trimmed these branches by now. It's become a hazard just walking here because those slackers never get their jobs done on time. They're too busy hanging around their other halves in

Nomi's garden!" he exclaimed. Forest Gemins were funny-looking little beings entrusted to be the protectors of all things green in the forests of Circa. Considering their diminutive size, it was hard to stay mad at them. Just then, two forest Gemins passed right by them, happily saluting the students with their signature greeting: "Gmonin, godafta, ganaayt!" Nohlan, however, was not in the mood to return the greeting.

"It's 'good morning' only! Not godafta, not ganaayt. Gmonin only! Do you understand?!" Nohlan scolded the innocent Gemins loud enough for the other students to turn their heads and watch.

"Shhhh!" Ezekiola nudged his friend's shoulder. But Nohlan couldn't contain himself.

"What kind of creature bids good morning, good afternoon, and good evening at the same time?" Nohlan continued, now making a speech to his audience, "It's only one at a time, depending on the time of day!" he cried out to the Gemins, who were further behind, in the hopes of starting a quarrel.

"Keep your voice down, Nohlan!" Ezekiola said, "You'll wake up the Furies, and then it really won't be funny."

Furies were tiny fairy insects that remained dormant in the Black Forest most of the time, but these innocent colorful wretches were not to be mistaken for good fairies. Despite being smaller than a bee, they roamed the Black Forest from one end to the other in search of strong negative emotions to feed on. Like moths to light, they were drawn towards anyone who became angry and would feast on their emotions, further agitating them by their mere presence. When attacked by them, many reported hearing voices inside their heads. The saying went that when you lost control of your emotions, the Furies had taken over. They had the power to drive you mad if you let them.

"I'll keep my cool for now, but regardless, those Gemins

should be reprimanded for their slothfulness. Especially Bopen, that wretched thief!"

"Bopen? A thief?" Ezekiola questioned him. Nohlan didn't answer. In an instant, a fight scene flashed in Ezekiola's mind, giving him the insight he needed, one where several blue plants were being tugged back and forth between Nohlan and Bopen, then Bopen making a run for it, his arms full of them.

"Oh, you can't be serious! He took all of your plants? That's why you were all dirty on ceremony day?" he said as the truth became clear to him.

Nohlan remained silent and continued to stomp ahead broodily, which made Ezekiola giggle.

"Don't you laugh! Those were my blue plants I worked on for years! That plant snatcher will have to answer to me one day."

Indeed, Bopen had stolen his experimental plants and hidden them somewhere. As a pastime, Nohlan had begun learning about botany and had spent three long years creating a new prototype of a plant with olfactory healing properties. They were almost ready for certification by Circa's agricultural ambassadors. It was a big deal to get that far. But when Bopen had been confronted, he had replied defensively that he had to protect the plants from "harm" and had never since revealed their location. Unfortunately for Nohlan, Bopen could not be reprimanded. They might once in a while steal someone's handiwork and, as Nohlan would put it, ruin someone's brilliant plans, but Gemins never laid waste to anything green and always ended up replanting the things they'd stolen, albeit not necessarily in their original location.

Suddenly, Nohlan looked like he was struck by a thought, and he stopped in his tracks, instantly forgetting his frustration. He turned to Ezekiola, who was keeping up with him, still hoping that he would eventually get an answer to his first question.

"Did you come across a hidden magnetic crossway like that?" he asked his friend point-blank.

"What? No. Not at all," Ezekiola lied.

"Was that why you were just standing there in the hallway before with a funny look on your face?" Nohlan prodded him further.

"Gather around everyone!" Professor Balthazar's voice broke into their conversation as it echoed through the forest. For once, Ezekiola was glad to hear the professor's voice, which had put an immediate end to a conversation that was becoming increasingly delicate. Nohlan shot him a dubious look as their teacher proceeded with his usual speech, and they made their way toward a translucent dome. Standing within it on a stage platform was the great Hercules, along with his partner in this labor, Lolaus, who was commonly known as the demigod's nephew.

Depending on which simulation they had to face, domains were set up accordingly with their principal and sometimes secondary characters. The Herculean domain was composed of twelve simulations, and each was designed to take place in different parts of it. In this particular instance, they were heading into the configuration of Scorpio, for the Lernaean Hydra was found within that sign. They had twelve steps to climb to get to the oversized circle-shaped podium, which would light up as soon as it sensed the weight of a foot. They represented the twelve astrological signs corresponding to the twelve labors that Hercules had to undertake.

The podium itself was adorned with beautiful geometrical shapes as well as astronomical configurations, tracing the paths the participants had to travel. The setting reflected the cosmos, complex yet orderly, and the symmetry of the drawn images was impressive even to experienced eyes.

"Now listen up. You have all done this before, but I must still go through the safety measures, as there are always some who end up with slight injuries of the mind."

The professor eyed a few of his students, hinting at their last Herculean simulation, where they had to conquer the Cretan bull under the sign of Taurus. Some of the students had come out of their attempt in a daze, unable to recall their names for long minutes after it had ended.

Everyone approached the center and circled the podium. They looked up at the bubbly magnetic shell in the image of Hercules' muscular build and ferocious look next to that of the more ordinary-looking Lolaus, both floating above them some nine feet higher up. These shell-like bodies remained suspended in a biosphere unaffected by time. Yet somehow, they never looked exactly the same from one simulation to the next, their appearance having been slightly altered between classes.

Nohlan, of course, always noticed every detail.

"Did you just give him a haircut, Professor?"

"Quiet, Nohlan! And don't you dare try to style him differently this time. Hopefully, you learned your lesson during your last foray."

Nohlan had been so impressed by Hercules' virility during the Cretan bull simulation that he had removed his own shirt and tied it around his neck to serve as a scarf. This little fashion statement had cost him dearly, as he had ended up hanging from a tree, his makeshift scarf having caught in one of the branches when the bull had swung him into the air. The students had been laughing hysterically when he came out of the simulation. It had served as a lesson to all about getting caught up in one's own aspirations at the expense of the mission at hand.

Nohlan already knew who his consort would be before he even stepped up on the podium. He had eyed his good friend Ezekiola on his way up, smiling happily at him. Ezekiola, for his part, would not have minded skipping this simulation altogether, as his mind was still lingering on the mysterious girl he had briefly met, but he knew he was about to get dragged into this quest no matter how he felt about it. Even though it was a simulation, there was always anxiety in the air. Depending on which character they were to enact, they would merge and become one with them before entering the dome. Physically, they became much stronger, but there was a drawback. Once the simulation began, their memories were virtually erased, including the one about how to conquer the beast, and they forgot everything except their mission. It was some kind of virtual amnesia, and only through the process of trial and error were they able to pull through each exercise. The objective of these tests was to prepare them for the real-life challenges they might encounter in outer dominions should they decide to venture outside of Circa. Professor Balthazar always reminded them that amnesia could occur when changing galactic landscapes, so déjà vu became your best friend. The more students learned during these simulations, replaying them over and over in their minds afterward, the greater their chances of overcoming challenges in the future.

Sensing the general tension, the professor's tone changed slightly. "Remember that, ultimately, there are no failures. Only the useless elongated passing of moments, or as I call myself, a waste of time. Let this be your guiding principle to remove any unnecessary weight you now carry on your shoulders so you may succeed the first time around, however unlikely. And good for those of you who do!"

He proceeded to read the guidelines:

"Rules for Observers:

1. *Students must remain within the outer vicinity of the podium at all times.*
2. *It is prohibited to throw any physical object into the dome.*
3. *Silence is golden in thoughts and words.*
4. *Trespassing rules will result in a felony under the Black Forest Governance Act.*

"Rules for controllers, principal, and secondary subjects:

1. *Entrance into the dome is permitted only through the use of body shells.*
2. *Controller must be present at all times during each simulation.*
3. *Keyword 'ABORT' must be used to exit simulation.*
4. *Be warned that pain and amnesia may ensue."*

Professor Balthazar was the mastermind behind the programming of each simulation. He wore magnetic gloves that were linked to each character, and with the use of a system he himself had developed, he could program the personality traits of each of these legendary characters depending on which student was controlling it. Each individual body shell was enshrouded in multiple vertical transparent layers of color that shone brightly, with each such color being associated with a particular trait. All he had to do was glide his fingers across the spectrum of colors to a designated shade to make the simulation task easier or more difficult to pass. He knew the strengths and weaknesses of his students and most often programmed the body shells in such a way that made it harder for them to be their usual selves. In hindsight, once the exercise was over, students would laugh at their own reactions to situations. By simply altering the shade of a color, Balthazar could challenge his students physically, emotionally, and intellectually. He especially liked to play around with the color orange, as it was associated with courage. He had once decreased its hue so much during one simulation that one student aborted barely a minute into his trial out of fear, having no courage left to rely on.

"Observers take your positions, principal and secondary subjects as well. Nohlan being the principal, you may choose your secondary subject as your assistant in this quest."

Nohlan smiled and, in his usual happy-go-lucky manner, said, "I choose not to die alone and take Ezekiola down with me," making it sound like the quest was more of a guaranteed death than a personal trial. Ezekiola stepped onto the podium halfheartedly.

"Please try to give him less of a sense of humor, Professor. Somehow, it always gets us into trouble," he pleaded.

"And try to give him *some,* please," Nohlan retorted, "his lack of humor might make it impossible for us to get through it!"

"Watch what you say, Nohlan. You chose me. Remember that," Ezekiola retorted.

Balthazar threw them both a stern look and, with a vengeful air, spiced up the program a bit, instantly sparking Nohlan's imagination as to what additional challenge might now be awaiting them. When he was done, the professor smirked as if Nohlan's failure was a fait accompli. The students gathered around the dome, vying for the best spot to watch the simulation. Some even placed bets on how long Nohlan would last. They waited impatiently for the professor's cue, which would allow them to have a panoramic view of the domain from above as they watched the legendary characters come into play.

"Quiet, everyone! The descent begins now." Balthazar spoke ceremoniously.

The floor of the dome opened up. In an instant, Hercules and Lolaus were thrust down into a new world's bubble.

Chapter 8

Lolaus, the Victor

Minds went completely blank at the start of each simulation, the participants' memories completely wiped away, only to return when the process was over. Once they merged with a mythological character, students would literally forget who they were. But Ezekiola was an exception. Having one of the strongest minds, he was able to defeat this feature every time. He would sound his name in his head so powerfully before merging with his character that it took him mere seconds to reconnect with a good portion of his memory. Once he remembered his name, bringing back other memories was easy to do. His personality, however, would undergo several changes depending on how his teacher programmed the characters. Sometimes, he would be too nice and too passive, and other times, more aggressive and impatient. But the mission itself was always clear: to conquer the beast.

"Nohlan! Nohlan!" he called out his friend's name but got no reaction from him.

"Hercules!" he tried.

Hercules, Nohlan's avatar, reacted to hearing his heroic name and turned to face his friend Ezekiola, who he saw as Lolaus.

"Lolaus!" he smiled, glad to see him, then looked around. "Where are we?"

They had both landed on rubble in the middle of a dense forest surrounded by lush, green foliage. Ezekiola was the first to pick himself up. Nohlan was sprawled further away in some kind of daze.

"We're in a forest, and we have to find the Hydra."

Nohlan took his first step and immediately stumbled, falling flat on his face.

"What in the devil is this?" He got up, and to his astonishment, his left foot was pointing backward instead of forward. This explained why he had toppled over while trying to apply pressure on the front of his foot. He had none.

"How did this happen?" he asked, confused.

Ezekiola realized what their professor had done in his last modification. His friend's snarky attitude towards Balthazar had come at a price. Making Hercules go through a simulation with a physical disability was cunning, if not outright insidious. There was no point in rekindling a bad memory, so Ezekiola didn't mention it. It would probably infuriate his friend. Instead, he led the way, contemplating a way to bring Nohlan's memory back if they were to succeed in their quest.

"I don't know. Come, lean on me. Let's head this way."

With Nohlan limping as he tried to adapt to his situation, they walked far and long, cutting through bushes in order to find the domain where the beast dwelled. What initially looked like an easy job of finding the creature turned into a strenuous, slow marathon with countless swerves, twists, and turns. The forest was filled with unexpected paths ending in forks, so time and time again, the duo had to choose a path only to discover later that it was the wrong one. Often, the road they picked brought them right back to the starting point, forcing them to now take the untraveled path, a pattern that would repeat itself several times. Needless to say, their journey did not go without quarrels, as the two bickered and blamed one another each time one of their decisions proved wrong. In their minds, several days had passed as they plowed along with as much notion of time as a common rock. Day would turn to night, and the cycle repeated itself, with the two warriors at times marveling at the peculiarity of their surroundings.

"That's an odd-looking leaf." Ezekiola suddenly came to a stop, thinking he might have found a way to stir Nohlan's memory. He bent down to prod a large spade-shaped leaf, almost half his size. It had spiked edges and was strangely colored, with shades of greenish silver visible in the thick veins that ran down the middle of each blade.

"This one has some kind of liquid filling in its veins," he said, pulling on it. The plant shook in defiance, snatching itself away from the intruder's grasp. A foul stench suddenly filled Ezekiola's nostrils. Thinking it came from the plant, he became even more curious.

"What's that smell?" he asked.

"I would be careful if I were you," Nohlan said. "These plants look intelligent."

"Oh please, they're just plants," Ezekiola replied, harassing the leaf intentionally this time while still keeping a small distance away.

"No, I mean it. They're not dumb. Stop picking at it."

"I just want to see something; what's wrong with that?" Ezekiola tried again nervously. The plant hissed and pulled itself back. He could not believe the plant was being this unfriendly. Most shrubs didn't mind having a few of their branches trimmed when their foliage became too dense.

Curious about the strange liquid coursing through the plant, Ezekiola took out his sword resolutely and chopped the leaf off, basically guillotining it. The plant began to close in on itself, finally giving Ezekiola a chance to observe the metallic-like substance, whatever it was, dripping slowly from the opening where the stem had been hacked. Ezekiola was so focused on the stem he didn't think twice about the severed leaf he was holding in his left hand. The gigantic leaf suddenly wrapped itself around his forearm, gripping it tightly. At first, he didn't know what to do. He felt nothing but pressure. Then a gush of heat ravaged his arm.

"Hercules!" he let out agonizingly. Fire rapidly spread from his arm over to the rest of his body.

Nohlan quickly rammed into Ezekiola and rolled him onto the ground until the fire was out. The leaf substance continued to burn for some time on the ground until it finally crumpled into ashes.

"What a foul, nasty, evil plant! Look at what it did!" Ezekiola stood back and tapered the rest of his clothes to put out any patch of fire left burning. There were large holes in his clothes, making him wonder what purpose they still served at this point. He took off his shirt and noticed his skin was smeared with charcoal-like burns, dirt, and blood. It did not make for a very heroic display. The strong stench he had smelled before filled his nostrils again.

"What's that stink?" he asked, ignoring his burns. Ezekiola began to wonder if the bad odor was coming from his friend instead.

"That's a fiery observation! I give you three pluses for that!" Nohlan gave a hard pat on his friend's freshly burned shoulders, ignoring his other question. He seemed ecstatic about some new discovery he had made as his knowledge of botany suddenly rushed back into his mind.

"I remember! This is the Lone shrub. It never mixes with other plants because of its finicky personality, if you want to call it that. It has to accept you before it lets you manipulate it," he smiled at his friend. He began exhaling on the plant and gently touched the edges of its roots enough to stir some of the soil around it. Then he hummed a strange tune. Ezekiola looked at him dumbfounded, wondering what he was doing. Astonishingly, the lone shrub opened its leaves in a welcoming manner. With a swift movement, Nohlan cut off a leaf from a small branch and held it in front of him. The leaf did not give any indication that it was going to try to burn Nohlan alive.

"The secret is in the stem, you see. When it's broken off with care, the leaf won't react. But traumatize the poor thing as you did. The silver-green coloring you see on the leaves triggers a chemical reaction that transforms them into fire. It's quite heroic, really, for it fights its last battle by serving a deadly blow to its attacker. And when you want the opposite to happen, you take the leaf and bunch it up in a ball like this, and then...."

"Stop! It's going to burn you!" Ezekiola warned his friend as his nostrils were filled once more with a whiff of the odd smell.

"Oh, little Lolaus, trust me for once. I know more than you," Nohlan said arrogantly.

He threw the leaf ball high up in the air and took Ezekiola aside along with himself. A loud explosion ensued, blasting every living thing around it. A shower of wooden branches, leaves, and dirt rained down on them.

"You see!" Nohlan said with satisfaction. "You have the perfect combustion weapon to conquer any beast with a single shot!"

"What do you mean?" Ezekiola asked.

"We'll deliver the right blow to this creepy hider as soon as we find it and be done with it," Nohlan said to himself as he went on gently picking as many Lone shrubs as he could.

"I don't understand. You want to throw shrub leaves at this beast?" Ezekiola asked again.

"That's right."

"But that thing has nine heads."

"I'm not wasting my time cutting one head at a time. That's ridiculous. I'll prepare enough of these fireball cocktails to blow the thing up with one hit."

"I'm not sure that's going to work," Ezekiola retorted. "It's nice to know about plants and shrubs, but you'll need more than that. Like thinking, for example, of a smarter way to go about it."

"How do you know? You haven't done this before, and I'm Hercules, not you. I'm the one who decides here. You didn't even know how to manipulate that plant and almost burned yourself alive."

"Well, I'm certainly not convinced that Lone shrubs are enough to conquer a nine-headed beast, no matter how carefully you manipulate them. It just seems too easy. Maybe we should think of alternative ways of dealing with that thing?"

Ezekiola's suggestion might as well have passed through deaf ears as if he were the one speaking nonsense. His disheveled and lackluster appearance didn't help him get his point through; he looked like the crazy one who lacked the ability for cognitive reasoning. Nohlan continued his careful harvesting, looking very much like a devoted gardener tending his plants lovingly.

"Little Lolaus," he said again, "do not ask questions and do as you're told. I'm the leader, and the most you have to do is follow me," he said without lifting his eyes away from his task.

Ezekiola shook his head in disbelief. His friend was barely paying attention to anything he said, and his cocky attitude was starting to get on his nerves. He thought it was time he stopped being nice and instead be blunt about Hercules' hygiene issues, which were wreaking havoc with his senses.

"Sure, I'll follow you. On the condition you stop farting every other minute since we started and keep that gas in. There's a limit to how much of your stench my nostrils can stand, you know."

"What?! You think I didn't smell it all this time? It wasn't me! Everyone knows that the first to put the blame on others for farting is the one who did it," Nohlan said, defying his friend's accusations.

"It wasn't me. It's your Mr. Vulcan's biscuits coming out," Ezekiola replied, "you always have problems digesting those, but you usually have the decency to walk away and distance yourself before you let loose. Apparently, you're not so courteous today."

"What biscuits? I never had any biscuits!" Nohlan couldn't even remember his real name, let alone any of his many morning snacks. "Why don't you, for once, admit it was you?" he countered.

"Because it wasn't me, stupid! And even if I admitted it, it won't make that horrendous smell go away. In fact, it's getting worse because it seems to be coming out of your mouth too!" Ezekiola shouted.

Suddenly, the sky above them grew dark as a swarm of bees hovered over them. Ezekiola took a careful look, and a tingly feeling overcame him. The heaviness in the air was unmistakable. He recognized the colorful bunch at once, these miniature chameleons heading their way: Furies! They dove down, reaching them instantly, and began circling the two right when Nohlan exclaimed, "Say that one more time, and I'm blasting your rear end off with this plant! I swear I'll free you from smelling anything ever again!"

"What did you just tell me?!" Ezekiola replied, aghast. Under the effects of the simulation, the two friends were reacting much differently than they normally would have. The Furies started doing what they did best, which was to make their prey's anger escalate, circling each of them, almost whispering inside their heads: *push him hard; he deserves it! How dare he; he's the foul beast!*

Ezekiola pushed Nohlan and said: "You dare do that, and it won't be one of the Hydra's heads rolling on the ground but yours!"

Nohlan pushed him back, and the two fell, rolling down on the ground, fighting. The Furies' presence made the voices get louder inside their heads: *Kick him! Punch him! Break his bones! Kill him!*

The two were so engulfed in their aggressive emotions they didn't realize which swamp they had landed in. They kept going at each other when an earsplitting shriek was heard. They both clamped their ears and stopped fighting.

"What was that?" Ezekiola asked.

Nohlan stood upright, drenched in mud. He looked closely at something disturbingly gooey in the swamp they were in.

"I don't know what it is, but I don't think it's good," he said.

A few feet away, they spotted a distinct slithering movement.

"What's that in the water?" Ezekiola stood frozen.

"I don't know," Nohlan whispered. In the silence that followed, what looked like a jittery tentacle splashed in and out of the muddy water, jerking the two intruders out of their frozen stupor. Nohlan and Ezekiola finally realized they had landed in the very pit where the Hydra dwelt.

Discreetly finding the beast after careful planning was one thing. But falling on it by accident somehow intensified the way it would have otherwise reacted. The untimely discovery of the serpent threw the simulation into disarray. The Hydra simultaneously activated all of its vicious defense mechanisms instead of taking the time to assess the threat. This included kicking her fowl stench up a notch, which almost made Ezekiola and Nohlan faint.

"Eww! Give me a shirt, something!" Ezekiola said as he held his hand to his nose, nauseous. His senses were taking a serious beating, and he didn't even have a shirt to cover his nostrils.

Not wanting to risk a breath to answer him, Nohlan simply shook his head, holding his own shirt over his nose. But he couldn't resist: "I told you it wasn't me farting; do you believe me now?!"

The grounds suddenly shifted. Their knees sank in deeper. Clearly, a mud bath had suddenly been added to their ordeal. They were about to take a swim in a stinky, rotting death swamp. Panicking, they tried to exit the swamp, shoving one another in the process.

"Stop pulling me back!" Nohlan said, right about when another deafening roar resounded from one of the horrific heads.

"It's not me!" Ezekiola yelled, half-petrified.

The serpent's slithering legs slapped Nohlan square in the face as it retracted into its shelter. Its gruesome tentacles had been disturbed by the boys' sudden arrival in its muddy domain.

"What are we supposed to do now?" Ezekiola asked.

"We have to kill it! You go first!" Nohlan told his friend.

"You're Hercules. Not me! You go first, you coward!" Ezekiola replied.

Without further thought, Nohlan took out one of the Lone shrubs from his satchel, made a ball with it, and with great precision, threw it into one of the beast's numerous mouths.

The head it belonged to swallowed it whole in just one bite and only partially exploded. Nohlan jumped up impressively, using only his right leg, and sliced off what remained of the head.

"See how easy this is!" He proudly exclaimed. But just then, two more heads grew where there was once only one. At the sight of this, he immediately scurried back behind his friend, using him as a shield.

"You just made it worse!" Ezekiola said. He was about to continue his ranting when a sudden distant memory came back to him. It had something to do with the heads growing twice when they were simply chopped off.

"I think we have it backward. Slice the head first, then burn the neck with fire so another two won't grow back. Try again!"

Nohlan tried again, but the Hydra had figured out what his next step would be. Like the cunning creature it was, it used its head to lure Nohlan deeper into its pit, and he fell right into the trap. His momentum slowed down to a turtle's pace as his legs sunk further into the muddy hole. Nohlan was stuck.

"I can't move! Help!" he yelled. Ezekiola had barely taken two steps into the muddy swamp when one of the Hydra's legs coiled around Nohlan's body, getting ready to feast on him. Luckily for him, Nohlan remembered what to do and screamed at the top of his legendary lungs: "ABORT!" Just like that, he exited the simulation.

Ezekiola now stood alone with just his sword and three leaves in hand. He thought for a moment about also aborting, considering the hero was gone. But apparently, this simulation was still going on since both the Hydra and himself were still alive. He had to figure out a way to outsmart this beast, for it was obviously smarter than he had first thought. So, he did what he thought was the right thing to do in these circumstances. He took his sword and his bravery and headed out to face the Hydra.

He had but three leaves and told himself there had to be a way to kill a few heads in a single blow. A thought then surfaced from the deep corners of his mind: there was another, more intelligent way to kill the beast besides chopping its heads off. But with no time to think about it, he relied on the same method his friend had used. He climbed up on a large rock and lured the beast towards him.

Just as the Hydra slid closer, Ezekiola jumped onto its upper back and severed three heads at once with his sword. The Hydra screeched in pain, then violently struck Ezekiola, who went flying into the air. Ezekiola fell hard on the ground, then struggled to stand up, slipping repeatedly in the slimy mud. Just when he thought he had regained his balance, the gigantic three heads he had just chopped off came tumbling down next to him, throwing him off balance again. He looked up and saw six new heads grow out of the very necks from which he had severed them. Ezekiola realized he had repeated the same mistake as Nohlan. In the deep recesses of his mind, he sensed once again that simply slicing the heads was not the way to conquer the beast, that there was another way to do it. But again, he was not afforded the time to think about it as the beast plunged at him, this time more viciously. Ezekiola resorted to slicing the heads one by one as fast as he could. It wasn't long before the Hydra's heads multiplied at a frightening speed, transforming it into an even more terrifying monster. Refusing to simply give up, Ezekiola kept chopping frantically at every single head that came at him, this time with an uncontrollable rage. It seemed as if he was fueling the beast with his own anger, which only made the situation worse. What he saw before him now was a nightmare, a horrifying scene filled with grotesque heads and open mouths all snapping at him. It was a question of time before he succumbed to the Hydra. When his sword was finally snatched away from him by the beast,

Ezekiola looked up to see more than a hundred furious heads coming at him for an easy kill. His only way out now was to say ABORT.

But just as he was about to pronounce the word, he heard a soft-spoken voice. Images flashed in his mind of a girl with a locket around her neck. He recognized her. *Leanne. What is she doing in my head?* Before he could answer his own question, images started flowing in the back of his mind at a pace he couldn't keep up with. He ceased trying to think, and suddenly, a single image became clear, shining ever so brightly. Ezekiola suddenly knew how to conquer the beast. Just then, he felt as though an outside power was running high-density voltage through him, and to his astonishment, his body took on a life of its own as if it had fused with a strange element that willed its way through him. The powerful charge that was whirling through him felt reminiscent of the energy he had felt when he had passed through the magnetic doors during his encounter with Leanne. Fueled by this force, Ezekiola went down on his hands and knees, fearlessly burying himself deeper into the mud in search of the Hydra's legs. In no time, he found the creature's slippery legs and grabbed them. Out of the filthy mud, using the last of his strength, he lifted the beast high in the air forcing the Hydra's heads out from the protection of the trees and directly into the sunlight. To his amazement, all heads vanished at once. A single tiny little head the size of an apple emerged from the neck, then fell off and came rolling down to his feet.

Ezekiola's surroundings drastically changed suddenly. He was now standing on a rock in front of a sunny field with mature trees and blossoming flowers. No longer was the ground mushy. He picked up the little dragon-like head that had fallen next to him and held it in the palm of his hand. It was alive and moving, but not menacing in the least. He stared at it, mesmerized, and wondered what to do with it. Somehow, though, he knew this head, too, could multiply if he allowed it and develop into the furious beast he had just conquered. Could it be that he had the power to control the Hydra but also turn it back into a fierce beast through his own lack of self-mastery? He was ruminating over what to do with the little head when he felt his body being violently snatched away, along with a voice he knew all too well. "Impossible!" he heard Balthazar say.

The Hydra simulation had come to an abrupt end when his teacher had stopped it preemptively. Ezekiola landed on the floor of the dome with a hard thump while the shell of Lolaus returned to its original floating position high above them. Ezekiola was dazed, but his classmates were electrified. They were beyond excitement recounting the way he had conquered the beast, something they had never before witnessed. Their state, however, did not match that of Professor Balthazar, who was unusually quiet, looking rather stunned. It was the calm before the storm.

"Class is exceptionally over for today. The rest of you students will run this simulation next week," he quickly wrapped up like he had some urgent business to run off to.

The professor had only one thought in mind: to speak to Headmaster Nomi immediately.

Chapter 9

The Strange Boy

"Where are you guys? I've been waiting here for half an hour, and the hostess is about to give our table away!" Andy was on the phone, pacing back and forth in the small, enclosed patio space outside The Bunkers' Inn, a Chester Town restaurant known for its lively spirit.

"We're almost there," said Leanne on the other end, casting a guilty look at her friend Bessie, who was driving. Bessie had still been showering when Leanne had shown up at her house half an hour ago.

"I wouldn't have come had I known you guys were going to be this late. I can't even sit at a table because the hostess refuses to seat people without majority show."

"Why can't you go to the bar instead?" Leanne suggested.

"Really? As in—by myself?" Andy was ever so mindful of never doing anything alone, especially at mealtime.

"Alright, alright, we'll be there in a few minutes. We can't go any faster."

"Well, be here soon. Otherwise, I'm leaving!"

Andy hung up and went back indoors to continue waiting in her hut-like corner amongst a particularly agitated crowd. There was some sort of pandemonium going on in the restaurant. She didn't mention anything to her friends, not knowing exactly what it was. She faintly heard a few customers complain about the room temperature. That probably explained why several people were standing outside taking some fresh air, or rather, cooling off. She was hot herself but thought it was because she had been standing and waiting for so long. No one could ignore the number of sweaty busboys rushing in and out of the restaurant, some carrying large amounts of ice bags through the side door. Whatever it was, it was probably some kind of electrical or water issue, she reckoned. No big deal. Regardless, having waited this long, leaving was out of the question.

Fifteen minutes later, Leanne and Bessie dashed onto the front porch as if on a life-or-death sprint to catch a departing train.

"Why are there so many people outside? Is there a special event tonight?" asked Leanne.

"When don't they have special events here? This place is always jam-packed for some reason," said Bessie. She then opened the restaurant door and was propelled backward by a powerful heatwave with the capacity to dry her wet hair in no time.

"Wow! What's up with this place?"

"The temperature is what's up." Andy swooped down onto her friends like a hawk snatching its prey. "You're finally here! Let's go sit. I'm starving!"

As they made their way in, the hostess greeted them and led them to a table.

Leanne scanned the restaurant to see what the crowd was

like. People had stripped off several layers of clothing while still remaining more or less decent. Despite the heat, the restaurant was incredibly rowdy. The hostess distributed the menus and took off.

"How come it's so darn hot in here? It's not usually this bad," said Bessie, removing her jacket and scarf.

"You better get used to it. It's been like this since I got here, and it's getting worse," Andy said.

Several minutes passed, and no waitress showed up. "Excuse me, miss!" Andy called out to one who was passing by, "Could we get some water, please?"

The waitress acted like she hadn't heard.

The girls sighed. "I'm going to the ladies' room; I'll be back," said Leanne, feeling the urgent need to do something about the sweat dripping down her back. She had unsuccessfully tried controlling the rise in her body temperature from the moment they had walked in.

Just then, Andy's eyes focused on something worth seeing further in the restaurant. "Don't look now, but there's a really cute guy at ten o'clock," she said. Like a night owl, Bessie rotated her head in every direction but the right one.

"Where are you looking? I said ten o'clock."

"Your ten or my ten?" Bessie was confused.

"Oh, just forget it!"

"Well, if you gave proper cardinal directions, I would find it." Bessie sighed. "Sorry, I think this heat is starting to get to me. I'm really dehydrated," she said.

"That's why we need water now," Andy said, looking around for their waitress, but she was nowhere to be seen.

Leanne came back from her bathroom break rather quickly. "It's a sauna in there. I couldn't go in."

"The waitress hasn't come since you left," Andy said, annoyed.

"Well then, anyone want anything? I'm going to the bar," said Leanne.

"Yes, please! Make your trip worthwhile. Get us as much water as you can carry and some drinks to last us the whole evening." Andy said.

Leanne headed to the bar and sidled towards the less crowded end. After a few minutes of waiting, she finally made eye contact with the barman, but he asked her to wait a moment. While she did, she cast a quick look around and spotted three young fellows sitting quietly not too far from her. The one in the center caught her attention. They looked too calm for the energy level of the place and were dressed rather out of style but still decently enough to blend in with the crowd. She found it odd that none of them had removed their jacket in this sweltering heat. They were slowly sipping their drinks in silence. There was something strange about them. She turned to watch the waiter rushing away with orders coming in from everywhere. He was extremely nervous, the sweat pouring down his forehead.

"I need more ice. The type that's frozen!" he yelled at the staff.

"But I just brought you a bag," answered one of the busboys.

"You call this ice?!" he pointed towards the sink, where a few paltry ice cubes floated in the water. Leanne looked away so as not to appear as if she was eavesdropping. Her eyes fell on the three guys again, but this time she locked her gaze with the one in the middle. He had been staring at her.

"Can you pass me some napkins, please, Miss?" he asked with a heavy accent.

Leanne froze, surprised by his striking resemblance to Ezekiola, the boy she had met and couldn't get out of her mind. It mesmerized her how she could meet two people who looked so much alike in such a short lapse of time. His eyes were different, though, like two inquisitive yet glittering black jewels. Despite feeling intimidated, she worked up the will to rouse herself out of the daze that seemed to befall her.

"Sure," she answered quickly so as not to give in to the effect he had on her and concentrated on grabbing a few napkins. As strange as he seemed, there was a wicked charm about him she felt she needed to guard herself against. With his accent and look, he was definitely not from her part of town. She leaned over in an effort to hand him the napkins. As she did so, her locket swung out of her blouse, delicately swaying back and forth. His gaze shifted to it.

"That's a beautiful necklace," he said.

"Thank you," she answered.

"Was it a gift?" he asked.

"No. I bought it myself."

He acknowledged this with a head gesture.

The barman interrupted them to take her order. While waiting for her drinks in her tight corner, she started sweating profusely. The heat was unbearable. She could have sworn it had risen by a few degrees despite the fact that she was standing in the least crowded area of the bar. She took hold of a few napkins and began fanning herself, unsure if it was to get the air circulating around her or to divert his stare.

"Are you hot?" he spoke again, smiling this time as if the obvious was not that obvious.

"Yes. I'm hot," she said. "It's like the sun's beating down on us in here."

"Oh, but it is," he said matter-of-factly. Leanne found that an odd thing to say, considering that he and his two stooges seemed unaffected by the heat; it piqued her curiosity. Why had none of them taken their jackets off?

"There are times when the sun should stay behind clouds

and not stir up chaos," he said in a somber tone. His fingers were fiddling with the cup of fresh ice that the waiter had just served him. Suddenly, the ice started melting at an unnatural speed. Leanne looked at him suspiciously for the first time. He was writing something on the napkin. She thought maybe he was writing down his name and number, but that wasn't quite it. Rather, it looked like he was drawing.

After a moment's reflection, she couldn't hold it in.

"Strange you would say that because, really, the clouds get in the way of the sun and not the other way around."

"A witty answer for a woman your age," he said without looking at her. He spoke as if he was much older, yet he looked not much older than Leanne.

"It's just logic, really," she replied, curious as to where he was going with this.

He looked up and directly at her this time. "You are correct," he smiled. "It's safer to stay within the confines of logic and not venture outside. Remember that," he said, making it sound like a warning.

She didn't reply at first, but the feeling that she was expected to not answer back bugged her. This was by far the most bizarre conversation she had ever had with a stranger. What an odd fellow he was.

"Why wouldn't it be alright to venture off sometimes?" she asked.

"The unknown is not a safe place. Heading into it can lead to disaster," he replied. She stared at him blankly, unwilling to continue a conversation like that. Her beverages could not have come at a better time. She happily took them and left without saying another word. She had barely taken a few steps when she felt something slip off of her.

"Your necklace fell," he said from afar. His voice held a mocking tone. She stopped and looked down in disbelief. Her locket lay split in half on the floor, exposing the paper with Ezekiola's name on it.

Since her hands were full, she saw him step down from his stool and walk over to pick it up. Standing tall the way he did, he seemed to draw attention from all around. She was right about him. He exuded a certain magnetism, and she wasn't the only one picking up on it. Others stared at him too. He slowly came over, closing the gap between them. He had the fierce commanding stare of an intruder approaching the thing he was looking for. Leanne was spellbound. Whether it was the conversation, the necklace falling, or his proximity, she couldn't tell. He bent to retrieve the locket and piece of paper off the floor, paused a moment longer to observe her, then came very near.

"A word of advice from someone who only seeks your safety. Don't wear this necklace," he said, close enough to whisper in her ear: "nor what's in it." Smoke suddenly rose from the hand which held the little paper. A moment later, the paper with Ezekiola's name on it had been reduced to ashes sprinkled on the floor. Leanne felt nauseous and thought she was going to faint. With her two hands busy, he took the liberty of slipping her broken necklace into the side pocket of her pants. She stood mute, barely hearing anything else except her breath mixed with the drumbeat of her heart. The sound of the crowd in the background had long seemed muffled to her. It took a loud bang to snap her out of that moment. A table had literally been turned over, and a fight had broken out not too far from where they were standing.

"Thanks, but I can decide that myself," she said defiantly and spun around to get back to her table as quickly as possible. His voice trailed behind her.

"My pleasure, Leanne."

There was something dreadful about him pronouncing her

name. Then it dawned on her; she had never told it to him. For an instant, she wanted to turn around and confront him, but she dared not do it in fear it would spark some kind of connection again. She could feel that he was still standing in the same spot, waiting. Considering her tray full of drinks, she carried herself resolutely towards the table where her two friends were waiting. She could still sense his eyes on her back. Who is he? How did he know her name? She suspected he knew more about her than he should. Why make such veiled comments about the sun, then stick to logic? How did the necklace come to fall off at that very moment? And what did he do to Ezekiola's name? Her mind was running wild. All of a sudden, Leanne felt the urge to leave the restaurant.

"Leanne!"

She finally turned her attention to her table.

"Look. The waitress finally showed up and got us drinks on the house because of the chaos in here," said Andy.

"I think we should leave."

"What? Why?" asked Bessie. "We haven't even ordered yet."

"Something is off with this place tonight."

As it turned out, the hostess went from table to table to let the patrons know that they were having electrical problems and the kitchen stoves were not working. Pandemonium ensued, with glasses shattering on the floor and hungry customers shouting angrily.

Frustrated, the girls packed up and left. Before exiting, Leanne cast one last look at the bar to see if the strange trio was still there. The three chairs where they had sat were empty. She quickly scanned the restaurant but didn't see any of them. She reckoned that they had left. She felt like a stalker keeping track of the whereabouts of strangers, but at the same time, she couldn't help feeling invisible eyes on her.

When Leanne got home and slipped into her pajamas that night, she rummaged through the pocket of her pants to remove the broken necklace. As she retrieved it, a tissue came out with it. She was about to toss it back when she saw the writing on it. She gasped. It was the restaurant napkin, the one she had handed him. He had managed to slip it in her pocket along with the locket. There were drawings of stars on it, as well as a weird shape she couldn't make sense of. It looked like a triangle. Beneath it was a signature, 'Zeke.' It sounded like a diminutive of Ezekiola. That must have been his name, she figured. And they looked frighteningly alike. Strange boy. Where did he come from? She replayed in her mind what he had done to the paper with Ezekiola's name. She looked back at the napkin and got the feeling Zeke wanted her to have his name instead. In sheer frustration, she shred it to pieces and swore to herself she would get her broken locket fixed, then put Ezekiola's name back in there again. Somehow, Zeke's attempt at depriving her of something had made her even more resolute.

She went to bed but couldn't sleep. The napkin boy, the star drawings, and those black eyes kept flashing in her mind as if she had studied them for hours. And no matter how hard she tried to switch her thoughts to Ezekiola, they kept reverting back to Zeke. At some point, she felt as if he was right there in her bedroom next to her. She tossed and turned most of the night, and it was only in the wee hours of the morning that she finally fell asleep, drifting into a disenchanted dreamland.

Chapter 10

Divining Session

The cafeteria located in the South Wing of Cypress School was packed with rowdy kids as if it were their first day back in school. Here, word got around about the feats of the week and who had performed what, especially during simulation classes. If it was spectacular enough, it would catch the attention of the Brown Robes, whose sole mission was to uncover nature's mysteries or, more precisely, to hunt down any student playing with the elements of nature in an unnatural way. And that's exactly why Borghis, a Brown Robe, thought it propitious to pay a visit to his little brother Nohlan that day. He knew how rare it was for a White Tunic to accomplish such an exceptional feat as had occurred during the Hydra simulation. There was something fishy about the whole thing. His friend Keenan, another Brown Robe, was also under the impression that something irregular had happened. For them, enigmas such as this one begged to be unraveled.

And as luck would have it for Borghis, his brother Nohlan had been involved. He was also the ideal candidate from whom to extract information. With no filter to his mouth whatsoever, answers flowed out of it like water from a fountain. Borghis still had to be careful, though, as his little brother could sometimes be mischievous. And then there were those friends of his he had to be wary of. Ezekiola and his mind-reading skill, and the very witty and deviant Atlas, who was able to stir other people's emotions by his mere choice of words. But Nohlan happened to be alone that day, having lunch quietly at his favorite table. He looked utterly content as he ate his usual hearty meal of peas, carrots, mashed potatoes, and steak. It was a most opportune time.

"Nohlan!" Borghis slapped his brother hard on the back, making his food shoot out of his mouth. "How is my little brother doing today amidst all the unusual things happening lately?"

Nohlan coughed out loud, and a few bits of peas dropped back onto his plate. He looked up at his lunch intruders. His brother and friend standing tall next to him contrasted heavily with the cafeteria background. Borghis especially, who with his impressive build attracted lots of attention, did not blend in the least bit with the crowd.

"What are you talking about?" replied Nohlan briskly. Annoyed at being interrupted, he took a bite out of his bread, swallowing it half-chewed, then took a gulp of his water to soothe his agonizing throat. Stopping the consumption of a meal was for emergency situations only.

"Something you would like to share with us?" Borghis asked to fire up the conversation. He cast a curious glance at what Nohlan was eating. Nohlan looked worried for a moment, and he glanced down at his food.

"You want to share my meal?" he asked, staring wide-eyed at his brother.

Borghis laughed. "Don't worry, little brother, you can eat all the food you want. That's not quite what I had in mind." Keenan chuckled at his remark.

Nohlan was relieved. "What then? Is Orgali in trouble again?" he asked, taking another big chomp of the food off his plate. Lately, their little sister had started taking after Nohlan a bit too much and getting into trouble.

"Orgali's fine. I'm thinking more of your Hydra simulation last week," he said.

Borghis was never sure how naïve his brother was or how much of it was a willful act of playing dumb. Nohlan always managed to confuse him, and with time, Borghis had become wary when dealing with his brother.

"What about the simulation?" Nohlan asked, "Professor Balthazar made me go first, that's all."

"That's all? Nothing out of the ordinary happened during the trial?"

"No."

"Like at the end, for instance?" Borghis hinted.

"No. I aborted before that slimy beast got the better of me," he replied smugly as if he had conquered the beast instead of bailing out prematurely.

"And what about after that?" Borghis pressed him further, losing patience. He was walking on a fine line, for he had to maintain his cool if he wanted truthful answers to flow out of his brother's mouth. Anger him, and it would sabotage his whole enterprise, as had so often happened in the past.

"Nothing," Nohlan answered plainly.

Borghis realized that his brother was genuinely naïve on this particular occasion. Keenan decided to intervene and took over, changing their line of questioning. "Were you flying solo in this simulation, Nohlan?" he asked.

"No, I had Lolaus."

"And did you get to pick a friend to act as Lolaus?" Keenan asked more carefully.

"Yes, it was Ezekiola," he replied. Ha! They had finally validated one of the points on their checklist.

"What's the big deal, anyway?" asked Nohlan, wolfing down a lump of mashed potatoes. He had already begun eyeing Mr. Vulcan's biscuits conveniently piled next to his plate to serve as his after-meal dessert.

"Well, what happened to him?" asked Borghis. His brother never seemed to get to the point.

"He aborted too like we all do in the end," Nohlan put his fork down and, with his mouth full, continued to speak. "Borghis, perhaps you've forgotten how these simulations work since you don't do them anymore at your level. It's also been a while since your last one, and I'm sure you didn't have as many as we do now, but most of the time, everybody aborts at the end," he proudly lectured his older brother.

Borghis and Keenan looked at Nohlan in disbelief. Borghis had to force himself to keep a straight face, unable to understand how his brother had even graduated to a Brown Belt with his low level of knowledge. At the Brown Robe level, the projects they had to do went way beyond simple simulations such as the ones they had in their beginning years.

"You're right, Nohlan. I haven't done them in a while." He faked a smile. "Would you like to tell us the story of how Lolaus aborted?" he asked.

Nohlan's face lit up as he remembered what he had witnessed on the podium after he had aborted as Hercules. He put his fork down as he readied himself to share his story. Borghis and Keenan huddled closer to Nohlan in order not to miss anything.

"Well, after I aborted, I think I saw Zek first throw a rock at one of the heads, which made the beast scream in anger."

He imitated the beast turning its heads left and right while making the gruesome sound: "Aaaaargh!"

This was not the part Borghis wanted to hear, but he continued to listen patiently.

"He then jumped on the Hydra and sliced three heads on his own. But then after, umm... something else happened." Nohlan stopped short. He went for another slice of his steak, immediately prompting another question.

"What happened?" Borghis asked impatiently.

"Everything happened at once... oh, I can't remember exactly," Nohlan said.

"What do you mean you can't remember?!"

"I think it was his sword, but then it got snatched away."

"What happened to the sword, Nohlan?" Keenan asked.

"Well, we couldn't even see it. It was blinding. Maybe it was him, not the sword. He almost disappeared at some point. Oh, I'm not sure. It's as if something...."

A loud thud resonated as Atlas dropped his heavy school bag in the center of the table, making everyone jump.

"Well, well, seems we have company today!" he exclaimed with delight. "Has a squadron of fawns decided to give us a visit?" he asked.

"Good mid-day to you, Atlas. You could be a little more discreet when you greet people," Borghis said, annoyed.

"We're in a cafeteria, not a library. Why would I be discreet? Especially when we can't even hear each other speak because there are so many of you in here."

Borghis and Keenan gave each other a disheartened look. They had lost their momentum. Sensing he had interrupted something, Atlas continued: "And for a moment there, I thought the cafeteria was having a vermin problem, with so many brown things hanging around."

Since the beginning of school, Atlas hadn't been on the

Brown Robes' good side. Having received red detention notes from them, Atlas now amused himself by defying their authority.

"We were just saying what an unusual week it's been for the star of your class," Keenan said. Atlas was just about to take the first bite of his sandwich. He stopped halfway as he realized why Borghis was visiting his brother.

"Where is he now, anyway?" asked Borghis. The fact that he had noted Ezekiola's absence made Atlas even more suspicious.

"What's it to you, Borghis? Have they assigned you the common task of supervising the cafeteria today? Have you been demoted again?" he asked.

"Watch your mouth, Atlas!" Borghis replied, pointing a finger in his face. "Haven't you been taught to show respect towards your superiors? Of course, we can't expect much from anyone being held on a short leash by the School Council for multiple forms of disrespect," he continued. "And to answer your stupid question, no, luckily for you, we haven't been assigned that task this week."

"Well, if you're not a supervisor today, then we don't have to answer unusual questions from your battalion of commoners," he barked back. "Now, if you don't mind, we have more important things to attend to." He looked back at his sandwich and waited for the Brown Robes to leave before taking a bite.

Borghis and Keenan took their leave, unhappy with the abrupt way in which their conversation with Nohlan had ended. In fact, Borghis was fuming at being interrupted by Atlas.

"Get something—anything—on that godless oaf!" he said to Keenan. "Something bad enough to get him suspended this time."

Atlas, in the meantime, started happily eating his sandwich

when he realized he would have to lie low and be on his best behavior for at least a week now. It gave him just the right incentive to find a way to get back at them for those red notes. He then forced himself to get back to the more important matter at hand. He needed to warn Ezekiola of what was going on. Whenever Atlas felt something was off with him, he usually waited for his friend to come forward on his own instead of probing into his life. But he was now beginning to harbor doubts. He turned to Nohlan and asked the question that was twirling around in his mind: "Where's Zek, anyway? It's not like him to miss three lunches in a row."

Chapter 11

Fusion

Nomi had been tending his garden peacefully that afternoon in his glasshouse, repotting his overgrown plants into their new habitats, when Balthazar arrived with a special memorandum clutched in his fist, requesting authorization to conduct an inquiry on a student's misconduct.

"A misconduct? On Ezekiola's part?" Nomi repeated the words on the special memorandum as if he was stuck on a word he did not understand. Balthazar felt an odd sense of satisfaction, knowing that, for once, he had caught on to something earlier than his superior comrade.

"That's right!" he responded. Like an agitated cat, he was unable to stand still and had been pacing back and forth. He recounted to Nomi with much detail Ezekiola's surreal performance during his simulation class and the almost nonexistent probabilities of such a victory on a first attempt. Nomi listened carefully, staring into the distance. He was trying to make sense of this account. He had wondered why Ezekiola had not come to see him yet about his Emerald Belt. Could it be that he had discovered something already? Yet Nomi could not probe too much. He remembered very well the instructions he had received from the High Council. He was not to interfere in any way and instead let the belt guide the way.

"But why would you want to open an inquiry? What did he do wrong?" Nomi asked.

"For Ezekiola to have succeeded in conquering the beast on his first trial, he must have meddled with something unworldly, perhaps even experimented with forbidden powers. I'm almost certain of it!" Balthazar concluded, with a distinct look of fanaticism perceptible in his wandering eyes.

Nomi was half expecting to hear something out of the ordinary concerning Ezekiola, but not so soon. He had much pressure on his own shoulders to report to the High Council everything that happened indicative of linking. When Emeralds linked successfully, they tapped into the Fountain of Fire, a tremendous source of power in itself, and there were always signs when that happened. The extraordinary feats Emeralds were able to accomplish was one of them. But linking during a simulation class in a simulated environment seemed unreal to Nomi. How could this occurrence be related? It didn't make any sense. Regardless, linking with the Fountain of Fire this fast was not possible. He was expecting much more time to pass and for Ezekiola to start his training lessons with actual Emeralds before such an event could occur.

"Perhaps there was a glitch in the system?" Nomi challenged. He didn't want to report an incident to the High Council, which they might deem insignificant.

"No, I assure you, I saw what I saw in a system that I built and calculated diligently. And this phenomenon was witnessed by all the other students, though they did not understand the nature of what they saw. Most students at his level revert to slicing off the heads, and on average, students need to go several rounds into the Hydra simulation to succeed in getting one head. After years and years of trials, students who are on the cusp of graduating to a robe level finally figure out how to conquer the beast by lifting it in the air and exposing it to the rays of the sun. It's a metaphor, really, to learn how to raise the lower aspects of one's self to the surface, exposing them to the light of wisdom. Ezekiola figured this out on his first try! Getting this far, this fast, is unheard of, especially for a White Tunic!" Nomi nodded, fearfully suspecting the very thing he was trying to evade.

"Well, as you know, Ezekiola is a gifted mind reader. Perhaps he read the mind of the beast," Nomi suggested.

"Oh, this is past being gifted. This is a rare portrayal of potency that requires something much more than just being gifted." Balthazar punctuated his statement by raising his index finger in the air. "The magnitude recorded was the highest I have ever seen for his level."

"So, this could be a first for an Emerald Belt then," Nomi concurred casually while mentally preparing himself for what was to come.

"Yes, but that is not the only thing that bothers me. There's something else," Balthazar paused and looked into the vine groves forming Nomi's garden. For a moment, he looked as if he was marveling at nature's beauty, but it was actually what was on his mind that engaged him so. His fingers fidgeted continuously as if he was playing some invisible instrument.

"After the trial, I replayed his dual many times on the Herculean hologram and saw his face light up right before he was about to abort as if something had caught his attention. I looked around the simulated landscape to see if there was anything, as sometimes Furies, changelings, and other creatures pop up. But there was nothing. And that's when he went down on his knees, plunged his arms and chest into the mud, actually dove into that filth, and lifted the beast effortlessly." The professor's gaze was focused as if the whole incident was replaying before his eyes in the distance.

"And what do you think he meddled with?" Nomi asked, interrupting Balthazar's apparent vision. He was anxious to know if Balthazar would guess the unimaginable. It was crucial, however, that Nomi keep this as private as possible, for he had been sworn to secrecy.

"I don't know, but I intend to find out, and that's why I came to see you."

"Come, let's go for a walk then," Nomi suggested, guiding him towards the outside gardens. Instead of remaining indoors, Nomi preferred to take walks, for walking and talking went hand in hand for him, keeping his body busy so his mind could contemplate in peace.

The two men strolled quietly at first until Balthazar finally broke the silence.

"How much can you tell me about Ezekiola's abilities?" he asked.

"Well, for one, he reads minds, as you know, but he's always done that. So that's not anything novel. He is excellent at guarding his thoughts as well, which is why none of us are able to pick up on them. If something was percolating in his mind, know this: he is a master shielder."

"A master shielder at seventeen, hmmm," Balthazar scoffed, playing around with these words, unsure of how to deal with them.

"Seventeen, yes, but don't be fooled. He has quite an agile mind. I would even go as far as saying he has far more age to him than several students combined."

"And that Emerald Belt of his, does it give him additional potency in any way?"

Nomi collected his thoughts for a moment before answering. He had to be sure not to say more than was necessary.

"Emerald Belts have greater freedom of movement as part of their training in traveling. They can actually exit Circa. Of course, they must first learn the theory part through various courses. This is a privilege of sorts to incite them to continue on the warrior's path. But I don't see how all this is tied to the simulation, Professor, especially since we are dealing with programmed forces," he said, hoping Balthazar would drop his suspicions.

"You see, I did not program any special abilities into his profile. He was enacting the part of Lolaus, after all; an accessory, really. That is the whole wonder of the situation; it almost looks as if he did it on his own, but I don't buy that either. I cannot conceive that, had he even mastered his level, that belt of his would enable him to leap into a power vortex, which is usually accessible only to highly trained Emerald Robes, who are much more advanced than a simple Emerald Belt. I am certain he merged with something, and I cannot put a finger on what just yet, but I intend to find out," he said resolutely.

Balthazar halted his stroll for a moment, then, with suspicion in his eyes, asked, "It almost makes me wonder if he hasn't secretly practiced other forms of arts, such as sounding the forbidden words in exchange for power."

"Ezekiola is not the felon of the universe that you want him to be, I assure you."

"Well, it could be a possibility, and I can't rule it out. It would certainly not be the first time some youngster becomes curious and tries something stupid we have to undo afterward," he insisted.

"He knows nothing of those words, Balthazar. In fact, if anyone knows anything about them, it's his friend, Nohlan. He learned a few basic ones in his Calling class last cycle, such as resuscitating small creatures into a balanced state of life. All of it is quite harmless, of course."

"Hmmm. So much for knowing words. That Brown-belted stoat was late for class again. I'm sure he didn't figure out the riddle. I don't know what he would do without those friends of his who save him every time."

"Have you thought of simply questioning Ezekiola about what happened?" Nomi asked, suggesting a quick fix to the matter.

"No, I won't do that. If he's up to something and I question him about it, then he might raise his guard further. On the contrary, I would rather make it look like it was a random occurrence and not give it too much attention so he doesn't think that I noticed anything out of the ordinary. If he's up to something, then, and if I'm right, he will undoubtedly continue. It's easier for me to track him and catch him in the act than to unravel what's in his head, especially considering his mind skills."

"I believe that is a wise way of going about it," Nomi agreed, humoring him. Balthazar paused. The two had walked the full square of Nomi's large garden and were now back at their starting point.

"I don't know what Ezekiola could possibly be up to, but we'll nonetheless keep an eye on him. I would not move forward with your student misconduct inquiry at this stage, for there is no wrongdoing on his part. I have discussion sessions scheduled with him. I'll see if he lets me in on some of his daily happenings. Often, by the sole nature of one's questions, much can be revealed," he said, comforting Balthazar.

Before letting him go, Nomi asked his colleague one last pressing question: "Have you spoken to anyone else about this?"

"No, I feared I might raise the wrong attention if I spoke to others prematurely."

"You did well. Keep it to yourself. Especially knowing that Ezekiola picks up on the thoughts of his teachers."

"True. Although there is one I might ask help from," Balthazar added.

Nomi appeared a little apprehensive.

"And who could that be?" he asked.

"Gerta."

"Oh yes, our librarian. I should have guessed. That's fine then. I doubt Ezekiola would suspect anything coming from her. Let's speak again soon to see what has unraveled."

Balthazar bid Nomi farewell but left with an unsettled mind. He thought he would have resolved more of this puzzle after discussing it with Nomi, not come away even more perplexed. He headed towards the library hall to find Gerta. On his way there, he couldn't help but notice the noise coming from the cafeteria. The kids must be very hungry, he thought, which was how it usually was on Fridays.

Chapter 12

Searching for Emeralds

Ezekiola acted as if nothing had happened, at least nothing unnatural or bizarre. In fact, he put great effort into making himself more sociable than usual to put any suspicion to rest. His efforts, however, only partially paid off. Some students merely gave him quizzical looks whenever they crossed him. Others, like Professor Balthazar, watched him like a hawk. Despite the added pressure, however, Ezekiola looked as calm as ever. But his mind was running wild.

He knew there was a connection between him and Leanne that had turned him into a savage beast during the Hydra simulation. He was now glad he had refrained from talking to Nomi about returning his Emerald Belt. He wanted first to find out what had happened to him when he had gone through that revolving door and then during the Hydra simulation when a simple flash thought of Leanne had infused him with an unfamiliar and most powerful energy. He had to know whether his belt had anything to do with it. *It won't hurt to hold on to it just a little longer,* he told himself. With that purpose in mind, he made maximum use of his free time by doing research in the library.

The library was enormous, with four large domes linked to a center square. Ezekiola was hoping to have a more productive library session than usual. But like every other day, he wasted half an hour ruminating before starting a real search. He walked from one dome to another, staring at the walls like he was in an art gallery. One wall was adorned with dictums. *Wrong questions lead to wrong answers*, was one of them. They had added that one after a student had virtually blocked an entire aisle with books, unsure about which one he needed. On the opposite wall were many drawings of mythical heroes overcoming all sorts of creatures. Ezekiola stood a moment longer, staring at his favorite one. It was of a hero holding a dragon's head high up in the air, a little like his conquest of the Hydra. Now he had a sense of how that felt. He was daydreaming about these mythical characters playing out their battles when he suddenly bumped into the librarian, Gerta Beck.

"What are you researching this time? You seem a little lost today strolling back and forth like this," she asked, looking him over carefully to see if he had a book in his hands.

Somehow, Ezekiola was creeped out by the way she observed him.

"I'm running errands for Nomi," he answered casually. He was annoyed at having to end his daydreaming so quickly because of her scrutiny.

"Really? Such as?" she asked, probing him further.

"He needs books on pottery," he lied.

"Pottery? That's strange. He's never made such a request to me in the past." Gerta's inquisitive nature was unusually strong today, Ezekiola noted.

"That's because he gets us White Tunics to do the job," he quipped. *What's up with her?* He wondered.

Gerta tilted her head sideways as she considered his answer.

"I'm sure you fancy that, running errands for the headmaster," she finally said. "Well, go on ahead now. Pottery is in the green aisle, next to the gardening section." Books were classified by color and theme and thus easy to find. Ezekiola now had to make a detour and add a search for a pottery book to what was supposed to be a productive session. Under her watchful gaze, he turned around and pretended to head towards the green aisle when a Gemin burst out of nowhere, scaring him.

"Watch where you're going!" the Gemin shouted at him. Ezekiola was stunned to be the one being scolded when it should have been the other way around. Those library Gemins could sometimes be insufferable. And lately, there were too many of them in the library. They had, in fact, become an outright disturbance, as they would suddenly pop up out of nowhere and then disappear, scaring the dickens out of anyone who happened to be quietly reading in the wrong aisle. Gemins working in the library were there to tend to the books, wiping them clean after they'd been used, dusting the shelves, and delivering parcels here and there. But as devoted to these tasks as they could be, they were a serious annoyance to the many users during the library's busier hours.

After grabbing a book on pottery in case Gerta was keeping tabs on him, Ezekiola finally began looking into books about belts and came across the master guide of them all: The Meridian Belts. Finally!

He pulled it off the shelf, sat down, and flipped quietly through the pages. His eyes scanned the words *Transitioning from grey to red ... grey to brown... grey to blue...* He went through the whole chapter and spotted the last paragraph: *from grey to emerald.* Like a devoted student, he read attentively.

"The transition from grey to emerald is a rare occurrence, for few choose the path of the warrior. Physical discomfort is reported upon initial wearing of the belt, its alleviation dependent solely upon the subject's capacity to adapt. Amongst the Meridian Belts, the emerald counts the highest in premature removals."

What?! *Premature removals?* There was no way Ezekiola would give it up. Even if it wasn't what he had expected, the last thing he would be able to handle was downgrading himself and remaining beltless until the School Council reassessed his situation.

He continued reading.

"The Emerald Belt allows for greater freedom of movement, with the added ability to explore different realms, in preparation for developing swift travel skills. A renowned bearer of the Emerald Belt was Meredus of Loggia. He had simultaneously developed his mind skills and the ways of the warrior, allowing him to infiltrate the minds of the Sons of the Night Sky and hunt several of their leaders down. Now in temporary retirement, it is believed he spends most of his time in the Limestone Mountains of Circa."

Meredus? Ezekiola had heard of that name before, but he couldn't recall when or where. Probably somewhere in Nomi's library, where he spent some time reading, he figured. He had heard of the Sons of the Night Sky as well, the last time being when he had visited the Brown Robe's lodge, but he had never studied them. Suddenly, he was looking forward to attending next semester's class on *Evils that can reign*. That is, if he held onto his Emerald Belt, for it was part of his beginners' training. Still, Meredus was an exception, and some believed him to be fiction altogether, for no one had ever seen him. The paragraph ended with a famous quote by Meredus: *'The belt shall bend to the will of the beholder.'* Ezekiola pondered on that for a while. *How could a belt bend to one's will? It's just a belt.*

As he skipped through several pages, there seemed to be nothing else written about the belt. In fact, the whole subject of the Emerald Belt and its owner's path was only referred to in vague terms. Perhaps that was intentional. The Emeralds attained such high levels of power that much of their knowledge could never be disclosed because of the dangers it could represent in the hands of untrained minds. He momentarily looked up from his book and saw Atlas nearby, staring at him.

"How long have you been standing there?" he asked, surprised.

"Long enough to watch you being way too absorbed in your lousy book to look up," Atlas replied.

"Are you stalking me?"

"Stalking? No. Simply taking pleasure in watching my friend becoming more and more of a recluse. I imagine you'll soon be joining our beloved Silence Keepers of Circa, keeping a vow of silence and spending all of your time reading," he said with a smile.

"Very funny," said Ezekiola.

Atlas dropped his bag next to the books scattered around Ezekiola and sat down.

"Well, let's see. You don't show up to our lunches anymore. You've been sporting that scary smile across your face that makes you look like you're possessed. You're sociable with everyone except your friends. And oh, we're being constantly interrogated about you."

"Interrogated? By whom?" he asked.

"Take a wild guess."

"Balthazar."

"No. Now why would you say Balthazar? Is he on your back, too? It's Borghis and his squadron of feisty know-it-alls. The Brown Robes have started an inquest."

He glanced at the open book in his friend's lap. "So, is this what you've been doing all along? Playing catch up with yourself. What do they say about Emerald Belts?" he asked before flipping some of the pages himself.

"Very little, actually."

"Really? And who's this?" Atlas asked as he saw a picture of someone in an Emerald Robe covering a full page in the book.

"It's Meredus of Loggia," Ezekiola answered. "It says here he took on both the Blue Robe and Emerald Robe at once, developing both his mind skills and the ways of the warrior."

They both examined the picture of Meredus quietly while Atlas read a little further.

The Meredus story was just a little too grandiose for Atlas to accept as real. "It's a myth. I don't believe it. It's too over-the-top to be true. They like to make up legends like this to motivate and recruit more students into the Emerald department," he reasoned. He flipped over the book to check the date. "See, it's from this year! They just upgraded this book. Cypress is not producing any Emeralds, and now they added the glamorous Meredus in there to attract students. He's not real. Don't buy into it, Zek."

"What? You can't be certain!" said Ezekiola. He seized the book back to stare at the picture of Meredus again and double-checked the date on the back of the book.

Atlas made a hushing sign to his friend as he saw two Brown Robes pass by. Luckily, they didn't turn into their row but instead into the one behind.

"I bet they're looking for you," he whispered, purposely teasing his friend.

They remained quiet so they could overhear the conversation taking place in the row behind theirs.

"Did you hear about the note?" asked one of the Brown Robes.

"I heard Balthazar requested a special meeting with Nomi."

"Do you think he'll be under inquiry?"

"For sure. He's up to something. They'll catch him soon enough. It would be nice, though, if we caught him before Balthazar does."

"He's in so much trouble!"

"That Emerald boy will have lots to answer."

"I heard that Borghis has a head start. That lucky falcon made inquiries before everyone else and apparently managed to get some answers."

"Really? What did he say?"

"He thinks that ..."

"Gmonin, godafta, ganaayt, I need this space here!" A library Gemin popped up where the Brown Robes were having their discussion, giving them a jolt.

"Is there no privacy here?" one of the Brown Robes burst out.

"Dis is my library, my job. Move!" the Gemin replied stubbornly.

Sighing in frustration, they put an end to their conversation and immediately left as the Gemin went about placing a book on one of the shelves.

"What's the matter with everyone? Are they seriously

holding meetings about me?" Ezekiola asked in shock, realizing the truth about his friend's comments.

"You tell me because so far you haven't told me a thing! And those Brown Robes are right. Borghis was actually inquiring about you to his own brother in the cafeteria. They're up to something. It leaves me no choice but to ask you: does all this have to do with what happened during the Hydra simulation?"

Ezekiola looked away, trying to avoid his friend's questioning stare, but he couldn't ignore his genuine concern.

"I think so. That's the only thing that makes sense."

"What do you think happened?" he asked.

"I don't know, Atlas. I'm trying to understand myself and how I did what I did. That's why I'm here, reading this, so maybe I can find out. I'm thinking it's the belt. Perhaps this is what happens when you choose the warrior's path. What else could it be?" he said, once again knowingly withholding information about meeting Leanne. He wasn't ready to share that yet.

"I'm not sure these books will tell you much. I thought Emeralds just got more freedom to do things. That's all. And I thought you said you were going to speak to Nomi about this mix-up with your belt. You were supposed to get the Blue Belt, not this green aberration!" Atlas said.

"I will. I just want to find the right time to speak to him," Ezekiola answered.

"Well, once you sort your problem out, everything will go back to normal, and this questioning frenzy will end," Atlas paused, suddenly remembering why he had come to the library in the first place.

"Alright, I have to get going. I have to find the most sublime book of all time before my next class: Boundaries of Logic."

"Oh! You should know I saw several of your red-belted peers in the library an hour ago," said Ezekiola.

"That's just great...." Atlas rolled his eyes, tossed his hair aside, and scurried away, knowing he'd have to fight his way to convince another Red Belt to share a book.

Suddenly, Ezekiola realized he, too, had to get going. Just before he closed the book, he recalled Atlas's words: "I thought Emeralds just got more freedom to do things."

He decided to take one last look to see if the book said anything about that. He quickly flipped through the pages and found what seemed like the next best thing in *Traveling on the Path of the Emerald Belt.*

"Although of rare occurrence, Emerald Belts may have access to Sporadic Doors, which come and go as part of Circa's orbiting movements. The notion of time varies for the one who has traveled through one of these doors."

A sudden thought about Sporadic Doors popped into his head. He thought he saw something when he was faking looking for a pottery book for Nomi. Maybe his detour had been a good thing after all. He headed to another section of the library and speedily took out a bunch of books. Ezekiola wondered if he should speak to Nomi that week about his belt but then hesitated again. He would purposely skip his meeting with him to gather more information. He was not ready to return the Emerald Belt just yet. He had too many questions buzzing in his mind that first needed answers.

On his way out, Gerta, the librarian, set Nova, her favorite Gemin, to send a parcel to Balthazar. In her commitment to keeping the professor informed, she wrote: "He took out almost half the books on Gemins." The information would leave Professor Balthazar more confused than ever.

Chapter 13

Strange Monday Mornings

For students at Chester High, nothing was more excruciatingly painful than sitting through an ecology class on a Monday morning. Today, however, promised to be more fun if such a thing could be said of that topic. It was the annual excursion. Unfortunately for some of the students, the field trip to a forest had been replaced by the exploration of Chester's schoolyard. There was untouched vegetation in the yard which served as a makeshift barrier between the well-manicured grounds of the school and the surrounding neighborhood.

Urda Vorsic, the ecology teacher, was about to take her class on a special journey; one that entailed the thorough examination of the very exciting life of a snail. There had been much rain the night before, and Urda was beside herself that morning as she guided her students outside, knowing that the snails would be out in platoon numbers. Some of the boys were also beside themselves, having a hell of a time jumping up and down in order to squash one snail after the other; their big challenge was to walk on as many snails as possible without ever stepping on snail-less ground. It didn't take long for Urda's ecstatic mood to change.

"I'm warning you, if I hear one more intentional crunching sound, you'll all start with a minus ten on today's report!" she threatened the class, scanning her students to find the culprits. She spotted Noah trying to hide his giggling.

"And that includes you too, Noah!"

"But we're not doing it on purpose, Miss," he retorted. "They're all over the place! It's impossible to avoid stepping on one."

"Noah, it's one thing if you're really trying to avoid them, but quite another if you're willfully squashing the poor things to smithereens!" she said. In truth, Noah had so far been one of the most active participants in the snail squashing competition. He kept quiet and continued walking, this time looking down in his first attempt at avoiding the tiny, viscous creatures.

"I can't believe this is the only thing she could come up with," said Leanne as she caught up with Andy. It had been a month since those strange happenings had occurred in her life. Meeting Ezekiola, even if only once, had brought her a high dose of excitement which had by now tapered down. Even though she had fixed her locket and put Ezekiola's name back in there, she had never seen him again. Neither had she seen that other strange boy, Zeke. Many times, however, she had wondered if maybe Zeke had done something to prevent her from seeing Ezekiola. Regardless, now it was slowly becoming a thing of the past, and a morning such as this one sucked what little motivation she had left right out of her.

"I know it's only snail-watching day, Leanne. You just have to pretend we're whale watching instead," Andy said, plodding along as if she was in a funeral procession.

"Why can't they just take us on actual trips, like going to a real forest for a change?"

"Cause their main goal is to bore us to death. God forbid we kids have fun, especially on an excursion day," Andy responded.

"To think this is Urda's definition of fun. Could you imagine what New Year's Eve must be like at her house?" said Leanne.

"If she invited me, I'd surprise her by bringing a batch of escargots as appetizers, but keep a live one in there," Noah butted in from behind, where he had been eavesdropping. The girls laughed out loud, catching Urda's attention.

"Miss Andy! Would you mind repeating what I just said?" Andy could not have been caught at a worse time. She had willfully numbed her brain for this excursion since there was nothing of interest in it for her.

"Sorry, Miss. I was too concentrated on looking for snails. I wasn't focusing on taking notes."

"We'll see how that turns out for you when you have to answer exam questions about what I just said," Urda responded and continued with her monologue. "As I was saying, snails are very unique in nature. Just like slugs, they are hermaphrodites, with both male and female organs."

"Eyuuuh ...," several voices sounded off. "...Gross!"

Urda ignored them and continued. "The selection process for choosing a mate is an interesting one. Since they're deaf with poor visual capacity, they use mostly their sense of smell and touch to get around. In addition, because they're able to recognize chemicals in the air, that's also how they communicate. Before mating, some species of snails use love darts, a structure of calcium or chitin, that they shoot out at their mate. However, snails have the capacity to self-fertilize, should they decide to do so."

"What?! ... How's that possible?" chorused a couple of students.

"And this over here is a red clover plant, which is why we have over a dozen snails on it. This is one of their favorites. Come take a look, everyone. This might be in your exam, so be sure to take notes."

Students started scribbling notes, forcing Leanne to do the same. Meanwhile, Urda noticed some students were leaving the path.

"Everyone, stay on the path and continue walking straight ahead. We'll next look for a snail nest. Oh! Here! We found one! We're extremely lucky! Right over here, we have a snail nest. Come everyone, take a look."

Several enthusiasts rushed forward to be the first to see, while the rest stood in line, waiting for their turn to have a look. Leanne was reluctantly waiting, forcing herself to be patient, when she suddenly heard two distinct voices coming from off the path.

"No, you is to plant it here, else the shrub is gonna multiply and take over. They'll be threatened by the newcomer."

"No, you lout. You can't put it here. These elm branches are sick as the devil and will cast a shadow. Then there won't be any sunlight."

"Sick elm branches don't harm plants, you odd hob! And it don't need much sunlight."

"It only needs three-quarters, and that's plentiful!"

Leanne's heart stood still. There, in the middle of the forest, were two strange, short, and stocky creatures arguing about the positioning of a plant that one of them held in his hands. Both were oblivious to the students standing close by. What were they? Gnomes? Leanne couldn't tell. They almost looked like they came out of an amusement park. They were clearly audible, so she looked at her classmates to see if anyone else had noticed the scene, but no one was paying attention. She turned over to her friend, who was taking notes while they were all standing still when the voices boomed even louder still as one of the creatures became defensive.

"If you plant this here and it disappears, I will receive five of your cherished Chorkin shrubs in compensation."

"Then a reward shall be justified!" replied the other one resolutely, "If it flourishes and survives, then I'll be prized with three of your Nebulas and six of your Disperses."

"Six Disperses? Have you gone mad as ole Gnewin's brethren? I cannot touch those! They're still protected and not on my turf. I can increase the Nebulas to five, and you can have two of my planting spades instead."

The other one nodded. The two seemed to have come to an agreement of sorts. They inscribed this odd exchange on a piece of wood with a dagger-like object. Leanne could not stand watching quietly any longer. She turned to her friend. "Andy," she said, whispering, "do you see something odd over there?" she asked, shifting her eyes towards the area where the talking creatures were standing.

"Where?"

"Over by the elm tree, the one that looks like the roots have been struck by lightning."

Andy looked over. Leanne noticed her gaze was exactly on the right spot, but judging from her reaction, she wasn't registering anything out of the ordinary.

"Well, I see the branches sprawled on the ground that were probably hit by lightning, and there are branches that are growing all around. What's so odd about that?"

Leanne understood in an instant that she was the lone witness to this scene. Neither Andy nor any of the other students could hear or see what was going on beyond the path. Ironically, they were just like the snails they were observing that morning, unable to see or hear. Leanne decided to play along so as not to look insane.

"No, I guess not. Well, maybe a little bizarre since the tree is still alive and branches are growing even though it's been hit by lightning," she said to give some credence to her observation yet mark it as irrelevant.

"Yes, it's Mother Nature, as they say, fighting her own battles," Andy giggled.

Leanne looked again at the spot, but the creatures were gone. She noticed that the plant that was the subject of their quarrel was now neatly planted underneath the stricken branch, making it naturally undetectable.

Her turn came to look at the snail nest. She could not have looked at the thing any faster. She was anticipating going back to that spot, curious to see if anything else was happening or if those dwarfish creatures would come back. For the first time that morning, she thought their exotic excursion a few hundred feet from their school wasn't so bad after all.

"All right, everyone, you have half an hour of free time to look around and take notes. You need to make five key observations concerning snails on your own besides those I have already mentioned. This observational segment of your report shall count for an extra five points."

Almost on cue, the students started talking amongst themselves. Urda called out, "This might be a free period, but you still have to do some work. I don't want to see anyone chatting away. Understood?"

The students dispersed, and Leanne hastened back to where she had observed the two brawling creatures. When no one was looking, she ventured off the path again to approach the new plant. It was easy to spot, as the soil beneath it was a darker shade of brown. It had been freshly plowed. She noticed the leaves had a bluish tint and stood marveling at them. She had never seen anything like this. Then again, she had never studied botany. She reflected there must be a myriad of plants out there that looked out of the ordinary. And there were always new species of things being discovered now and then. She then noticed the footprints right next to the plant. It comforted her to see that what she had witnessed was definitely not a hallucination. Surprisingly, they were much larger than she had thought they would be, especially for such small beings. In addition, the footprints showed that they were not wearing any shoes but were, in fact, barefoot. She counted the toes on each footprint, then recounted them several times. Four. They only had four toes and not five, she mused. Surely these footprints would be detected by everyone since they were visible to her.

She knelt down and touched the blue leaves. They had a smooth surface and felt soft on her skin. The plant was very small, enough not to draw too much attention. She scanned her surroundings to be sure no one was around and bent lower, crawling on all fours to take a look at the roots. While kneeling to better observe, her locket swung freely from her neck and went right through the split tree's bark. Reflexively, she immediately pulled back and stood in awe. She could have sworn she heard a swooshing sound in the midst of all of this. She questioned herself as to whether her necklace had simply hit the bark, and she hadn't heard it. She took hold of it and, this time, came closer to the bark where her locket had passed through. She swung it, and her locket went right through the bark again as if she'd dunked it in water. She could no longer see it, the only visible part of her necklace being the chain around her neck. There was that swooshing sound again, too. She backed away and looked around to take a moment's break from this extraordinary finding.

"Unbelievable," she said in a whisper meant only for her own ears. This was some special tree, not dead at all. She then wondered if there was something about her locket that created a connection with the tree. After all, she had found it in a book on trees, gnomes, and healthy greens. Could these talking little things be gnomes? she wondered again.

A few faint voices reached her ears, but no one came near her. She bent back down again to touch the bark, this time with her hand. It slipped right through. She glided it back and forth, examining the strange phenomenon. As she made one final attempt, she dunked her arm in fully and was suddenly swallowed up completely by the bark. She barely had any time to process what was happening when she was ejected and fell sideways on the ground.

She stood up immediately to observe her surroundings. She was in a noticeably different environment. There in front of her was a healthy, undamaged tree. The blue-leaved plant was not there, but the footprints she had seen were continuing further away into what seemed to be a plusher field of green foliage. Leanne looked around at her surroundings from eye level. *Plusher fields of green foliage?* she wondered. *More like a majestic forest!* A myriad of trees surrounded her, with unusually large circumferences the likes of which she had never seen before. They all seemed freshly grown and young, not withering in old age the way they should be, considering their immense sizes. The forest wasn't just green. Some trees had golden leaves, and, amazingly, some had blue leaves. Leanne stood staring at these, marveling at their color. She reasoned that the blue plant she had been observing in the back of her schoolyard probably came from this place. There were a few sounds coming from chirping birds, but not a single student's voice could be heard. Clearly, she was the only one in her group to have landed in this place. It smelled different here, too. The Chester schoolyard definitely did not have this smell. Her senses were at their apex when she suddenly heard a melody coming from further away, followed by another coming from another direction. The latter sounded different, almost as if it were answering the first one's call. For a while, she kept hearing a symphony of sounds at odd intervals, always one followed by the other, just like whales singing to each other as they communicate underwater. It was a sweet symphony. She then heard a buzzing sound from above and looked up. She saw rainbow fireflies or colorful bees, she couldn't tell what they were, but they were very lovely, nonetheless. For an instant, an insane thought crossed her mind that they might be little fairies.

Leanne put an end to her observing and quickly came to her senses to assess what had just happened. It seemed as though she had changed location literally through a tree. This place was nothing like the terrain in the back of her school, a place that at the moment was dimly lit, still draped in morning dew filtering the sunshine. Over here, the air was rather dry and serene, as if all living things had already been awoken by the glowing sun. A dirt path was clearly visible among the foliage, with cobblestones aligning the sides. Other stones in the shape of arrows were integrated into the ground, pointing off into the distance. Leanne followed the arrows with her eyes and, further ahead, saw a junction where two paths crisscrossed. There was a wooden sign where she thought she could read 'Towards South Wing.' She looked back at the tree she had exited from and touched her finger to it to test it once more. Just as before, it went right through. She figured she could go back the same way she'd come. She decided to acclimate herself briefly to her surroundings. She untied her ponytail and placed her red elastic by the side of the tree so she could locate it again. There was no way she would miss the stark contrast in color.

"Oh, hello, my lady!"

Leanne's body jolted in the air like a startled cat's. She turned around instinctively to face the voice that had just scared the dickens out of her.

A little boy was standing in the middle of the path with his arms full of branches. By the looks of it, he looked like he was stockpiling wood. Leanne stood dumbfounded as she stared at him, unsure of what to say. The little boy looked back at her innocently, his head tilted to one side. He stood quiet for a moment as if to let her speak first but then realized she was just standing stock-still.

"Are you lost?" he asked.

Leanne couldn't bring herself to answer. Her whole environment had instantaneously changed drastically, and conversing with a stranger, albeit a small, innocent-looking boy, was still a little too extraordinary for her at the present time. She remained quiet, staring at him as if she was a statue.

"Dear me! We usually don't see Cypress Ladies in this section of the Black Forest unless, of course, they have special tasks to undertake. Your part of the forest is much nicer to be in than ours," he said.

Suddenly, the boy's white outfit struck her as familiar, and this made Leanne snap out of her daze. He was wearing a white tunic with a gray belt. She had definitely seen the likes of his uniform before.

The boy thought it best to speak further since Leanne had still not said a word.

"We haven't made introductions. My name is Virgil. What's yours?" he asked politely.

Because he was at least friendly, as well as a little boy of no more than eight, she finally decided to break her silence.

"Leanne. My name is Leanne," she responded.

"Well, it's nice to meet you, Leanne," he smiled. "That's a beautiful name," he acknowledged quietly to himself. "Leanne," he said again.

"Thank you. It's nice to meet you too. Virgil, was it?" she asked, unsure.

"Yes. Although most of my friends call me Virgo."

Leanne nodded. Another unusual name, she told herself. Where could he be coming from?

"Did you say this is a forest?" she asked.

"The Black Forest," he corrected her, "Where we are now is usually the restricted pathway, but don't worry, I won't tell anyone. I was only crossing here because I needed more dead branches for the school's firewood reserves, and the main roads didn't provide me with enough. The Gemins probably cleaned them all out as usual. Then I saw you and came closer. I swear that's why I came. Otherwise, I don't venture into this part," he pleaded honestly.

"That's alright," answered Leanne. The last thing he needed to do was to explain to her why *he* was there. It should have been the other way around, she thought. *And what's a Gemin?* She wondered.

"Would you..." she hesitated, wanting to ask something about his outfit, which was nagging at her memory too much to dismiss it as irrelevant. She finally gathered her courage to ask.

"Would you happen to know someone here by the name of Ezekiola?"

"Why yes, I do!" Virgil answered wholeheartedly. "He's now of the Emeralds. You know him?"

Leanne's heart leaped. "Yes, I met him recently," she said, feeling excited for the first time.

"He's been quite popular lately; everyone's been talking about him."

"Do you know if he's close by?"

"Yes, he's having his second breakfast. Would you like me to fetch him for you?" he asked eagerly. He was too enthusiastic for Leanne to refuse such an offer. Might as well make the most of her stay here.

"Sure. Is it far from where we are?"

"No, not at all! The cafeteria is in the South Wing, and it's not far from here. I won't be long. Stay here. I'll be right back," Virgil hastily dropped his entire bundle on the ground and went running like a mad dog in the southern direction, turning back once to give Leanne a blazing white grin. She couldn't tell if he was more excited about fetching Ezekiola for her or about having seen her. She was going to see Ezekiola again and now felt nervous about it. Everything had happened so fast, she hadn't foreseen this moment. What was she going to say to him? How have you been? Where did you go? Why did you disappear? What is this place? How did this happen? Maybe she would just let him speak first and see what happened. Her thoughts were suddenly interrupted by a sound she heard far off in the bushes. She was frightened for a moment and rushed to hide behind the trunk of the tree from which she had entered. A strange little horse came out of nowhere, walking about on the pathway. She relaxed as she realized it was only a horse, albeit a wild one, and nothing more. But then something else came out of the bush behind it, and the sight of it made her heart pound faster. It was a green-looking creature, similar to the ones she had seen in her schoolyard. This one, however, was greener than the rest. It went calling after the horse. "Noyay! Noyay!" Both the horse and the stumpy little guy could barely run.

He stopped where Virgil had dropped his bundle, collected all the branches one by one, and stored them in his travel pouch. He then strapped the whole thing onto his miniature horse's back and continued on his way. Leanne realized that was probably the creature Virgil was referring to as a Gemin.

She remained crouched behind her tree, wondering if something else would come out of those bushes. How long Virgil was going to take, she had no way of knowing. Having no idea what time it was, she did not want to take the risk of getting lost in these uncharted territories. She leaned without thinking on the tree to help herself back up, and just as she did so, that simple act thrust her right back into the Chester High yard. It was then that she seriously began thinking about the time. What time was it? She looked around to see if the others were around, but saw no one. Was class over? She disentangled herself out of the odd bushes and ended back in the large yard of her school when she noticed that her fellow students were already halfway towards the entrance door. She was the only student left behind. She saw Andy walking last and looking back with a frown on her face. She sprinted and cut through the field. Andy turned around to see Leanne running like a fox that had just been flushed out of its hiding spot.

"Where have you been? I was looking all over for you! I didn't tell Urda anything not to raise suspicion, but I checked everywhere."

"Let's just say I wandered off the path," Leanne answered. She was dizzy and out of breath. Her blood was pumping from an array of things at this point. Not seeing Ezekiola, although he was probably rushing to see her, was one of them. Now she couldn't wait to get back to the schoolyard. Who would have thought that a snail safari could turn into the excursion of a life-time? Madame Camille had been right. Leanne had never stopped wearing her locket with his name in it. She was happy to have found a way to see Ezekiola again. Nothing else was on her mind for the rest of the day except getting back to that split tree trunk and venturing off the path and into the unknown. She didn't care to look back, but in a dark corner of those woods were a pair of dark eyes watching her leave, fiddling with the very red elastic she had left behind.

Chapter 14

Virgil Tells a Tale

Early that Monday morning, the constant deciphering of his professor's abominable puzzles had taken its toll on Nohlan. He decided he had had enough of this riddle fest. For far too long, he had entertained the thought of doing something about it. And today was going to be his special day. Each time Balthazar prepared a riddle for his students, he had one of his devoted Gemins post them on the bulletin board. There were three such Gemins, according to what Nohlan had been able to monitor over time, and each had its own time pattern. Nohlan thus sat on a bench in the South Wing of the school, halfway between the cafeteria and the main hall, pretending to be studying one of his gardening books. He waited patiently, looking up every now and then into the distance towards the board. He had an overpowering urge to see a Gemin slap a piece of paper on that board.

He had barely waited fifteen minutes when Luprin the Tall walked past him, heading towards the main board with a brown satchel under his arm. At two feet four, Luprin towered over the other Gemins by several inches. He was not only known for his height but also for his imposing weight, which was entirely concentrated on his protruding belly. Most Gemins had a rounded midsection, but his was shaped differently because it started right below his neck. Luprin took his time, which made watching him unbearable. But Nohlan remained uncharacteristically patient. Opening his satchel, Luprin delicately pulled out a thin sheet of parchment. From afar, it looked like a memo with special calligraphic writings on it. Nohlan was certain it was Balthazar's handwriting, which was recognizable from miles away since he often wrote in a manner that made his riddles look like artifacts that were at least enjoyable to look at. And in this particular instance, Nohlan couldn't wait to get his hands on it. Luprin manipulated the memo with a pair of thin tongs, careful not to touch its surface and risk smudging a word or two, for the ink was still fresh. In fact, he was handling that piece of paper as if it were the purest diamond, worthy only of a master cutter's expert touch.

When Luprin had finished and left, Nohlan quickly made his way to the main board. Making sure no one was looking, he gently peeled off the only copy of the day's riddle, then made his way discreetly back to his hidden observation post. Without even glancing at it, he vigorously shredded the memo to pieces. It was a well-deserved end to its short-lived life. If he couldn't figure out the location of his classrooms because of these pointless riddles, then no one else would either. He wanted Balthazar to face an empty classroom for once, and Nohlan would revel in his victory. He found a trash bin outside the school and recklessly discarded the shredded memo. He told himself it was the best depository for such an abomination. He got momentarily distracted by a small piece of paper that flew off into the wind but wasn't able to follow its course. It was probably nothing, he thought. Satisfied, he quickly gathered his belongings and headed to the cafeteria, where his fellow students were having their second breakfasts.

When he got there, the crowd was bustling. It took Nohlan a moment to locate his friends. From afar, Atlas and Ezekiola looked like they were engaged in a serious conversation.

"So what's the one sitting in the northeast corner thinking?" Atlas asked quietly.

"I already told you the thoughts of three of them, yet you want more? What are you up to again, Atlas?" Ezekiola asked, struggling to maintain his patience as he faced once again the insistent requests from his friend to read other students' minds.

"Nothing. I just want to know."

Over a dozen Red Belts were seated at a long rectangular table across from them, and Atlas was curious to find out what was on each of their minds.

"Fine. This is the last one. I won't tell you which one it is, but one of them just thought about your sister. How about that?" Ezekiola teased.

"My sister? Helva? Who *doesn't* think about her!" Atlas dismissed Ezekiola's observation like it was common knowledge. Helva was Atlas' older sister and a Brown Belt. There was a goddess-like beauty to her that made every head turn. "Ha! Unfortunately for Borghis, he's clearly not the only one to have a crush on her! The competition will surely beat him," he added, chuckling.

Ezekiola's brow shot up at hearing Atlas make such a comment.

"Borghis has a crush on Helva?" he asked. "Now that's news to me. How would *you* know such a thing, Atlas?"

But before Atlas could say another word, Ezekiola read right through him. Atlas knew it was too late to make up a story, so he grinned instead.

"Oh, I can't believe it!" Ezekiola said, shaking his head.

"You didn't. How could you do that? That's bad. Really bad. You better wish on the moons of Circa you never get caught!"

Atlas had gained leverage on Borghis when he learned, through reading the latter's missing journal, that he had a deep crush on his sister. He had read it, not once, but twice, and had uncovered Borghis's very deep feelings for Helva.

"Now hold on, Zek. Half the students here would say they have a crush on her, so Borghis fits right in with the others. Didn't you notice the way he was looking at her when she came over to congratulate us at our ceremony?"

"You know what they say, Atlas ... you see what you want to see. Every move he makes simply fulfills your expectations, doesn't it? Borghis is a very private person. Don't try to pass off his feelings for your sister as being a meaningless thing like everyone else's."

Atlas rolled his eyes and was about to offer a rebuttal when Nohlan arrived, but before anyone could say another word, their conversation was cut short.

"Ezekiola! Where is Ezekiola!" Came a commanding voice through the crowd, drawing the attention of everyone in the cafeteria.

"Ezekiola! Ezekiola!" followed a frail little voice behind it.

Ezekiola stood up. "Yes?" he answered. A little boy emerged from the crowd. It was little Virgil, followed closely by a Brown Robe, Gordi, who happened to be one of Borghis' best friends. He was holding Virgil by the arm as if he had caught him doing something wrong. Surprisingly, he was carrying his personal staff in his other hand. Indeed, Brown Robes carried their staffs only on rare occasions and only in certain parts of the Black Forest. Seeing Gordi alongside Virgil made for quite a confusing scene, as Virgil, contrarily to Gordi, was beaming with joy.

"Go ahead, tell him!" commanded Gordi.

"I saw a girl, a girl...." Virgil was still trying to catch his breath. By the looks of it, he had been running not too long ago. Gordi had probably caught him running and stopped him in his tracks, as Brown Robes usually did.

"A girl? And?" repeated Ezekiola, not sure what this was about. The crowd wooed as if an important secret had suddenly been revealed. Everyone gathered closer to hear more of what Virgil had to say.

"Yes, a girl, for you. She's waiting for you!" replied Virgil enthusiastically, like he was delivering a royal message.

"A girl waiting for me?" Ezekiola asked again, this time amused, but Gordi cut his amusement short.

"Yes," he intervened, "tell him where."

"In the Black Forest," replied Virgil.

"Not just that part, you fool. Where were you exactly?" Gordi pressed.

Virgil became a little nervous. "In the restricted part of the forest," he swallowed hard, then switched to a more pleading tone. "But I already told you why I was there. It was only because I couldn't find enough sticks, and I just ventured off a little." Ezekiola immediately understood why Gordi had his staff.

He was about to say something when Atlas cut in.

"What's all this about?" he asked. "So what if Virgil saw a girl on his way?"

"Right!" Virgil continued awkwardly as if it was his turn to speak again. "She said she wanted to see Ezekiola and asked for him, and that's why I was hurrying to the cafeteria."

Gordi, however, wasn't convinced.

"You will be reprimanded for this, Ezekiola," he warned, "you know very well it's forbidden to set meeting times with Cypress Ladies during school hours, especially in any of the restricted parts of the forest."

"What?!" Ezekiola jumped at his words. "This is completely absurd! I never set a meeting time with any girl!"

"If you were up to something, the time to tell me is now. This will have an effect on the consequences of your actions."

"Here we go again, Gordi," said Atlas, "another failed attempt by the Brown Robes to try to blame something on us. Either you convinced Virgil to tell this fable, or he's deliberately lying."

"But I'm not lying!" pleaded Virgil. "She's still there now, waiting. Her name is Leanne, and she was wearing this odd uniform I've never seen any of the Ladies wear."

Ezekiola's expression changed abruptly as if he had just been transported to another world. He stared at Virgil in shock, not knowing what to say at hearing her name. Could this be true? It didn't help that his cheeks had turned scarlet red. Atlas suddenly realized that this was altogether another matter he was not aware of. It amused him that he was suddenly now the one to uncover a secret about his friend.

The boisterous crowd became silent. Atlas was not the only one reading Ezekiola's mind, but everyone else as well, as if Virgil's tale had suddenly become truthful.

"Let's go see!" came a voice in the crowd.

Noticing a hint of panic on Ezekiola's face, Gordi quickly seized his opportunity. "Lead us to her, Virgil. Now!" he said with an obvious feeling of pride.

"Go ahead, Gordi," Atlas chimed in, "lead us to her, so you may see that Virgil, here, is telling a tall tale and that you can't, for the life of you, discern truth from fiction, not even from an eight-year-old!"

Ezekiola took hold of his friend's arm. "Don't!" he said in panic.

"Trust me," Atlas whispered, barely audible.

"Whoever wants to follow us, come with me! And you can

witness with your own eyes that there's a girl waiting for Ezekiola in the very zone where it's forbidden to stroll," Gordi lavishly boasted, like a hero commanding his army.

A crowd gathered to follow Gordi outside. Atlas stood up on a table and applauded, drawing everyone's attention back to himself as if he was about to plunge into some special speech.

"Now that's a demonstration of leadership! Bravo Gordi! Bravo! Lead all of us to the very restricted part of the forest where we're forbidden to go. And when all of us White Tunics are being questioned on our whereabouts, why some students were late to class or even absent, we'll tell the truth and say exactly where we were and point to the culprit who led us there. You, Gordi! A Brown Robe. This will look great on your weekly report! You'll make your brothers proud!" he shouted.

Gordi's expression slowly changed. He had not calculated this part of the equation when making his boisterous statement. He took Virgil aside and mumbled something in his ear, then turned around to everyone and said: "Okay. Everyone, stay here except for Virgil. I'll see if he's telling the truth. Then I'll decide on the outcome."

"Well then, I'm coming too," said Ezekiola, "since all of this is just a ploy to accuse me of wrongdoing. I have the right to witness this for myself and see if there's any truth to it."

Gordi hesitated at first, taking a long moment to answer. "Fine then. Come along. Everyone else, finish up and go off to your classes."

Gordi led Ezekiola and Virgil to the exit door. The cafeteria being in the South Wing, it was quite an embarrassing walk for Ezekiola to get to the North Wing in order to access the Black Forest, with all the curious faces observing him and his mismatched crew. A twenty-two-year-old Brown Robe strolling with an eight-year-old beginner and a seventeen-year-old Emerald Belt made for a curious trio. When they arrived at the gates of the Black Forest, Nohlan and Atlas suddenly popped up behind them.

Gordi turned around and saw them.

"What are you two doing here? I said only Ezekiola could come!"

"Well, we're certainly allowed to follow. My brother always lets me follow him. And class hasn't started yet anyway," replied Nohlan with the utmost innocence.

"Yes, I'm sure he lets you follow him, Nohlan, considering you're such a faithful follower. But I'm certain he doesn't let you follow him into the restricted parts of the forest."

"Well, up to this point, we haven't ventured into a forbidden area. We're just strolling," Atlas said as if he was out for a sunny walk, both hands in his pockets.

"That's such a remarkable change in your discourse, Atlas. That's not what you were saying a minute ago, was it?"

Gordi knew what they were up to.

"How about this then, Gordi," Atlas stopped him in his tracks, "if Virgil is right, then you can put in a reprimand on all three of us. I believe you'd be in your right to do so," he challenged.

Gordi gave serious thought to that proposition. It sounded very alluring. He stared Atlas down as he did so, weighing the younger student's words. He would be glad to get all the honor on this one, being able to hold Atlas responsible for trespassing, as so many Brown Robes were still furious with him. Items had gone missing from their dormitory, and the Brown Robes were certain Atlas was the culprit, although they couldn't prove it. How best to pin the theft on him emas the real challenge. This might be a good opportunity. Gordi would be exalted to a higher status amongst his brothers for reprimanding three White Tunics all at once. Regardless, he had nothing to lose.

"It's a deal then," he said finally.

Atlas' challenge did not sit well with Ezekiola, who had sweat running down his brow. He was nervous about what to expect and how he might handle what he found. *Nobody knows who she really is.* It would make a great scandal indeed if a Brown Robe found out the truth about Leanne. *How did she even get here?* Being in the restricted part of the forest was the last of his worries. *Gordi can't find out. He must not!* Ezekiola quickly devised a plan about what to say or do in a worst-case scenario.

The boys stopped when they reached the closed wrought-iron gates marking the entrance to the Black Forest. The gates had a set of three exquisitely carved leaves on each door representing the Cypress School crest. Gordi opened the doors and signaled the others to follow him. Not too far in was a wooden signpost giving directions. Each zone of the forest was clearly delineated, all the way to the domain of the Cypress Ladies, where the female division of Cypress School was found, its limit being past the northernmost section of the forest. The northeast side was the restricted zone, where passage was forbidden to White Tunics.

All the boys walked North for a while until they arrived at the Willow Tree Lane. There were a hundred willow trees, perfectly lined up, casting giant shadows on the path which defined the entrance to the forbidden section of the Black Forest. Walking past them took a while, for each tree was over a thousand years old, and as big as several normal trees combined. At the end of the long lane of trees stood a wooden sign that was impossible to miss: 'Restricted Zone. No Trespassers Allowed.'

They silently walked past it while Virgil enthusiastically led the way. After a few minutes, they finally came to a stop.

Virgil hesitated and turned around as if he had forgotten his way.

"What now?" asked Ezekiola. "Was it here?" He had never felt this impatient before about meeting his fate. His friends took note of his mood.

"No, wait," Virgil mumbled to himself. "I laid it down here and turned around this way..."

"Laid what down? There's nothing here," Ezekiola remarked sharply.

"The branches! I had accumulated a bunch. I was almost done. Somebody must have," he scratched his head, uncertain about what had happened. "See, she was standing over there, right in the middle. Somebody must have picked up my stash!"

"Oh, here we go again ..." Atlas had had enough. "Virgil, this is not the first time you've made up a story."

Virgil's gleefulness suddenly disappeared. "But I'm not lying! She was right over there. I saw her, I swear!"

"Really, Virgil? Just like when you told your brother you saw that a willow tree had miraculously planted itself with the others in the Willow Tree Lane, and everyone made their way to see it, but the number of trees was exactly the same. One hundred."

"Because it had moved again! The other trees didn't welcome it!"

"It's what happens, Virgil," Atlas continued, "when you work too hard picking twigs. You had a hallucination. And now it's become your favorite pastime—to make up tales."

"But I'm not making up a tale! She was over here, and somebody must have picked up my stockpile of sticks; it was lying right in the middle of the path."

Nohlan and Ezekiola giggled for the first time since leaving the cafeteria.

Atlas couldn't get enough: "I'd like to have your sense of

sight and hearing one day, Virgil. I think I'd have so many more tales to tell than my own boring stories."

Virgil's face turned red while Gordi's became bereft of any amusement. "You may all laugh now, but I'll be watching you three very closely. Don't think you'll get away with this. Especially you, Ezekiola," he cast him a vicious glance, "you're up to something, and we all know it. Mark my words, it's just a matter of time. I'll figure it out. I will. Get to your classes, all of you," he ordered and took Virgil by the arm to escort him back.

Like an honorary emissary, he turned around, the edge of his robe shuffling the ground and raising dust. He was angry enough to forget to escort the three friends out of the restricted zone, focusing only on the youngling. The boys silently watched him depart like a ship going on a long voyage.

"That Gordi is like a crazed falcon," Nohlan observed, "just like my brother gets sometimes."

"They're all the same, completely deranged birds," Atlas said.

"I don't think Virgil was lying," Ezekiola interrupted, still staring at the spot where Virgil said he saw Leanne. He walked slowly towards it.

"What?" they both asked in surprise.

"Of course he was!" Atlas argued. "How can you say that? You saw what Gordi tried to do. Since our last meeting with Borghis and Keenan, they've been itching more than ever to accuse one of us of something. This was just another lame attempt. Funny enough, for a moment there, when Virgil made his big announcement in the cafeteria, I thought he was telling the truth. How ridiculous of me!"

Ezekiola walked towards a particular tree and observed it for a moment.

"What is it?" asked Nohlan.

Nohlan approached the tree his friend was scrutinizing and

noticed something. He bent down to touch the ground and picked up a few things. "Empty pumpkin seed shells. A bird probably feasted here," he declared, but there was a note of uncertainty in his voice.

Ezekiola pondered this and replied. "You know, Gemins pick up sticks all the time. If Virgil laid down a bundle in the middle of the road like that, they might have picked it up in no time."

"What about this girl, Leanne, then?" asked Atlas. "Who is she?"

Ezekiola remained quiet as if in contemplation.

"Well? Do you know of a girl named Leanne or not?" Atlas persisted.

This was the moment, he realized, to get things off his chest.

"Yes, I do," he finally answered.

"So, what's the big deal, anyway? Did you ask her to meet you here?"

He shook his head.

"So, she likes you and just wanted to see you."

"There's something else," he said. "I don't understand how she made it here."

"What do you mean?" asked Atlas.

"She's not from here, and that's why Virgil said she was wearing a strange uniform. And I'm glad Virgil didn't realize who she really was," he said, almost to himself.

Nohlan laughed. "You mean you met a girl outside of our school?"

"Not just from outside of our school, outside of Circa," Ezekiola said, weighing whether he should tell his friends everything.

"Well, then, where is she from?" Atlas asked, growing more curious.

Ezekiola hesitated. But it had been torturing him for so long now, and he had spent way too much energy concealing it.

"She's from Planet Blue."

"What?! That's impossible. They can't enter Circa; we're veiled. Isn't that right, Nohlan?" Atlas turned to his friend and asked, knowing that Brown Belts had greater knowledge about entering and exiting different realms than he did.

Nohlan looked like he was brewing things over in his mind. "Not entirely," he said, surprising both. "Is that why you asked me about Sporadic Doors?" he suddenly recalled and looked up at his friend.

Ezekiola nodded.

"And is that how you met her?" he continued in a mix of excitement and disbelief.

Ezekiola nodded, relieved. "The day after our ceremony."

"Did you tell her you're from Circa?" he asked.

"No. It didn't cross my mind. She was as confused about meeting me as I was."

"How do you know for certain she's from Planet Blue?" Atlas asked again.

"I was able to read her mind. She knew nothing of me or of our existence."

"I still don't understand. Aren't all entrances to their kingdom barred, and only Emerald Robes and much higher can access their world? How sure are you about entering their world?" Atlas asked again.

"I just knew," Ezekiola gave them his customary response, "I looked around and realized how unfamiliar it was for time to go by so fast. Our time was so short. The books I read in the library spoke about the sensation of time being short when passing through Sporadic Doors," he recalled.

Nohlan interrupted, "How did this happen exactly? Tell me everything!"

Ezekiola then recounted his experience, leaving nothing out.

Atlas tried to make sense of the whole thing. "Wait, if Sporadic Doors can open just like that, wouldn't this happen more often?"

"I'm not sure," Nohlan answered. His knowledge of this topic was limited, and he thought of how his brother was much more knowledgeable.

"This must have something to do with the Emerald Belt, then. It can't just be a mere coincidence that right after our ceremony, you met her. Freedom of movement, remember? That's what your belt brought you according to that book we looked over in the library the other day," Atlas reasoned. Then something else dawned on him. "So that's why you didn't return your belt to Nomi right away," he said, figuring out a piece of the puzzle.

Ezekiola gave him a faint nod.

"But the books don't say much about the belt. They make it sound like a mystery you have to figure out by experiencing it!" he said, his frustration evident in his voice.

"Well, now we know how you got there. But then, how did she get here?" asked Atlas. He looked at Nohlan for an answer.

"I'm not sure, but I have an idea," Nohlan said reflectively. "Sometimes my brother loves to brag to me about his 'great' knowledge. I'll ask him a bunch of stupid questions and see if I can pull anything out of him about Sporadic Doors." He took a handful of the empty seed shells in his hand and looked at them closely. "I wonder about these seeds as well. They might also be a clue. Leave it to me. I'll find out more through Borghis."

"I wouldn't bet on it," said Atlas, knowing well how Borghis handled his brother. He certainly hadn't appreciated their last encounter.

"Don't tell your brother anything about what I just said

concerning Leanne," Ezekiola warned. "Find out whatever you can from him as indirectly as you can. Knowing them, the Brown Robes will get the whole school involved if they learn of a human crossing from their planet over to our world."

Nohlan nodded. It had been a while since he'd felt this excited about something. The special bell suddenly chimed, cutting their conversation short. This particular bell tolled for urgent announcements only.

"Oh, what is it now?" Atlas asked.

"To all students partaking in Professor Balthazar's Platitudes class, take note that the class will be held in *The Seven Moons* classroom."

"Oh, good news then! That means we don't have to figure out any riddle today. I had completely forgotten to check the board, too," Atlas said, relieved.

How could that be? Nohlan thought, his ecstatic mood shifting suddenly. The location of the classroom was not supposed to be disclosed. Balthazar was supposed to think that his riddle was on the board, and his students were trying to solve it. Why did his teacher announce the classroom location, then? Something was amiss. Things had not gone according to Nohlan's plan at all.

As fate would have it, failed attempts at mischief always came at a cost. Nohlan would soon learn that everyone was about to pay the price for his deviant behavior.

"Take your pens out and put your books away, everyone," Balthazar said with a strange look of defiance on his face, even though most students had barely settled in their chairs. Nohlan and his friends had run like racehorses to make it to class on time.

"Since all of you are looking for rapid progression here, I thought you'd enjoy having a quiz today to see how far you've come in your learning."

"What?!" several students yelled out.

"You heard me correctly. Take your pens out and clear your desks," he ordered.

"But that's not fair, Professor! You didn't tell us we had a quiz today. We haven't even studied for it."

"The more you huff and puff and ask asinine questions, the more time you waste, the less you'll have to use your brain. Now it's your choice how long you want to drag this out."

"Since when is it legitimate to run a surprise test without any notice or preparation?" asked a student.

"Since when does life give you notifications for upcoming challenges? Do you think you get a special memo from your guiding stars advising you weeks in advance whenever a problem is about to hit you?" Balthazar replied.

He handed out the exam papers on which there were two squares: on the left was a single picture of a warrior, whereas the one on the right only contained empty horizontal lines for which to write on. On this particular occasion, Atlas was the one to speak out, as Nohlan had shrunk further into his seat and was unusually quiet.

"This quiz has nothing to do with our Platitudes class, Professor. This almost looks like psychometric to me."

Balthazar shot him a deadly look.

"The way I see it, Mr. Pleione, my position as a teacher comes with certain liberties. School requires you to absorb many topics, not just one. Unless, of course, you doubt your own capacity and would like to argue in favor of it, your brain should be equipped to handle that."

Atlas shrank back down and shook his head. He had fought enough battles for today. Nohlan then overheard a conversation behind him which filled him with dread. A classmate was describing how Gerta, the librarian, had crossed Balthazar in the hallway and shown him a torn piece of his memo in the palm of her hands. How could that be? Nohlan was sure he had disposed of all the pieces in one of the closed bins outside the school. Suddenly, a devastating image emerged in his mind: that lone shred of paper flying up in the air, carried by the wind. The professor had not wasted a moment and made the announcement that class would be held in the Seven Moons classroom that afternoon. The quiz was another one of his intentionally confusing type of questions:

Describe which principles apply in the following situation: a warrior hesitates to kill his opponents in battle when it is his duty to do so.

Nohlan scratched his head. The most plausible answer he could come up with was: *Where are the opponents? I don't see them in the picture,* as if his professor was supposed to draw an entire battlefield. Suddenly, the logic of it hit him: *There are no opponents here. They're all gone. That's why the warrior is hesitating. There's no one to kill.*

His answer would soon become the source of rollicking laughter in the classroom. Balthazar always read the most ridiculous answers out loud right after the quiz. He took his sweet time doing it, too, keeping Nohlan's answer, the 'best' by far, for the last. By doing so, he successfully set Nohlan ablaze with rage.

Chapter 15

Dark Moving Cloud

Ever since Leanne had discovered the locket in Madame Camille's shop and a gateway into another world, she wondered what other treasures lay hidden in the old woman's store. Until she figured out a plan on how best to enter Ezekiola's world again, she decided to spend more time at the shop. In fact, she volunteered to help the shop-keeper at every opportunity she could. With Madame Camille working all by herself and boxes stacked up in the back of the shop, it didn't take long for Leanne to get herself hired. After working one evening and a weekend, Monday night was special because Madame Camille was leaving early and, for the first time, asked Leanne to close up shop.

"It'll be a quiet evening for you but not for me! All my grandchildren are coming over tonight!" Madame Camille blurted out joyfully as she gathered her belongings and searched for her keys.

"There's a double lock. Remember to first lock the knob on the door handle before you exit and then also lock the door from the outside with the key. We're not in a fancy mall, so I lock double. Oh, and don't forget to switch the sign from *Open* to *Closed* fifteen minutes before nine to give yourself time to close up."

Leanne nodded patiently. It was the third time Madame Camille had repeated herself on the lock-up procedures.

After her boss left, Leanne fiddled around with the radio until she landed on a music station she liked. She went into the back of the store and glanced at the latest shipment of boxes delivered the day before. She calculated about thirty of them in different sizes, all bunched in one corner. She brought down a few that were hard to reach for Madame Camille and cut through the tape to see what each contained.

"This one sucks," she said. It was a box full of vases.

"And what's in this box?" she asked out loud as she sliced open another one. It contained mostly books. She scanned a few and put one aside that looked interesting. She was about to cut through a third box when she heard the little bells on the front door. She sighed and went out front. Two customers had just walked in. She served them as quickly as possible to get back to her boxes, but halfway through, more clients walked in, and then even more. In no time, the store was as crowded as it was on a Friday night, leaving Leanne with no time to return to the storeroom.

With no choice but to stay close to the cash, Leanne got into the beat of serving one customer after another, some who bought items, others who sold, and then, those who simply browsed and asked questions. She didn't feel time pass by until she felt her first pang of hunger and wondered where she had left her apple. In between serving clients, she had taken two bites out of a crispy, juicy apple, only to have put it back down somewhere in the store. She was sure the apple had turned a dismal shade of brown by now.

It was almost closing time, but there were still three people left, all waiting to pay. Leanne was punching numbers mechanically on the cash register when she heard the little bells sound once again at the door. She glanced at the clock up on the wall. There were ten minutes left to nine. She should have switched the store sign from *Open* to *Closed* as Madame Camille advised, but she hadn't had time. While punching her numbers on the cash register, she quickly glanced at the last-minute customer. Her heart dropped like lead into her stomach. He didn't look at her but walked around casually as if he'd just entered a museum.

What's he doing here, shopping? This was the first thought rushing into her head.

Momentarily, she doubted herself and looked up again in his direction. The light cast on him revealed high cheekbones and highlighted his unmistakable features. They looked so much alike. Him and Ezekiola. She watched him for a moment as if in a trance. The store lights danced on and off him, casting shadows on his face each time he moved. She now had a better view of his clothes. He wore dark breeches, a jet-black tunic of some sort, with velvet integrated around his broad shoulders and back, and a fabric of a different texture with markings wrapped around his waist. It looked like a gallant uniform from another era. At the sight of his belt, she recognized the strange triangular shapes he'd drawn on the napkin he had given her when they first met. It was definitely him. That strange boy, Zeke. Butterflies suddenly filled her stomach.

"Excuse me, Miss, but you charged too many sixes in there," the customer in front of her stole her attention away. Leanne looked at the cash register. She had punched the same number twice.

"Oh, I'm sorry. Just give me a second here." With sweaty palms, Leanne fiddled around with different buttons on the register to reset the numbers, but they remained frozen.

Like a dark moving cloud that needed to be watched from afar, Leanne kept an alert eye on every one of Zeke's moves. While attempting to reset her buttons, she saw him picking at items, browsing through books, and putting them back on the shelves. He ran his fingers across wooden shelves, tables, and carvings, even delicately tracing the edges of paintings, touching the second-hand clothes on the racks.

"And this here is four dollars, not five," the client impatiently corrected her again on another item punched in wrong. Leanne couldn't remember the last time her heart pounded so hard, not even during her worst exams. Despite fiddling around with the cash register to make a correction, she was unable to erase the whopping total of nine thousand six hundred and sixty-four dollars she had punched in for a teacup, saucer, and pan.

She ran her hands through her hair. "I'm sorry, ma'am, my cash register is frozen. How about I do this by hand?" She turned the items over and looked at the prices. Despite there being three items, she couldn't seem to add them up mentally. The numbers refused to stay in line in her head, vanishing at an incredible speed.

"This can't be too hard. This here is worth six dollars and fifty cents. The teacup is sold for—"

"It's okay. I got this!" Leanne threw the client a stern look. Too embarrassed to count on her fingers or a piece of paper, she just grabbed the calculator from the drawer to end her fit, and it dropped on the floor. She sighed and went to pick it up when her locket swung in midair. She stood crouched for a moment, realizing the reason behind his visit. *It can't be.* Instinct told her to remove and hide the locket. In a hurry, she yanked her locket necklace with Ezekiola's name in it off her neck and stashed it somewhere behind the cash register as she rose to face her customer.

While she continued serving the remaining clients, from the corner of her eye, she saw him sit down on a conference chair. He slowly pivoted from side to side as if trying out the chair for comfort. He then stretched his legs on a stand nearby, tilted his body to face the cash, and glued his eyes on her. By the time Leanne finished with her last customer, her cheeks had turned a flaming scarlet. Under his prolonged gaze, she bagged the last of the items and headed towards the exit to help her customer out and switch the store sign. He followed her with his eyes. Even with her back turned, she could still feel them on her.

When she got close to the door, she was about to switch the store sign to *Closed* when she saw that it had already been switched. Her heart started pounding again. Did he switch it? She had a sudden urge to run. But this was Madame Camille's store, and she had responsibilities tonight for the first time. She had to lock up even as she felt he was still looking. Waiting. She took a deep breath, turned around, and resolutely walked towards him.

"Excuse me, sir, but we're closing," she said in a voice much sterner than the one with which she usually addressed her customers. Their eyes met. It took all the power of her will to act neutral and not give in to his magnetic effect. A menacing gleam danced in his eyes. They seemed darker this time, despite the light in the room. A knowing look crossed his face, one which said he realized she was pretending like she didn't know him.

"There's five minutes left," he said, pointing at the clock by the cash registry. He was right. She had checked the time quickly when the last customer left.

"Yes, but this is not a lounge; you can't just sit here. If you have nothing to buy or sell, I'm going to ask you to leave, please." She kept her stance, her back rigid and hands clasped tightly in front of her like a teacher.

"I'm trying out the chair for now," he said with a mischievous smile and pivoted from side to side.

Leanne's attention was suddenly drawn towards the stand where his feet lay. There was her apple, the one she'd forgotten. He followed her gaze.

"Is this yours?" he asked, pointing to the apple. The apple had browned on one side, as she had suspected.

"Yes," she said. She came closer to take it, but the apple quickly rolled into his hands instead. She looked at him, mystified. The motion was anything but natural.

"Here you go." He held it in front of her, offering her to come and take it from him. Leanne stood frozen.

"On second thought, no, thank you. I don't want it anymore," she said.

"Why not?" he asked, tilting his head sideways.

"It's darkened on the side. Just throw it away," she answered. There was no way she was going to take the apple from his hand.

He rotated the apple with his fingers. "You shouldn't throw this apple away. Don't judge a thing by appearance. Don't you know that the dark side is as good as the light?" he asked, never taking his eyes off her. "I say it even tastes better," he added. To her astonishment, he took a bite out of the browned end. Leanne was about to speak up but then chose silence. There was something eerie about his behavior. And much like their last conversation, she sensed every one of his words had double meanings. She decided it would be best to ignore him.

"You have five minutes, sir, then the store is closed," she said and walked over to the cash. She opened the wooden counter panel that acted as a barrier between her and her customers, and she let it close with a bang. Despite her heart beating too fast, she was going to carry on and finish her shift as usual. She was going to count her money, put it in the safe, and act like he was just another last-minute customer. He'll have to leave when his time is up.

"It's a lovely store you have here," he said as he took another bite out of her apple. Leanne shook her head and continued taking money out of the cash register as fast as she could, slamming it closed at the very end—out of anger or nerves, she couldn't tell—but she got some satisfaction from the sound it made.

"I'm sure you find many treasures here," he continued. "On second thought, I may have something to offer you," he added and stood up.

Leanne continued to ignore him. She opened the safe and stashed the money without counting, and slammed it shut. Step one, done. She stood up and was startled to see him already standing by the cash register in front of her. She had barely heard his footsteps.

"What do you want to sell?" she asked in a quick short breath. He stood there silently for a moment and leaned closer.

"This," he said and delicately placed something small in front of her. Leanne glanced at it. Up until that moment, she had managed to handle him as coolly as possible. But at the sight of an elastic that looked so mundane at first glance, her stomach balled up in knots when she realized what it was—the red elastic she had left behind by that tree in the Black Forest, the special one she had discovered when she ventured off path during her school trip. It's where she met Virgil and came so close to meeting Ezekiola again in his world. And it's where she was planning to go again. She looked up at Zeke, and their eyes spoke. She knew that he knew.

"I'm sorry, but we don't buy elastics here," she said as noncommittally as she could.

"Oh, no?" he asked, a little bemused.

"No, you can try somewhere else. I already closed my cash, so you'll have to leave, please," she repeated more firmly this time. He looked at her, and to her satisfaction, she saw his jaw clench. She turned her back on him, pretending to do something other than engage with him. By ignoring him, she told herself, he'll just have to leave. She bent to take the garbage out of the trash can. She was replacing the garbage bag with another one when she heard the wooden panel creak as it lifted. Her body jolted back up.

"What are you doing? You can't come in here," she said.

"Oh, am I not allowed to venture here, Leanne?" he asked, saying her name for the first time in their exchange, breaking what little barrier was now left between them.

"No, you can't come on this side, sir," Leanne answered, motioning with the sweep of her hand to indicate the cash register area. She didn't dare say his name, in fear of what she couldn't identify.

"So, I'm venturing someplace I shouldn't, hmm?" he asked in a mocking tone. Leanne couldn't think of anything to say, rather shocked at what he was alluding to—their last conversation in the restaurant and his vague warning to not venture off someplace.

"Yes, you should be on the other side."

"I see. Am I breaking your rules?" he asked as he slowly edged closer. "Rules for thee, but not for me." Her heart beat faster as she saw him close the little space that was left between them.

"I don't know what you're talking about. Your five minutes are up. Leave now. Otherwise, I'm going to call security," she said, her chest rising with every breath she took.

"Tell me, Leanne, why wouldn't it be alright to venture

here?" he questioned, ignoring her threat. He moved closer until her back finally hit the cash register. The phone was too far in the back room. The broom was on the opposite side of the cash register, closer to him. Leanne's heart pounded hard enough that she feared he might hear it. Her forearms rested on the edges of the counter, and she wondered if she should just make a jump for it. Her hands glided towards a metal stapler not too distant. He closed the gap further and looked hard at her.

"I wouldn't do that if I were you," he said as if reading her mind. He grabbed the stapler first and moved it closer toward him. She tried to move sideways, but he blocked her way, cornering her back in her spot.

"Tell me, where did you put your necklace, Leanne?" he asked in a somber tone.

"What necklace?" Leanne answered almost too quickly.

"The one you were wearing when I walked in," he answered.

In a flash, she thought of where she hid her necklace behind the cash register. Incredulously, his eyes shifted to that corner. In a swift movement, he leaned over and pulled it out. He swung the locket like a pendulum in front of her. She went to grab it, but he swung it out of her reach.

"Who are you? What do you want?" she asked, unable to contain herself.

"You know the answer to those questions."

Leanne shook her head. "No, I don't."

"You're playing with fire, Leanne."

"What? How is wearing my necklace playing with fire?" she challenged in a last bid to remain cool before screaming.

"Would you like to know?" his eyebrows shot up. "Because there's something that I, too, am dying to know," he said and looked deep into her eyes, searching for something on the far horizon. "Maybe you and I can exchange information," he proposed, "and then I promise I'll leave."

Leanne looked back at him, confused, weighing his words.

"What information?" she asked. Nothing he said made any sense.

"Just look me in the eye. It's that simple," he said, and she found herself doing just that, in part in defiance, in part, because he had a hypnotic effect on her like he did the first time they met. From the corner of her eye, Leanne saw him tug at his belt and wrap his wrist around it. Being this close to his face for the first time, she noticed black markings around his eyes. It was eyeliner tracing the contour of his eyes. They grew somber like dark clouds gathering. She suddenly felt a piece of cloth wrap swiftly around her wrist, binding both their hands together and the palm of his hand compressing into hers. It was feverishly warm. She wanted to withdraw from his grip, but he squeezed tighter, sending a ripple of heat coursing through her body. She tried to shift but found herself paralyzed. She realized her body wasn't answering to her will. Strangely, his touch eased all her muscle tension, immersing her whole body in an almost unbearable heat, not enough to burn but enough to deplete all her energy. Her head suddenly felt light and began to spin. Her eyes shifted and were suddenly out of focus.

"What's happening?" she asked in a frail tone.

"Stay with me, Leanne, just a moment longer," he whispered and lifted her chin up. She gazed back into his eyes again, into the deep, black recesses of his pupils. Drops of sweat trickled down her temples.

"Where did you go? What did you see?" he asked.

"I... I..." She couldn't speak. Her thoughts were muddled. In fact, she couldn't think at all. No two words could come together. Her mind was a black canvas where he took all the space. Her lids became heavy, and she struggled to maintain her sight as it blurred. She blinked a few times but to no avail. Darkness crept into her vision from the sides, closing on the little light she could see. She had never fainted before, but now she wondered if that's where she was headed. He pressed himself against her, and the heat emanating from his body burned her inside. She blinked a few times to get her sight back, but the only thing she could still see were his eyes. Dark and foreboding. The last of the light she could see then dimmed. She was finally caught underneath the dark cloud that had been threatening her since he walked in. Suddenly, her breath shortened, her head tilted back, and her knees gave in. That's when he caught her, and they merged.

Zeke had never known what the essence of the fountain was like. He had only heard rumors about it, some tale in old writings passed down through the ages. But merging with Leanne now, he was about to have a taste of what others had only dreamed of. The essence was in her and the other boy, he could feel it. Still, he wanted to be sure. He needed to see for himself if the rumors of a certain fountain coming alive again were true. He searched within Leanne, penetrating deep within the recesses of her mind to access her memory. Her life flashed before him. He saw Leanne meeting Ezekiola in her classroom, wrapped in an emerald belt, he saw Leanne talking with Madame Camille, putting Ezekiola's name in her locket, he saw the night they first met at the restaurant, the conversation they had, and how he consumed her thoughts that night. He then saw Leanne crossing over to Circa, meeting Virgil. His mind then shifted to Ezekiola again, and the resemblance struck him. He realized who Ezekiola was and that there lay an opportunity he had never imagined. He saw the link Leanne created with Ezekiola. He continued to concentrate on it until he hit the mark. There it was, pure and shining, the Fountain of Fire, and being so close to it, he'd never felt so alive. He ached to merge with it. But the fountain was weak in her still, not yet fully developed. He knew Leanne wouldn't last long if he continued to fill her space this way. She had already stopped breathing. If he wanted to access the Fountain of Fire and merge with it, he had to find the boy first. And knowing now who Ezekiola was, a plan started forming in Zeke's mind. There was only one way to get what he wanted; an ancient ritual practiced amongst the Sons of the Night Sky. He willed himself to stop. He unwrapped his belt from both their wrists and tied it back around his waist.

"Breathe," he whispered as his lips brushed her ears. Leanne didn't move. Not a breath of air entered or exited her body as she lay in his arms. He took one long breath, then blew air on her neck and slowly moved to her face.

"Breathe, Leanne," she finally heard him say. Despite hearing him speak, Leanne was unable to breathe. He brushed a few strands of her damp hair away from her face. He took an even longer breath, opened her mouth, placed his lips on hers, and exhaled inside of her. Leanne sensed a wave of crisp, cold air ripple through her. When a few more breaths were pushed into her, she slowly returned to her senses and found herself with an acute chill like she had just been dunked in cold water. She started breathing with his help, but he kept his mouth on hers longer than needed, inhaling her soft breath in turn. Towards the end, he pressed his lips differently on hers, kissing her. She was conscious that his lips were parting hers. She gasped and took her first lung-filling breath by herself as if she had just exited an airtight container.

With shaking hands, she reached up and touched her face, her mouth where Zeke's lips had just been. Her clothes were stuck to her skin as if she was caught in torrential rain. Panic filled her. Her arms and legs had gone slightly limp, lacking their usual strength.

"What happened?" she asked.

"You fainted, and I helped you breathe again," he answered, his mouth curling ominously at the edges. She looked up at him. Something had changed in his eyes. He looked at her differently. Everything suddenly came back to Leanne, including their recent exchange.

"How did I faint?" she asked incredulously. "You did something, didn't you?" she said, rubbing the tender spot on her wrist. He offered his hand to help her up, but she pushed it away, recalling the intense heat that came out of it a moment ago. She grabbed the counter instead and lifted herself up.

"I won't hurt you, Leanne. You can take my hand," he offered again with a charming smile, though Leanne could see his sudden gallantry masked something dangerous.

"No. You said you'll leave. Now leave!" Leanne said as she got up, gathering her strength.

His face suddenly darkened. He stood still as if contemplating his next move.

"Listen to me carefully, Leanne. I don't want to be chasing after you for this, but if you care about your life, don't venture into that school forest of yours again. This will be my last warning. And don't ever wear this again," he said as he laid a melted, deformed locket on the counter in front of her. Leanne looked at what had once been her prized possession.

"What did you... get out!" she ordered. Fury engulfed her. Though she was glad to see him move away from her finally, looking at what he did to her necklace, it didn't seem right for him to just leave in victory that way.

"Whatever you are, you can't decide for me," she suddenly exclaimed.

He spun around. "If you cherish your dear friend's store, you'll do as I say because next time, I won't let you put the fire out," he said in a somber tone, then walked away. She watched his demeanor as he made his way to the exit door, and yet she couldn't hold back.

"What fire? The invisible one you think I'm playing with?"

Zeke stopped midway. He turned around, a wicked smile curling his lips.

"Oh yes, I almost forgot. This was your part of the information I had to exchange," he said. He clapped a few times in a particular sequence that made Leanne wonder what he was up to this time. When he finished, he turned around and walked out. Silence filled the air. His gestures didn't make any sense. Leanne lifted her arms in the air and was about to yell after him when a hint of smoke suddenly filled her nostrils. She spun around, trying to figure out where the smell came from. A faint glimmer of orange on the bookshelf then captured her attention. Like lightworks, Leanne watched a spark spread itself rapidly on a bunch of books, wooden tables, displays, paintings, clothes, and everything Zeke had touched in the shop and that carried his scent during his grand tour. She gasped and quickly grabbed the fire extinguisher from the back store. Within a few minutes, she put out the fire that had started. When the last of the flames were extinguished, the stench of smoke permeated the whole shop and every single item in it, many of which were damaged.

It would be the last time Leanne worked at Madame Camille's store.

Chapter 16

Ye Ole' Brown Staff

Circa's Moon Festival was just around the corner. This was a holiday celebrated to mark the day all seven moons shone their brightest in the night sky. On the eve of the holiday, Nohlan's mind was already swarming with ideas on how best to execute the plan he had devised. In his quest to find out how Leanne had crossed over into Circa, he was convinced birds were behind it, and he needed to get more information from Borghis on the matter. He went to see his brother very late at night to discuss with him the mundane subject of trees and birds. He knew his brother could handle only so much of him, so he had thought of the best approach and decided indirect questioning was a good way to start.

"I've already told you that three times, Nohlan, birds don't use Sporadic Doors in order to transport pumpkin seeds. Why do you keep insisting?" Borghis tried yet again to answer his brother's odd inquiries.

"But you said before that some bird species, or other

animals, can shift in and out of our domain by using Sporadic Doors. Why can't they transport pumpkin seeds?"

"They don't transport the seeds because they obviously don't need to. Circa provides enough," Borghis replied impatiently.

"So pumpkin seeds can never be transported and never change lands," Nohlan summed up his understanding of their whole conversation.

"No, that's not what I said, Nohlan," Borghis sighed. Conversations with his brother always weighed down on him. Nohlan would summarize things in the wrong way, applying logic in his own painfully distorted fashion.

To make his conversation easier to bear, Borghis concentrated on polishing the wooden table he was building for the Brown Robes' lodge. Carpentry was his passion, and wood, his love. Since most of his time was spent learning theory, creating and polishing wood at least made him feel useful. He momentarily tuned his brain off and out of the conversation with Nohlan. It was his only means of staying sane during these endless sessions. Noticing the several wooden staffs aligned against the side wall in his brother's carpentry room, Nohlan strategically changed the topic.

"You make those, too?" he asked.

"Yes, a while ago, they're our old staffs."

"Really? They look brand new."

Nohlan drew closer to get a better look.

"Don't touch them!" Borghis warned. "I just refurbished them, and they're almost finished. They'll be brought to our lodge later tonight. We have newcomer brothers starting next week, and they need staffs for their first initiation. We recycle our old ones for this purpose."

This was interesting second-hand information Nohlan had been unaware of. He had never seen his brother use his staff, but knew that each Brown Robe possessed one. They would use them as prescribed in their rule book and only carry them when mandatory. He made a mental note that they recycled the old ones.

"So, to get back to my theory, is it true then that pumpkin seeds can't be carried through Sporadic Doors?"

Borghis sighed, deciding just then that he'd give his brother one last explanation to get rid of him.

"How is this so important, Nohlan? Pumpkin seeds, like anything else organic, can be transported through several types of tree portals. What's odd is you going on and on about birds doing it."

"So what animal would you attribute that to, then?"

"Not exactly an animal," he answered, shaking his head. There was only one way to get rid of Nohlan, he thought, and that was to simply share his knowledge.

He looked up at Nohlan. "More like Gemins," he said.

"Really?" Nohlan was surprised. "Can they use Sporadic Doors in restricted parts of the forest, too?"

"Yes," he sighed, "I'll let you in on something, and perhaps you can leave me in peace after that," he said.

"Take Bopen, for example. His satchel was recently inspected by Keenan in the restricted zone of the Black Forest, and he had over two handfuls of seeds in it."

"Inspected? Why would Keenan do that?" he asked cautiously.

"Because there have been many instances of the Black Forest being littered lately, especially in the restricted parts, and Keenan was trying to find who's behind it. And so Bopen, like everyone else found in the restricted parts of the forest, got his belongings checked."

"Then Bopen was caught?" Nohlan asked with glee in his voice.

"Bopen said he needed those seeds as compost for the special blue plants he's planted in different areas of the forest. We think he was lying. Those plants had been tossed so recklessly in his bag, Keenan was sure they had all died."

"What?!" Nohlan yelled, aghast. His breathing grew heavy as if he was witnessing a horrific scene.

Borghis stopped his polishing for a moment and looked up at his brother.

"You're really strange, you know that, Nohlan? I let you in on something, and you react as if something horrible was happening in front of you," he paused, "and what's so shocking about that, anyway? Gemins love pumpkin seeds!"

Nohlan's mind had completely shifted to the blue plants that Bopen had stolen from him a while back. Could it be that he might find them again? With great effort, he got back to the subject they had been discussing.

"So if he was caught with so many seeds, could it mean that he'd carried them through a Sporadic Door and left empty shells nearby?" he asked, searching for a ray of hope.

Exasperated from the questions and wanting to put an end to the conversation, Borghis gave in: "I'm not supposed to tell you, but since you'll eventually learn about their travels soon, yes. It's a clue we learned on how to locate Gemin passageways. And it enables us to find and enter them with the use of our staffs without having to spend hours looking for them." He sighed again. "Talking to you exhausts me, Nohlan. It's late, and I need to finish my work."

"Then it was Bopen," Nohlan spoke his thought out loud. He had gotten something far greater than what he had come for. His evening session had been very fruitful. He left his brother with a plan in mind. To find that Sporadic Door, enter it and search for his plants. He then thought perhaps that was where Leanne had come from, too, since it was so close to where Virgil had seen her. It had to be the same tree!

On the night of the Moon Festival, Nohlan was pacing back and forth in the dormitory in front of a brightly lit fireplace while Atlas and Ezekiola focused on their schoolwork. The decorative emblem leaves of their school engraved within the stone fireplace shone like golden flames.

"We've found *the* tree! We should go back to it. No one will follow us there. Everyone will be feasting in one place or another. And it'll be dark outside," Nohlan declared.

"I don't know. They have Brown Robes stationed at each entrance of the Black Forest, except the North, of course, because you can only enter it through the school. They've locked all the school doors, and you can only unlock those from the inside," Atlas said, flipping through a book he was supposed to be studying.

"Not the main entrance," Nohlan replied.

"What's the point of just going to see the tree anyway?" he asked.

Nohlan's eyes twinkled with a golden light as if the flames he had been watching continued to burn in his eyes. He lowered his voice as if he was about to reveal a great mystery to his friends: "What if I told you that Gemins enter trees, not only in their zones, but in the restricted parts of the forest as well, and the way to locate those trees is to follow the pumpkin seed trace they leave behind," he said, closely watching his friends' faces to note any reaction. Since neither Atlas nor Ezekiola reacted in any way, he continued, "And right there, where Virgil said he saw Leanne, is where I found a bunch of seeds!"

"So what?" Atlas said. "Even if we know it's *the* tree, what difference does it make?"

"Because that tree is a Sporadic Door, and we can try

entering it ourselves!" Nohlan blurted out, unable to contain his excitement.

Both Atlas and Ezekiola stopped what they were doing and looked up.

"Nohlan, what happened to me was a onetime thing," Ezekiola told his friend, "I read in the Meridian Belts book that—"

"Yeah, yeah, I know: Sporadic Doors are caused by the orbiting movement of Circa, and it's an extremely rare happening," Nohlan quipped. "But now you have to think beyond that, my friend!"

"Why are you so enthusiastic, Nohlan? And why this sudden urge to find Sporadic Doors? I've never even heard you talk once about them before," Atlas retorted.

"This is why! My brother told me they caught Bopen with loads of pumpkin seeds stashed inside his bag. He's been littering all over the forest's restricted zones, and there was a big pile of seeds where Virgil said he saw Leanne. Borghis also told me it's a trick they used to locate Sporadic Doors instead of trying a myriad of trees one by one to see which one is a Sporadic Door. They just look for those seeds. Bopen must have used that same tree to transport himself. And finally, Virgil brings us there." He paused to see if this was registering with his friends, then exploded when he saw that it didn't. "Don't you realize we found THE tree?"

"You actually think that was the Sporadic Door where Leanne came from?" asked Ezekiola, suddenly alert. He remembered some of the information on Sporadic Doors he had read in the library books he took out on Gemins.

"Yes! And it's common knowledge that Sporadic Doors remain open for a short period of time after a Gemin uses it. Leanne must have crossed through the same tree right after a

Gemin did," Nohlan said, ecstatic that someone was finally catching on.

"Nohlan, I don't want to put a damper on your hopes. It's one thing to say Gemins can do that. But we White Tunics can't and don't, excluding Zek's rare incident, which probably only occurred because of his Emerald Belt," Atlas reasoned.

"That's it, though! It's because Zek has the Emerald Belt that I think we have a chance at this." Nohlan grew agitated just talking about it.

"I'm not sure it'll work. It sounds too easy," Ezekiola suddenly jumped in.

"How can you say that? You managed to enter a Sporadic Door at least once without even trying. Now imagine if you *do* try this time. We just have to figure out how to make it happen."

"And how is he supposed to make that happen? Just run into the tree?" Atlas asked. "Nohlan, you're starting to sound just like Virgil and his crazy stories," he added, flipping a page of the book he was pretending to read while avidly following the conversation between his two friends.

Nohlan was trying to play his cards smartly, dying to get just one of his friends onboard so he could try that Sporadic Door and see if his stolen plants were on the other side. It would be a great way to hit two birds with one stone, he reasoned.

"Don't worry, I thought about that too. I made a copy of my brother's incantation notes so we can succeed at this," he said.

Atlas finally looked up. "Are you serious?"

"Yes! You sure wouldn't want to miss this, would you, Atlas?"

"It's pouring rain outside Nohlan, the forest ground is soggy, and you want to go outside to cast incantations at trees to see if you can enter Sporadic Doors?"

"Yes!"

"You're as crazy as your falcon brothers!" Atlas said, shaking his head.

"What if it works?" Ezekiola said. "Maybe it's not as crazy as it sounds."

Nohlan jumped up enthusiastically, excited at having one person on board.

"It's okay, Atlas. You don't have to come," he quickly said. At that moment, the flames seemed surprisingly high in the fireplace. Atlas, who looked as comfortable as a cat resting on a windowsill watching the rain fall, didn't look like he was going anywhere. But then he suddenly slapped his book shut.

"Well, I'd like to see that happen if it does, which I strongly doubt it will. But no, I wouldn't want to miss that opportunity. The one where I get to tell you *I told you so.*"

Nohlan didn't care why Atlas was tagging along. After all, he had his own personal agenda. They exited the dorm, leaving their differences behind, and headed towards the main entrance of the school.

As they walked closer to the main door, Ezekiola came to a halt. "Oh no, look, they have Ariad stationed there."

"What's a gardening Gemin doing there? Standing guard?" wondered Atlas.

"Probably. I guess they wanted most Brown Robes at the festival and not on duty."

"I can't believe they put her there. What are they afraid of? Students entering their own school?"

"You know I never liked Ariad," Nohlan said. "She's always with Bopen."

"Oh, come on, Nohlan, you can't dislike her just because of that," said Ezekiola in the Gemin's defense.

"It's just the way she carries herself, pretending to be all-knowing and the best gardener among us."

In the midst of their discussion, they saw Ariad let a student out with a few books in his arms. "Thanks, Ariad. See you later tonight," they overheard him say.

Atlas stopped his friends short. "What's this? Students are allowed to go out?"

"With books, it seems," answered Ezekiola.

"Let's go then. Follow me," he said.

"Let's think for a second here," Ezekiola said, but Atlas ignored him and made his way resolutely toward the school entrance.

"This is our school! Just walk on," he said confidently.

"Good afternoon, Ariad," said Atlas as he walked past her.

"Gmonin, godafta, ganaayt, where you lads off to?"

"Library, where else?" he answered.

"Oh am sorry, dears. Library is closed today. Sorry about that. You will have to come tomorrow," she said.

"Actually, Ariad, I just remembered our books are not in the library, but in our study room. We need them for our project tomorrow," Atlas said, realizing that the student exiting before them had probably done just that.

"Well, I cannot have you three go in there together. You're too many!" she said.

"That's fine," replied Atlas, surprising his friends. Nohlan and Ezekiola shot him suspicious looks.

"I'll simply go and get them myself then," he said.

"What? As in, you alone?" asked Nohlan.

Ariad looked at Nohlan worriedly. "He'll be alright, dear. I'm here, and if he doesn't come out in a few minutes. I'll fetch him."

The situation had suddenly become worse, as now she was going to wait for Atlas to come out.

"Yes, I'll go alone. You guys can leave. I'll get your books too, don't worry. See you back at the dorm."

Nohlan looked crushed and turned around to leave with Ezekiola.

"Oh, wait!" said Atlas as he was about to enter the school from the main entrance. "Can you take this with you? I won't need my cloak, it's not raining much." A flash of anger lit Nohlan's face. As he snatched his friend's cloak and school bag, Atlas whispered something in his ear. His expression immediately lightened up. They then parted ways, and Ariad resumed her position standing guard.

Atlas calculated he had no more than five minutes. Else, he would raise suspicions. He entered the school, ran full throttle to the study room, grabbed a few random books he saw sitting on a table, and ran all the way to the West Wing. Once there, he opened the exit door from the inside and used one of the books as a doorstop. He then ran back and waited about a minute to catch his breath, so Ariad would not suspect anything. He finally exited the school calmly, saluting her just as the student before him had done. He walked out of the main hall the same way he had entered, then made a sharp turn to head towards the West Wing. Nohlan and Ezekiola had already let themselves in and were waiting for him.

"Great thinking! I couldn't even have come up with such a plan so quickly!" said Ezekiola as he greeted his friend with a smile at the West entrance. The three then began a quiet run down the hall. But Atlas, for all the times he had been reprimanded for running, made an astonishing dash through the hall, beating his friends to the finish line. They exited from the back door leading into the Black Forest.

"All right, give me back my bag and cloak," said Atlas to Nohlan. The three put on their hoods and secured their cloaks shut with leather belts. Looking like night travelers out for an adventure, they headed into the woods, not knowing what would come of their outing.

They headed North and walked past the several cottages occasionally used as study rooms when Nohlan suddenly came to a stop.

"Wait here," he said and turned around, "I need to get something quickly from the Brown Robe's lodge. Don't worry, no one's there," he reassured his friends.

For what felt like several minutes, the pair huddled under the roof of the Ye Ole' Brown Lodge, sheltering themselves from the rain, which had started pouring even more intensely, wondering what Nohlan had forgotten. He finally appeared, holding a long stick.

"What's that?" asked Atlas.

"A wooden staff," answered Nohlan proudly, motioning his friends to pick up the pace to further themselves from the cottage.

"But you don't own one!" Atlas remarked.

"I know. I'm borrowing it," Nohlan answered.

"And you think now's the right time to steal a wooden staff?" Atlas asked, incredulous. Their list of offenses was getting longer by the minute.

"Come on, Atlas, this is not stealing. It's borrowing. My brother was polishing it just yesterday, and it's not fully refurbished yet. Look here, see?" he pointed towards the back end of the stick where the carving of a falcon, the emblem of the Brown Robes, was faded from overuse.

"The symbol of the Brown Robes is almost erased, and there's no name on it," he said as if it somehow made it legitimate for him to take it.

"Regardless, they won't be coming here today. The Brown Robes are all heading to the festival, and they have other things to do. No one will notice that a recycled staff is missing."

"Are you sure about this? Staffs belong to their masters, and if this one belongs to Borghis, even if it's still unfinished, it'll mean trouble. I think you should bring it back," said Ezekiola.

"No, like I said, it doesn't have a master, and it doesn't belong to anyone anymore. He told me it's for someone's initiation, on a trial basis only, because they have newcomers coming next week. Nobody uses it anymore," he reassured his friends. "Besides, we need it. It'll help us get through the Sporadic Door. I'll just put it back once we're done."

"So, we have a broken-down, overused staff," cut in Atlas. "How can this be of any use to us?"

Nohlan stopped in his tracks. "Atlas, a minute ago, you had no interest in it, and now you're worried whether the staff will be enough. Why should you even worry if it's all the same to you!" he said, annoyed at his friend's meddling.

"Quit it, you two!" Ezekiola snapped at them. They walked silently for a few minutes until Nohlan could not remain silent any longer.

"Has either of you ever seen one in action?" he asked.

They both shook their heads.

"Have you?" asked Ezekiola curiously.

"Sort of. I've actually used something much smaller in our motions class to move things around and speed up vegetable growth."

"But you've never tried entering a Sporadic Door?" said Atlas to make his point.

"No."

"This will be your first time, then," he said.

"Don't start again, Atlas," cut in Ezekiola. "We decided to give this a try. If it works, it works. If it doesn't, it doesn't. We'll just go back. At least we won't sit on regrets and dwell on what we could have done." *This answer should satisfy everyone,* he told himself, and more importantly, quench his own curiosity.

They passed the simulation zones under the rain, sticking

to the manicured path until they finally came to the signpost where they had last been with Gordi. They walked past it in search of the tree where Virgil had led them to. As the night sky set in, visibility dwindled.

"This way," Nohlan said, turning right.

Atlas stood still, not following his friends for a moment. "No, it was this way," he said, motioning his friends to continue walking ahead.

"No, I think Nohlan's right. It's this way," corrected Ezekiola, pointing to the other direction.

Atlas looked around, and every direction suddenly looked the same. He tried one last time to convince his friends, but in vain. Outnumbered and doubting himself at this point, he decided to follow them. Besides, he was in this for the ride, he told himself.

Nohlan headed towards a tree that looked just like the one they had seen before. He searched around the trunk for pumpkin seeds but saw none. Maybe the rain had washed them away. Not wanting to accept the possibility that Atlas might be right, he reassured everyone, including himself, by announcing: "This is the tree."

"Are you sure?" asked Ezekiola, sensing his hesitation.

"Yes, I'm sure. It's the one that had the thickest trunk, you can almost hide behind it."

"So, what do we do now?" asked Atlas.

"All right, hold this for me," Nohlan handed his staff to Ezekiola and pulled out the numerous sets of scribbled notes he was popularly known for keeping in his pockets. He pulled the right one from the lot and stuffed the others back in his pocket. The three of them looked at the crumpled piece of paper.

"This is Borghis's study notes from his Incantation class," he said.

"You have to read all this?" asked Atlas, mesmerized by the length.

"No, I already went through it, we just need the incantation part."

"It should be easy then."

"I'm not sure about that. Incantations are never simple readings," Ezekiola said. He pointed to something in the notes. "Look here, Borghis wrote, *'the staff will answer to the command of the one calling, for as long as it is sounded on all three.'* "

"What's that supposed to mean?" asked Atlas.

"On all three," Ezekiola contemplated out loud. "Those must be the levels. Do you remember what Nomi taught us in one of our classes? Incantations have to do with the sending of words to higher levels, and vocalizing them with purpose is only the start."

"All right then. How does the staff come into all this?" asked Atlas.

"Let's try it. Here, hold the paper, and hand me the staff." Nohlan took the staff awkwardly as if he was in dire need of practice. He held it in front of the tree according to the instructions, touching its tip to the trunk. Like a student who is forced to read out loud in class, he recited the incantation without a hint of rhythm.

"Within the radius of Circa I stand
And firmly sound forth this note,
Forge might into this shaft,
Open the doors to mansions abound,
Let us free to explore the paths."

The three boys watched closely where the tip of the staff touched the tree to see if something would happen. Atlas and

Ezekiola then noticed the staff start shaking. They looked at Nohlan's hands holding the staff, and they were shaking, too, naturally vibrating the piece of wood he was holding.

"Are you moving the staff or is it moving by itself?" asked Atlas, as skeptical as ever.

"I don't know," answered Nohlan nervously. Nohlan touched the tree, and it stood hard as the dense wood it was made out of.

"Well, it clearly didn't work. To be honest, Nohlan, your chanting sounded half-hearted at best, like you were trying to open the doors to your closet," Atlas observed.

"Shut it, Atlas. Try again, Nohlan," Ezekiola pressed him. "You have to try again. But put more of your intent in there. I think you have a good understanding of the incantation, and that's the first level, which is the speech part. Now put your will behind it. Remember, it has to be sounded on all three for it to manifest. Feel and think your words beyond the speech part. Bring it up a notch higher and then higher still. Make it come alive!"

Encouraged, Nohlan tried again, uncertain about how to sound 'on all threes.' He simply said the incantation ferociously louder this time, and by the time he got to the last verse, he was virtually shouting it. "LET US FREE TO EXPLORE THE PATHS!"

The boys eagerly waited to see if something happened. The tree stood still, and all but a few leaves shook from the wind. Some fell from the rain that was beating down on them.

"That last one sounded like you were angry at your cat, Nohlan. Maybe you need to do it a little softer," said Atlas helpfully.

"Try again, Nohlan. Try a softer version, like Atlas said, but stronger on the inside. You must connect with the words with heart and mind. We'll get there, just try one more time," said

Ezekiola, hoping Nohlan wouldn't give up despite several failures. The prospect of seeing Leanne was powerful in his mind. He, too, wanted badly for this to happen.

Nohlan tried again, and again, and again. He tried softly, calmly, roughly, frantically, to the point where it became too much for Atlas to simply sit back quietly and watch his friend's many attempts.

"Goodness Nohlan, you tried so many times I learned the whole thing by heart," he blurted out. That last comment was one too many for Nohlan. "Well then, you go ahead, and you try it, Atlas! You're driving me mad here, chatting away the way you do. I can barely concentrate! Here!" He shoved the staff in Atlas' direction. "You do it. My turn to criticize!"

"You know very well I don't have these skills. In fact, I don't even believe this thing can work. How do you even want me to try?" Atlas said, backing off. Far from his field of logic, he well knew it would be close to impossible for him to make such a thing happen, especially when he held little belief in the matter. Yet he kept sticking with the very friends who could possibly prove him wrong. Entering into discussions and heated arguments of this sort was a side effect of these friendships he cherished.

"Here, give it to me," said Ezekiola, realizing they weren't going anywhere. He took hold of the staff and touched its head.

"Give me a moment, please," he asked his friends. They stood back, curious and oddly hopeful as to what he would do differently. Ezekiola went for a small stroll around the tree while gripping the staff and muttering to himself. He came back around and, this time, laid his hands on the trunk of the tree. He closed his eyes, leaving his friends to wonder what he was doing exactly.

"Nohlan, give me your incantation notes, please," he said, suddenly opening his eyes, then, to the surprise of all, added,

"Atlas, I need you to stand a little further away from us, just for the moment. In fact, please go for a walk and don't think of us."

Atlas looked slightly offended. This was the first time he was being asked to step aside and keep a distance from his friend. He was about to say something but decided against it.

"You probably don't remember, but it's just what Nomi said," Ezekiola said apologetically. "To manifest something in the material world, one must work at casting away the shadow of doubt. If this is to work, then I must try it in an atmosphere where doubt is completely absent, and your presence is casting many doubts."

Atlas stood away. Not angry, but unexpectedly intrigued.

"Fine then. I'll go for a stroll. Come fetch me when you're done."

Ezekiola stood next to Nohlan and mindfully sent forth his thoughts. He then looked at the incantation and, with a focused mind and to the best of his ability, read it out loud, taking a few breaks in between the verses to feel each word. It was surprisingly heartwarming to sense them on all the levels he could manage to attain.

When he reached the last word, the tip of the Brown staff dipped right into the tree, making Ezekiola almost fall forward if it hadn't been for Nohlan grabbing him.

"Whoa! Did you see that?!" Nohlan was amazed.

"Go get Atlas. Quick!" Ezekiola told him. Nohlan hurried to find their friend.

"Well, I'll be sprinkled with the stardust of Circa!" Atlas said from where he was standing. He dared not come closer at that point, in fear his presence might make the phenomenon end.

"It's alright, Atlas, come closer. I think we have to go into the tree now that it's opened."

"Who goes first?"

"We all do. Hold the staff, everyone, and walk right through. We won't have much time from what I read about these doors. Some close faster than others, right Nohlan?" His friend nodded quickly.

They walked right through and heard a swooshing sound as they exited from another tree. They quickly scanned their new environment. The first thing noticeable was that there was no rain. It felt like the sun had just set. As if it was a few hours behind Circa.

"Ha ha! We did it! WE DID IT!" Nohlan was ecstatic, raising his staff in the air, believing in it even more. He had just had his first experience of going through a Sporadic Door. Not only that, but he did it with his friends, not by learning it in class. It was a first for him on many levels.

Once their initial excitement had died down, they wandered about, exploring the forest they were in. A few minutes into their new environment, Atlas asked the pressing question that was on everyone's mind: "So, where are we exactly?"

"A forest, it seems, where Leanne came from," Nohlan answered. Only one path was visible.

"Well, let's see where this takes us," said Ezekiola. He was extremely glad for their successful entry into this unknown land and would not have imagined for a moment that they were not the only ones lurking on this path.

Chapter 17

Mirhas the Oracle

The boys walked cautiously, taking in their surroundings one tentative step at a time. Traveling to a new world was a novel experience for them. As much as they were eager to make its discovery, they kept eyes in the back of their heads, searching for anything out of the ordinary. The forest was dense, more so than their schoolyard. The foliage here, however, was chaotic, not as orderly or trimmed as what they were accustomed to. It was surprising that a path had been cleared out, although it was filled with dried leaves as if fall had come and gone. What struck them the most, though, was the silence. Besides the sound of their footfalls and the cracking of a few branches, nothing else could be heard. No birds chirped, no bees buzzed, no squirrels squeaked. Ezekiola sensed something was amiss.

"Everything is so quiet. Almost too quiet," he observed. "Nohlan, do you know exactly where this incantation took us?"

Nohlan's excitement suddenly dampened. He was growing wary of his environment. "I'm not sure, really. I would think it's where your lady came from."

"She's not *my* lady," Ezekiola said, smiling.

"Yet!" Atlas finished his friend's sentence, making them all giggle.

"Could we have chosen another tree than the one she came from?" Ezekiola asked, coming back to his initial observation.

"No, I'm pretty sure this was where she came from. Otherwise, it would not have worked, right?" Nohlan responded with some hesitation.

"Well, it's not as if you tried your recipe on one of the trees I was heading for," Atlas said. "You can, therefore, not be certain of your answer, Nohlan. Who knows if this would have worked perfectly on another tree?"

"I feel movement," Ezekiola said suddenly, freezing in his tracks.

"What? Where?" Nohlan asked. He looked right into the trees to try to detect something.

"No, not around, but underneath the ground."

He lifted his foot and saw the leaf underneath it shake slightly as if something was either hiding or trying to make its way out.

"I just felt it, too," said Atlas, 'there's something beneath us."

Atlas dug into the ground with his foot to toss away some of the leaves covering the surface and felt the movement increase. He dug in further still to see what was causing it. Suddenly, everything beneath them was stirring. What should have remained dormant had been awakened and was coming out of every possible hole in the ground.

Snakes! Snakes everywhere.

"Get off the path!! Quick!" Atlas yelled.

Atlas, Nohlan, and Ezekiola sprinted off the path into the denser section of the forest. The trees overhead blocked most of the light, making it harder for them to see where they were going. In no time, darkness descended on them.

"They're following us!" Atlas yelled, pushing away the branches that kept hitting his body as he ran. "Nohlan, what is this place? You brought us straight into the land of serpents!"

Snakes were coming out of everywhere, making their way to greet their visitors. The boys continued to run as fast as possible when Ezekiola halted unexpectedly.

"Wait! That's it. You said it right, Atlas. We're in the land of serpents. That's it! I know where we are!" he told his friends.

"Really now! And where do you think we are? Leanne's paradise?" asked Atlas. He began to regret his decision to follow his friends.

Ezekiola continued walking instead, letting the snakes catch up to him. "No, we're not in Leanne's world. We definitely entered the wrong tree. There are many worlds outside Circa. We must be in Master Sohan's domain. I learned about this from one of the books in Nomi's library. I'm almost certain," he said.

"Master who?!" Nohlan asked, bewildered.

"Master Sohan. Wait, you must stop running. It's not what you think," he said to his friends who thought he'd gone loony.

"Stop running and stand still!" Ezekiola yelled louder this time. "Running away from them will simply make it worse."

But they wouldn't hear of it.

"Are you mad? Who in their sane minds would stand still when they're being swarmed by snakes? What do you intend to do, pet them?" Atlas was petrified by the idea of being chased by hundreds of snakes, some of which he could have sworn had come out of thin air.

"There's just too many! Let's just go back," pleaded Nohlan, frightened at the monstrous horde of slithery critters gathering around him. A few snakes poured down from above, falling on Nohlan's and Atlas's heads with a dreadful thump. They shrieked and shrieked.

"Nohlan, where the hell did you take us with that staff of yours?!" Atlas was beyond himself now. While the two were busy tossing snakes off their heads and shoulders, Ezekiola slowly walked past them deeper into the darker woods.

"What are you doing? We better head back, it's getting worse!"

Ezekiola turned around and glanced back in the direction they had come from. "Actually, I don't think so. We must go forward. Behind us is no longer an option anymore," he said.

The two looked back and saw a mountain of snakes building up at lightning speed. Like an avalanche, the mass was headed in their direction.

"RUN!" Nohlan screamed while swinging his staff into the air, trying to toss the snakes off of it.

"If you keep doing that, their number will increase. Just stay calm," Ezekiola warned them again. The two friends then noticed that Ezekiola was not surrounded by any snakes. Instead, they slithered aside to let him walk past them. Some even followed by his side as if they were all part of some ceremony.

Ezekiola continued to walk calmly, yet Atlas and Nohlan could barely keep up, as they were too busy removing the snakes hanging off of them.

"Ezekiola, this is not funny anymore! We need to get out of here!" Nohlan shouted. He had even begun using his staff as a bat, striking as many snakes as possible that came his way.

"Keep walking, don't hit them. Just walk and don't focus on them. They will only hurt you if you fear them. We're getting close," he said.

"Close to what?! We need to leave NOW!" Atlas said, panting.

But Ezekiola ignored his pleas and began talking to himself.

"Where are you? I know you're here, you're waiting for us, aren't you? I'll find you," he said as he looked above and beyond the snakes around him. He approached a ditch, where he noticed a coiled red snake that seemed to be sleeping. He knelt down and remained still.

Suddenly, all the snakes slithered towards the ditch where the red snake lay, merging with it until it became larger than the three boys combined. Nohlan and Atlas were mortified, wondering if they would ever be leaving this place alive. The red snake stood upright, opened its eyes, and spoke:

"Greetingsss, Ezekiola of the Emerald Belt. What brings you into my domain?" he hissed.

"Greetings, Master Sohan, I came to seek your help and guidance," Ezekiola replied courteously, showing no outer fear whatsoever. But then, he was an expert at masking his feelings. Ezekiola extended his hands towards the serpent. To the shock of both Atlas and Nohlan, Master Sohan also extended a pair of hands to receive Ezekiola's. He then noticed Ezekiola's entourage and fixed his gaze on the boys behind him. Atlas and Nohlan stood frozen like statues, wondering if they, too, had to extend their hands.

"Goes sssame for your compatriots? Ssso full of fear they are," he hissed, "They make my sssnakes fall upon them like rain from the sssky."

Atlas and Nohlan stared back dumbly at Master Sohan, clueless as to what to do. The words reverberated in Atlas's mind. "They make my snakes fall from the sky." *What does he mean by that? How can we be the ones making them fall from above?*

"Yes, my friends seek guidance, just as I do," replied Ezekiola.

"And what is it that you all ssseek?" asked Master Sohan.

"We seek the path back to where we came from, the domain of Circa," Ezekiola replied.

Master Sohan looked at him intently for a long moment, making the others wonder if the snake was attempting to hypnotize his guest and penetrate his mind. They were thankful they were not standing in his place. Yet Ezekiola kept his cool just as he had when he greeted Master Sohan.

"You ssseek to go back, then why come here in the first place?"

"We got lost, actually," said Atlas suddenly from behind. The serpent's head could not have moved any faster as it abruptly swerved towards Atlas, who became still as a rock. His heart froze as Master Sohan approached him, almost touching the tip of his nose.

"Atlas of the great stars, how is it that you follow your friends with a heart full of doubts?" All at once, Atlas realized that Master Sohan had been reading Ezekiola's mind while staring at him. Now he knew his name as well. He felt the gaze of the snake penetrate a deep place within him and felt himself become an open book as if nothing could be withheld from the reptilian master.

"I followed because I trust them," he said truthfully. "They usually steer me in the right direction."

To his surprise, he was able to face the snake better than he thought he could and, ironically, found comfort in being direct with him. In the face of his fear, it was his best armor.

"Ssso you trust them, knowing they will make mistakesss. You are a sssolid friend to them," he said while keeping his gaze focused on Atlas. "Ssstill, allowing such a fear-filled imagination to govern your mind can sssteer you away from reality.

Learn to master your fearsss, Atlasss of the great stars, for they are magnified beyond measure in my domain," he ended his conversation with Atlas by turning to Nohlan.

"And finally, the leader of this troop guided by temptation, tell me, then, what made you bring your friends into my domain?"

Nohlan blurted out the words before he even had a chance to think: "We were trying to find a way into a Sporadic Door using my brother's old, worn, down staff and wanted to enter the very same door we thought a human girl from Planet Blue had come through. We just wanted to try, but we ended up here instead."

"A human from Planet Blue? Interesssting. I have not seen one in many cycles," he said. "You made a mistake, went through the wrong door, and took that risk knowingly, from what I can sssee. You have much heart, I must sssay."

He then slithered back into his ditch and stood upright to look Ezekiola in the eyes.

"In the face of fear, you govern yourself with courage, Ezekiola of the Emerald Belt. A noble ssskill. Follow me, and there where I find my other half is where you shall find your way back home."

In an instant, Master Sohan transformed himself from a serpent into a dove. The contrast in his animal forms had a striking effect on the trio. From a state of sheer terror, the boys quickly found themselves in a state of sublime hope. They barely understood what Master Sohan meant by meeting his other half but, having no other option, followed him nonetheless. Thankfully, there were no more snakes on the ground. The light grew more intense, and it became bright as midday. Master Sohan flew high into the sky, making signs with his head, motioning the boys to continue along the path in the direction he was flying.

The white dove soared ahead, taking breaks from time to time to allow the boys to catch up. They barely spoke a word, and the only times they stopped were to catch their breath. Finally, after crossing what seemed to be a thicket of dense foliage, they finally emerged onto a prairie-like path where the sun beamed down onto golden fields. Master Sohan picked up speed, calculating that his guests could see him well enough in the clearing, a stark contrast to the labyrinth they had just left. They ran faster until they finally saw the dove come to rest on a lone tree in the middle of nowhere. They looked up, fearing they might miss Master Sohan's next move, and were momentarily confused when they saw another dove soaring ahead.

"Either we're seeing double, or this is some wicked game he's playing," said Atlas.

The second dove came down to rest next to its partner, and like a mirage, the two merged into one, then vanished into thin air.

"That must be his other half!" Nohlan said.

Atlas, who was the first to arrive at the lone tree, sat down to wait for his friends. He looked around and noticed crumbling huts, the remains of what may have been a village. *Where are we?* he wondered. He couldn't wait to go back home. Never again, he promised himself. This type of unplanned adventure was off-limits for him from now on. Just then, Nohlan arrived, staff in hand, readying himself to use it. Ezekiola, however, took his time wandering about the fields and derelict habitats. The place looked long abandoned.

"Would you like a biscuit while you stroll? We might just make it for dessert when we get back home for the festival," said Atlas, hinting at his friend's snail's pace. He was sure they had missed the festivities by now. "Let's just hurry and get out of here."

Ezekiola shook his head. "Something's not right. Master Sohan didn't give us a straight answer."

"Why do you say that? Here's the tree. This must be the Sporadic Door," Nohlan said.

"Alright then, go ahead. Try it," he told Nohlan.

"I think you should do it. You were better than me."

Ezekiola took the staff and, just as he had done before, went ahead and said the incantation out loud.

Nothing happened. With a frown on his face, he went at it again a second, then a third time, but to no avail. He turned around to Nohlan: "I think you should try now. This door is not responding to me."

Nohlan tried, his incantation sounding more like a plea than anything else. Again, nothing. After several attempts, the desperation was such that Atlas took the staff and gave it a try. His calling didn't work either.

"That foul, wicked serpent! What a liar!" exclaimed Atlas. "I can't believe we all fell into his trap."

"What do we do now?" Nohlan panicked, realizing for the first time the possibility he might be stuck in a place he didn't want to be.

Ezekiola spoke up. "Master Sohan doesn't lie, he only hints. I think we should search the vicinity and see if there's anything else around here. We can't be too far off," he said reassuringly, nonetheless thinking there had been something odd in the way he had led them here.

They strolled about, looking for what could possibly be a Sporadic Door.

"This place is a dump," Atlas said, kicking at a pile of bricks, the remains of a ruined house.

"I wonder why the inhabitants left this village," Nohlan said.

"This place is completely forsaken. Who would ever want

to live in a rut like this?" Atlas added, pointing to the desolation all around them.

"There might be more to this place than meets the eye. Don't be too quick to judge," said Ezekiola. "Remember, we're not in our own domain. So don't rely on appearances," he said, remembering his reading escapades in Nomi's library. Amongst some of his interests, Ezekiola sometimes liked to read about worlds outside of Circa.

"Don't rely on appearances? Let's be realistic, Zek. We're standing exactly where vultures shop for food. Let's hope none of them see us as their next meal," Atlas said.

"Nah, I don't think even vultures would come here, there's nothing to eat. Speaking of which, I'm hungry," Nohlan said, looking around as if he might find a table with food on it.

"Well, one thing's for sure. This place can put anyone on a diet," Atlas said, laughing.

"Maybe that's why everyone's disappeared. There was no food." Nohlan continued, stuck on the topic of food, as he walked alongside his friends in no specific direction.

"I sure hope we find our way back soon. Otherwise, Borghis will realize his staff is missing, and he'll..."

They suddenly stopped talking. There in front of them was a little girl picking flowers, quietly sorting them, then adding them to a bunch in her hands. It was an odd and surprising sight to fall on in such an austere setting. Ezekiola became wary just at the sight of her. The boys approached cautiously, not knowing what she was doing there all alone. Although she didn't fit the least bit with her surrounding, she continued very naturally, truly focused on her task, her back towards them. Ezekiola motioned to his friends to stay where they were, then softly said, "Hello."

She jumped around, startled, but then her face warmed with a gleaming smile.

"Hello," she responded. She was a pretty little girl of no more than five, he reckoned.

They stared at each other, with Ezekiola unsure exactly of what he should say. He had been trying to read her thoughts, but her mind was completely blank.

"We didn't mean to frighten you. Do you live here?" he asked.

The girl nodded.

"Can you tell us where we are?" he then asked.

"You're in the Mistress' domain." *The Mistress' domain? What was that?*

"And which Mistress would that be?" he asked.

"Why, the only one in this domain: Mistress Mirhas."

The name sounded vaguely familiar, but he couldn't recall where he had read it. It must have been in the same book he had read about Master Sohan. The two must be connected somehow.

"We're from the domain of Circa, and we're looking to find our way back home. Do you think you can help us?"

"Perhaps my Mistress can help," the little girl answered enthusiastically.

"Can you tell us where we can find your Mistress so she may guide us?" Ezekiola asked as Nohlan and Atlas made their way to stand behind him, wary that the girl might be more than she appeared to be.

"Why yes, but she mostly hides since she has been cast away. Our whole village has been, as you can see."

"Great, now what?" whispered Atlas to Nohlan. "We switched from the domain of a serpent master to that of a hiding mistress."

"Quiet, Atlas. She's trying to help," Nohlan whispered back.

"I can bring you to her dwelling, she will be happy to greet you. She has not been visited for many ages," she said sadly.

For a moment, Ezekiola pondered her words. Why had the mistress been cast away? And her whole village at that? Had her domain been invaded by nomads who had destroyed everything and everyone as they passed through? Yet from what the little girl said, her mistress was still alive and in hiding. To think that no one had paid her a visit all this time.

"Follow me," the little girl said lightly and hopped over a crumbling pile of bricks that had once been the foundation of a building. There were weeds growing from odd corners, providing a minimum of greenery to this desolate environment. The only trees left standing were naked, with frail branches pleading to the sky above. At one point, Nohlan sidetracked when he saw something unbelievable: a white rose growing behind a tilted barrel. Under the disapproving look of his friends, he walked towards it and unashamedly plucked it. The last thing this village needed was the removal of the last glimmer of beauty left in it. Nohlan shrugged and mouthed, "Sorry." He handed the rose to Ezekiola instead, motioning him to give it to the girl. Ezekiola took the flower from his hands and sighed. As they walked quietly amidst the rubble, it seemed each footstep they took added to the desolation, further crumbling whatever was still left standing. Ezekiola couldn't help but feel a pinch of sadness that such a place had once been thriving and now seemed utterly abandoned. *What had this place been before?* He was itching to ask her. Whatever it was, it seemed to only be wilderness now. As intriguing as it might be to unravel more about its history, his priority, however, was to get him and his friends out of this place.

She brought them to a large brick hut.

"You may wait here. I'll go get her."

She walked through a makeshift veil serving as a door entrance, and it immediately closed behind her.

After a few minutes of waiting, the boys grew impatient and began wondering what was going on. No noise came from the hut, and the girl hadn't returned. How long could it possibly take to see if there was anyone in such a small space? The three looked at each other and became suspicious.

"This is taking too long," noted Ezekiola.

"Maybe we should call her," Nohlan said.

"What was her name?" asked Atlas.

"We didn't ask. She said Mistress Mirhas lived here," Ezekiola answered.

"Ask then. We can't just linger here forever!" Atlas pressed.

"My lady? My lady, are you still in there?" asked Ezekiola, hunching forward to bring himself closer to the curtain door.

There was no answer.

Ezekiola shrugged, not knowing what to say next.

Nohlan came close to the entrance and yelled louder: "We would like to see the mistress of the house, please. Mistress Mirhas?"

Nobody came out. Silence persisted.

"That's it. I've had enough." Atlas tossed the curtain aside and walked right in. Nohlan and Ezekiola followed cautiously behind. The place was as rundown as a home could be, and the little girl was nowhere in sight. Broken pots, vases, and tools were scattered on the floor; the foundation was worn, and the layout of the house was barely distinguishable. A faint circle made of rocks could be made out in the center of the hut. There was a room on the right with dirty bedclothes and other rags tossed in a corner and a living space on the left with one standing chair, but the rest was just broken furniture scattered here and there. At the far end of the hut was something that looked like a kitchen. Judging from its size, this dwelling could house only one or two people at most.

Something hanging by the kitchen window grabbed Ezekiola's attention. He walked over to it and touched the only item that seemed to have survived the crumbling of this place—a glass ball hanging delicately by a string. He looked closer and fixated on what was inside the glass: the image of a moon and several stars floating about. He could not shake off an intuitive but nonetheless worrying suspicion that there was more to this place than met the eye. And yet, the little girl was still nowhere in sight. Atlas was getting visibly jumpy and turned to Nohlan.

"This place gives me the creeps. Where did that little girl go? She came out of nowhere, and she looks like she doesn't belong here. I mean, where are her parents? I'd be worried about leaving her in this place."

"How can anyone live here at all?" Nohlan added.

"Maybe there's a village nearby," said Atlas.

"Maybe there isn't, and this is where she really lives."

"This place is odd, for starters, and I'm not sure Sohan knew where he was leading us. For the love of Circa, how will we get back home?!"

While Atlas and Nohlan were raising all sorts of questions, Ezekiola shook the glass ball out of curiosity to see if the moon and stars would move. A gigantic rock suddenly rolled into the opening of the door, giving them a fright. It blocked the entrance of the hut. The light coming from the front door was gone.

"What's happening?" Nohlan asked and moved closer to grab hold of Ezekiola's cloak. He then noticed Ezekiola holding a glass ball in his hands.

"Did you just shake that ball?" Nohlan asked, wondering if that's what had caused the rock to block the entrance.

"Yes, I did," said Ezekiola, starting to feel claustrophobic. He let go of the glass ball, which began turning in circles.

"You shouldn't have touched that ball! How will we get out now?" Atlas said, convinced that Ezekiola shaking the glass ball had put them in this situation.

To their horror, the walls around them began to close in, further shutting out the small rays of incoming light. They stood in the dark, their backs against one another. Then the floor they were standing on rotated, knocking them off balance. They ran for the exit but couldn't get out. The rock would not budge.

"She's ready to see you now," the little girl's voice was heard through the dark.

They spun around, only to find no one there.

"What is this place? Let us out!" Nohlan yelled.

Out of the darkness came the sound of rushing water.

"What's that?" Atlas asked, huddling closer to his friends. "Ezekiola, Nohlan, if you have any tricks up your sleeves, now's the time!"

"My feet are getting wet," Nohlan said.

"It's just water," Ezekiola said, trying to maintain his cool.

"Yes, just water, AND it's rising!" Atlas retorted. "Goodness, it's up to my knees already! Nohlan, quick say something with your staff!" he insisted.

"This is what he meant, his other half," Ezekiola muttered to himself.

"WHAT?!" both asked.

"That's it! I just remembered!"

"REMEMBERED WHAT? I don't want to drown here!" Panic had now grabbed Atlas by the throat.

"Something I read that just came back to me now. Master Sohan sometimes appears as a master of fears and teaches through illusion. That which appears real is not."

"So what are you saying, that this is not real? We're outside of Circa, and we haven't figured out how to get back home. How can this not be real?" Atlas said, panting heavily.

"Oh, now you believe, don't you, Atlas?!" Nohlan said. He picked the worst possible moment to say such a thing. He couldn't hold it back for all the mocking he had endured up to this moment. Ezekiola continued as if he had never been interrupted: "We're in the domain of his other half, his feminine opposite! She's the forgotten one because of the unseen forces she works with. That's why she was cast away, for no one believes in that which they cannot see. We must believe in her and invoke her presence. It's the only way to save ourselves."

As he spoke, the water kept rising and was now up to their necks.

"We're going to die here!" Atlas exclaimed.

"Whatever happens, stay with me," Ezekiola said. He instinctively undid his Emerald Belt and, without any further thought, took hold of his friends' wrists, attaching them one by one, linking them all together. The water then engulfed them. They began gasping for air and soon began swallowing water. It would be a matter of time before they drowned.

With the last breath left in him, Ezekiola gathered all his strength and mindfully sounded her name:

"MIRHAS, HELP US!"

The little girl that had guided them suddenly appeared underwater and took hold of the end of the Emerald Belt, dragging the boys deeper underground where the circle in the hut was positioned. They entered a tunnel and emerged in a cave adorned with miniature waterfalls gushing from gleaming rocks. It appeared they had been ejected from a makeshift water bubble onto hard land. Ezekiola was lying on the floor when he instinctively looked up to see where they had fallen from. He saw that the cave had a wide opening from above through which all the stars and moons of Circa shone brightly.

He looked in front and noticed his belt was in the little girl's hands. He looked around for his friends and found them lying on the floor, immobile. This rapid change of environment made him dizzy for the first time. Worried about his friends, he got up and went over to see them. "Don't worry," he suddenly heard her say, "they're only sleeping." He leaned over to see, and indeed, Atlas and Nohlan were in a deep slumber.

As she walked ahead of him, the little girl changed appearances, rising taller than Ezekiola. Her robe changed colors, too, from the damp gray-white to an indigo blue. She was still holding his belt in her hands. Ezekiola was then surprised to see that she also held the white rose that Nohlan had given him earlier. He had let go of the flower while in the hut. At this odd moment, the thought crossed his mind that ladies truly did like flowers. She turned around to face him, and he took a step back, mesmerized. He had never seen anything like it. He could only see eyes on her face and no other features. Her eyes shone like beacons in the darkness, and she was reading him like an open book.

He picked up on her thoughts immediately as she welcomed him. He had never before met someone with the ability to see through him so effortlessly. He locked his gaze with her and slowly fell into a slumber himself, letting her sink into his mind.

"Who are you?" he asked.

"I am Mirhas, the Oracle."

Her voice seemed to come out of the walls. He then heard several voices speaking at once: "The Fountain of Fire has come alive in you, for you have created a link. Yet, the one you linked with is in danger. And so are you. You must face the one who will seek to crush you and dominate him. I bless your belt, for it shall be of aid to you in your coming battle."

After hearing her speak, he gathered the little strength left in him to ask her the question pressing on his mind.

"Will you always remain in exile here in this wilderness?"

"This era of my life is coming to an end. My nature will soon be acknowledged and understood. My village will thrive once more."

He wanted to continue talking, but his eyelids closed.

"Be good and journey well, Ezekiola of the Emerald Belt." It was the last thing he heard her say before he fell into a deep sleep.

Chapter 18

The Falcons Awake

Borghis, Gordi, and Keenan were having a good morning after a lively night celebrating Circa's Moon Festival. And it had just gotten better as they stood staring down at the three boys they had stumbled upon blissfully asleep in the restricted zone of the Black Forest.

"Look at them, with half of the school worried sick," Borghis said deviously to his friends as they circled around their catch.

"I knew we would find them here," Gordi said.

"They've had a good night's sleep, it seems," Keenan added, noting the boys' peaceful faces. Indeed, there was an air of serenity about them, as if they were having delightful dreams they didn't want to wake up from.

"GET UP!" Borghis yelled, clapping his hands close enough to their ears to yank the three younglings out of their slumber.

Nohlan was the first to open his eyes. After all they had been through, he had completely lost his sense of reality. For a moment, his surroundings could not have been any more surreal: him on the ground, his clothes covered in an unusual amount of dirt, his brother Borghis and Brown Robes Gordi, and Keenan all looking down on him. Worse yet, Borghis' wooden staff was in his hands, the wood darkened from having absorbed so much water. As Nohlan slowly shifted his body around, his brother suddenly cried out, "IS THAT MY STAFF?!"

"What? This?" asked Nohlan stupidly. He was desperate to buy himself some extra time to come up with a credible answer.

"YES! What else, you fool? Give that to me!" Borghis jerked the staff out of Nohlan's hands. By then, both Atlas and Ezekiola were up, staring wide-eyed at the scene. They noted it was morning; they had ended up asleep in the forest, completely missing Circa's Moon Festival. Borghis touched the staff and realized it was much rougher, different from its last polished state, with a noticeable piece of wood missing from its edge.

"Nohlan! It's been chipped," he said incredulously. "I just polished this, and now it looks like it's got a year's wear on it! What did you do to it?"

Nohlan looked at him with a blank stare. "Nothing," he said. "It's just that the weather and the rain didn't help. Like you said, it's an old staff, anyway. How could it possibly not have a year's wear on it?"

Borghis stood with his mouth open at hearing his brother's answer. He snapped back at all of them: "You three underlings better have an explanation for all this. I don't even know where to start with you deviants. From what I can see here, you're up for some hefty sanctions. You've broken a load of rules! Stealing a staff being the first on the list!" he said.

"Well, good morning to you, Borghis," yawned Atlas as he walked past him onto a sunnier portion of the path, like a cat settling into a warm spot to nestle. He was visibly relieved to be on familiar ground once again.

"Don't you walk away, Atlas. You, too, will be escorted back to the school premises, along with your mates. Be assured this incident won't go unaccounted for. All of your actions will be reported to the headmaster!"

"Report what, that we slept?" Atlas asked nonchalantly, laughing at the simplicity of his own question and answer. Nothing could bother him at this point. He had found great relief after being lost for so long. The only thing that boggled his mind was that he could not remember how he got back.

"Laugh all you want. This time you won't get out of it so easily. I'll make sure of it."

"Borghis, it's as simple as that. We simply spent the night in the forest and woke up under this tree. And why do you always have to overreact to everything I say?" asked Atlas, his mind as calm as a tranquil sea despite the fact that he knew none of the answers he gave would satisfy Borghis.

"Overreact? For your information, when you three didn't show up to your dorms last night, a general search was organized to find you." Borghis blurted out. Keenan and Gordi were nodding in agreement next to him. Gordi then turned to Ezekiola.

"Now I know that Virgil was telling the truth about you, Ezekiola. You're the culprit leading this wolf pack," Gordi added.

With barely any time to wake his senses, Ezekiola shot back, "The culprit leading his wolf pack? You've clearly lost your mind, Gordi. For one, I'm not a wolf, and you know very well nothing came out of Virgil's made-up stories," he said, whisking the dust off his clothes. Brown Robes trying to get the better of them was the last of his worries. His mind was occupied with other things. He was craving to debrief everything that had happened in the presence of the oracle with his friends. He had been robbed of that precious moment by Borghis and his cronies.

"You mind telling me what happened here, then? Just a few days ago, Gordi caught Virgil coming out of this very same restricted section of the forest where you were set to meet a lady, and now we find you here again, with the added element that you spent the night here!"

"We just got lost," Nohlan blurted out.

"You got lost?" asked Keenan.

"I'll run you through how everything happened," Nohlan said, having planted the introduction to his story. Atlas cast a worried glance at Ezekiola, not sure how Nohlan's story was going to turn out. Nohlan related how they had volunteered for the task of fetching additional wood for the bonfire the night before. Under the questioning glares of the three Brown Robes, it was astonishing how much he detailed every small path they had supposedly taken into the Black Forest to find each piece of wood and how they had fixed a few worn-out arrows on their way as an act of goodwill. Atlas and Ezekiola were delightfully surprised to hear Nohlan tell his story with such precision, to the point it would have sounded convincing even to them if they hadn't known it was complete rubbish. To their dismay, Nohlan's story then took a sharp turn when he got to the point where he said they got lost because of heavy rains, followed by flash flooding and mudslides, leaving them no choice but to stay put.

"Flash flooding and mudslides in this forest? Really?" Borghis repeated his brother's words. His face could not have worn a greater expression of disbelief. "So, you opted to stay outdoors, actually sleeping outdoors, to avoid muddy floods."

Atlas was about to intervene to save the story, but Ezekiola threw him a cautious look.

"We were waiting for the storm to calm down, but it got worse. So, we just camped out here," Nohlan concluded.

Borghis turned to look at the rest of his brother's friends to see if anyone was going to embellish the story to make it more plausible. He was met by neutral faces. He turned back to his brother with a determined expression: "Do you know, Nohlan, why it is forbidden to walk all by yourselves, let alone sleep in the restricted zones of this forest?"

Nohlan shrugged. He didn't know what the reason was, except that some areas were reserved for the more advanced students.

"There are things out there that are outside of your grasp of knowledge, dangerous things that could put your life at risk, and you wouldn't know what to do."

Borghis' educational speech was too much for Atlas.

"And let me guess, Borghis. Unlike us low levels, you and the Brown Robes would know exactly what to do. Correct?"

"Don't mock me, little fool. Come enough times into this restricted part of the forest, and you'll have a taste of what I speak of. Perhaps it's exactly what you deserve at this point."

"What a blatant fable. Why not tell it as it is, Borghis? That in the end, it's not our safety that truly concerns you, but rather that liberty you claim to have of being the only ones capable of lurking in these parts of the forest without harm. And the fact is that we just took that liberty away from you by spending an entire night here and coming out unscathed," he said defiantly.

"That's enough, Atlas," Keenan stepped in. "All of you gather your belongings. We have to bring you back and report you. Keep your foul explanations for Nomi's ears. See if your story flies with him."

Ezekiola, Atlas, and Nohlan slowly put on their cloaks, gathered their bags, and made their way toward the main path.

"I'll suggest a well-deserved suspension. Who knows, you

might get something worse," said Borghis, a smile curling on one side of his mouth. He had never been able to prove Atlas was behind the theft of the items missing from the Brown Robes' dorms. He had only heard rumors that Atlas was the culprit, and he believed them to be true. So any which way to make Atlas pay was a means for Borghis to get even with him. When dealing with transgressions of this sort, the School Council seriously considered everything put forth by the Brown Robes.

The White Tunics walked slowly. Nobody was in a hurry. No one spoke again, and the only sounds heard were the ones coming from the forest. At one point in their silent march, Hilga appeared with her miniature horse, Jostan. Nohlan was fond of Hilga, for she was one of the few Gemins knowledge-able on the subject of herbalism, and so he decided to chat with her, exacerbating the Brown Robes' annoyance. This was supposed to be a time for them to reflect on their offense in silence, but Nohlan made it look like he was on a social outing. Nohlan welcomed Hilga's presence as a break in their solemn procession. In her hand, she carried thyme to plant close to one of her favorite shrubs to help it grow. Somehow, the scent emanating from the thyme enhanced the growth potential in some types of shrubs. Being a student of botany, Nohlan was always intrigued by the Gemin's unconventional knowledge.

They laughed loudly together, making the three Brown Robes sneer.

As Nohlan elaborated on his experience with plants of Nomi's that had produced foul smells, Jostan, the horse, grew agitated.

"Come here now, woooo, calm," Hilga tried to calm Jostan down, but the horse grew more agitated, veering off the path and into the woods.

"Jostan!" Hilga yelled and started trailing after the horse.

Then suddenly, she dropped all her belongings on the ground and wailed as if she was in deep pain. Nohlan froze with genuine concern on his face. Ezekiola drew closer to see what was happening while Atlas remained behind. Hilga's wailing grew louder as she wandered aimlessly off the path and into the forest, touching trees wherever she found them.

"What's going on?" Borghis asked from behind as he observed the scene. "What did you do to her?"

"Nothing!" yelled Nohlan, frustrated by his brother's accusations. "She just went off with her horse all on her own! I didn't do anything."

"You shouldn't have spoken to her, Nohlan! You have a knack for provoking catastrophes, you know that?!"

"But I didn't do anything!" Nohlan pleaded and bent to pick up Hilga's belongings, including the thyme she had left behind.

They then heard a choir of wailing sounds as if the forest itself was playing a symphony of lament. This sudden outburst of keening was bone-chilling, and it brought the whole group to a dead stop.

Keenan looked up and scanned the trees above. "But it can't be, we just did the count," he said.

Atlas turned and asked Borghis what was going on? But the Brown Robes just stood there with confusion on their faces. Hilga suddenly stopped next to a tree and, in the blink of an eye, disappeared as if she had been pulled into it.

"Well, maybe the count was done wrong," said Gordi.

"No, it was done correctly," retorted Keenan, "I double-checked it myself, and the Forest Stewards confirmed it. This cannot be happening. None of them were on the verge of dying. They were all healthy and strong. And anyway, Gemins don't cry when a dying tree is passing on. They cry when it happens to a healthy one."

A thunderous bang was then heard. Several birds flew off from where the wailing sounds were emanating, which was close to the Willow Tree Lane. The winds picked up speed as if nature was preparing itself to speak. Borghis quickly shouted out his orders. "Gordi, stay with them, Keenan, you come with me."

Borghis and Keenan walked towards the area from where a massive thudding sound could be heard. The wailing got louder as they approached. Nohlan noticed that his brother had taken the worn-down staff with him.

"There's resistance in the wind," Keenan said sharply.

"Resistance? Where is it coming from?" Gordi looked around in panic.

"From the North," said Keenan after raising his head skyward. Some leaves spun and twirled madly, rising in the air.

"Something is amiss. We have to report this immediately to the Forest Stewards!" Gordi exclaimed. He was always the one to cite protocol when they fell into an unexpected situation. Although his nervousness was palpable, the three White Tunics themselves were calmly assessing the situation.

"Stay put, Gordi. There's no need for reporting. Just look after the boys while Keenan and I go take a look at what's going on," Borghis said, taking charge. "We'll see if we need to take another path."

While the two left them in the middle of the forest, Ezekiola began feeling the oddest sensation on his waist. It was a new one, and he looked down at his belt warily. Everything looked normal, yet he felt he had a ring of fire around his waist. When he tried to shift his belt around, he felt a burning sensation. He checked underneath his shirt to see what was going on, but there were no signs of anything unusual from the outside. He then wondered if his skin might be burning from the inside, if such a thing was possible. He wiggled his body a few times, hoping to shake the sensation off. But the burning feeling only increased.

"Gordi, what does it mean when there's resistance in the wind?" asked Atlas, curious about what Keenan meant by that. He didn't like being left in the dark and was already pacing in circles instead of standing still as he was told to do.

"The winds respond and react to things. When it resists, it's a warning sign. Either something is taking place right then, or it's about to, but it foretells nothing good."

"Shouldn't we be making our way back faster, then?" he asked, getting a déjà vu moment of being in the hut in Mistress Mirhas' domain. He was not looking forward to another accidental detour into the unknown.

"Stay put, Atlas. You heard what Borghis said. Everyone stays with me and follows my..." A strong gush of wind rammed Gordi's body and almost knocked Atlas off his feet. He never got to finish his sentence, as his words were sucked into the whirlwind.

"This is ridiculous! You want me to follow your instructions when there's a windstorm building up around us?" yelled Atlas. "We should be heading back NOW!" He suddenly regretted having walked so slowly.

"I told you we'll follow Borghis' instructions," Gordi reiterated, looking over his shoulder to avoid being caught off-guard. But despite his efforts, this time, he got knocked off balance and had to actually grab onto a tree. Meanwhile, Ezekiola fiddled with his belt while being swayed by the wind as the heat around his waist increased, becoming unbearable. Finally, Nohlan, unable to stand still and wait either, had taken it upon himself to somehow find Hilga to quickly give her back her belongings. He looked like a lost squirrel as he tried out every tree in the hopes of finding the portal she had used, knowing they only remained open for a short time after Gemins used them.

"I think Atlas is right, we should hurry back, the wind is getting worse," Ezekiola said.

"I'm in charge here! And I decide what we do. We follow Borghis and Keenan in that direction," Gordi finally said, deciding on a course of action. He veered around determinedly in the hopes he was exuding an air of leadership to his disenchanted charge. Atlas threw his hands up in the air, not knowing what to say anymore. They were already in enough trouble, and confronting Gordi over everything he said or did might just make matters worse at this point. They were clearly heading in the direction of the wind, and if it wasn't for their belts holding their tunics tight, they would have blown off by now.

"What's wrong with those trees?" asked Nohlan. "Are they on fire?" They all looked up to see smoke rising from the top of some of the trees located further away.

Gordi looked up, but he didn't say a word. His face couldn't conceal his state of panic.

"Let's just find Borghis and Keenan," he quickly reiterated his instructions, as much for himself as for the three others. Another loud bang was then heard, and the wailing sounds increased. Meanwhile, Ezekiola's belt was growing more and more heated. He had the urge to remove it but didn't want to draw any attention to his situation, so he instead fidgeted as if he had ants in his pants. A sudden flash came to him. His dream with the green snake and the heat rising around his waist.

"What's the matter with you?" Atlas asked after spotting his friend's discomfort.

"Nothing, I just need to go do my business," he lied, rushing into the woods as if he had to relieve himself.

"Wow! You sure found a perfect time for that! Make sure you don't do it against the wind. I won't forgive you if I feel a drop on me!" yelled Atlas from behind.

As the wind picked up both speed and strength, a small tree too frail to withstand the force of the wind fell in the very direction where Ezekiola was headed, forcing him to make a detour.

"This is the worst timing, Zek. Can't you just hold it in?" Nohlan said. Gordi turned around to see all three of them lagging behind.

"What are you doing!" He yelled at them. "Pick up the pace, all of you. This is not a leisure walk anymore!"

"Gordi, if it wasn't for that ugly outfit of yours, I'm not sure if I wouldn't...." But another strong gust of wind came crashing through their conversation, and the rest of Atlas's words were drowned out. They were barely able to move forward. It took all of their energy to confront the wind's magnitude. Yet strangely, Ezekiola could have sworn his skin was burning. He reached his hands under his tunic and touched his skin to see if it was intact.

"Are you alright?" asked Nohlan, observing his friend's queasiness. Ezekiola nodded immediately, not wanting to make matters worse by raising another issue. Lest the belt actually set him on fire, he told himself he would suffer the discomfort in silence. He recalled reading about the discomforts an Emerald Belt could cause in the beginning. *This must be my first episode,* he thought.

As they neared the crossroad ahead, they heard familiar voices, followed by screaming and shouting, along with several unfamiliar voices. They drew closer and finally came to a halt when they saw Keenan's leg stuck underneath a thick branch and Borghis trying to free him while protecting himself and his friend with the use of the recycled staff in his hand, with unknown men watching them a few feet away, laughing.

There in front of them, in this restricted part of the Circaean forest, stood another trio of young men wearing black uniforms with unfamiliar belts. Just then, the heat from Ezekiola's belt became unbearable, and he pulled it off. It was at this most inappropriate moment that a quote from Meredus of Loggia whispered in his mind: *"The belt shall bend to the will of the beholder.*

His belt was now on fire.

Chapter 19

Son of the Night Sky

Leanne spent most of her time at school thinking about how best to pass through that magical tree again. Her incident with Zeke deterred her from trying, but only for a short time. Although she didn't see him again, at times, she sensed invisible eyes on her. But her desire to see Ezekiola was a flame she just couldn't put out. She quickly overcame her fear of encountering Zeke and decided the time was right to try once more. It wasn't easy. Every time she attempted to explore Chester's restricted zones during school hours, there were always kids roaming nearby. Worst yet, surveillance was at its height during lunch breaks. The lack of privacy made it difficult for her to get close enough whenever she had some free time.

One glorious Friday afternoon, she gathered all her courage and decided to put into action the plan that she had devised. This time, though, she had company. She had confided to her friend Andy about what had happened to her on the day of their snail safari. After keeping the incidents with Zeke to herself for so long, she shared her strange encounters with him and what he did the last time they saw each other. Upon hearing her tale, Andy couldn't believe her ears. She was intrigued and now wanted nothing more than to embark with Leanne on her quest to find out more. The girls were hungry for adventure. When school was finally over that afternoon, Leanne and Andy made their way to the furthest end of Chester's schoolyard. They then strolled about until they found the tree trunk Leanne remembered so vividly. Leanne was quick to locate the blue plant beneath it and noticed that the soil in which it was planted was darker and moister than the soil surrounding it.

"It looks like it's been watered recently. I'm sure those creatures were here again, tending to this plant," she said, showing it to her friend.

"This little blue plant was what they were arguing about?" Andy asked, surprised.

"Yes. And this right here is the tree I was telling you about," Leanne said, taking a step further and crouching on the ground to approach the tree without touching it. She looked around cautiously to see if there were any students lurking close by. There was no one.

"You ready to try?" Andy asked. She had been curious to witness the phenomenon Leanne had spoken of.

Leanne nodded.

Leanne gently stroked her fingers on the tree, and her fingers slipped right through the tree bark.

"Oh, I can't believe it!" Andy gasped.

"I told you so! Here now, you try," said Leanne.

Andy tried, but her hands collided with the hard wooden substance. "It's not working," she said. She then put both of her hands around the tree and gripped the trunk in its entirety to see if an opening would emerge, but nothing happened. "This thing doesn't work for me, just you!" she said, heavy with disappointment.

"Wait, give me your hand."

With their palms held together, Leanne stroked their knuckles lightly against the tree again. This time, both hands went through. Andy gasped and covered her mouth. She was ecstatic.

"It works!" she said in a whisper. "Leanne, this is amazing! You must have some special power. I've never seen such a thing before."

Leanne said nothing but sensed that her locket with Ezekiola's name in it might have something to do with this new "power" of hers. She was glad to have found a new one after Zeke destroyed the original. A thought suddenly sprung into her head. *What if Zeke knew what I was about to do?* But as quickly as it surfaced, Leanne chased the thought away and moved into action.

"Are you ready for this?" she asked Andy, in a hurry to get going.

"Wait, so when we go through, are we going to fall down or something?" Andy asked, trying to prepare for what awaited her on the other side.

"Yes, but not too hard. We'll be in a place that looks just like here, but it's a real forest with big trees. It's much grander. You'll see."

"Okay. And how do we get back?" Andy asked.

"The same way we go in." Leanne smiled in anticipation. "Ready?"

Andy nodded.

Holding her friend's hand, Leanne fearlessly pushed herself right through the tree. The girls both exited on the other end, falling down on the grounds of the Black Forest. Andy was amazed. She looked around in awe, like a two-year-old at the zoo. Everything was far taller and larger than what she was accustomed to.

"Look at the size of those trees! It's like the Amazon here. So, this is where you ended up last time while we all suffered through Urda's excursion class?" she said with wonder in her voice.

"Yes, and that boy Virgil I met, he was standing right there." Leanne pointed towards the center of the road where Virgil had been.

"He said this was the restricted part of the Black Forest, whatever that meant. He then ran in that direction to go to his school cafeteria to fetch Ezekiola. You can see a wooden post further down where it says 'South Wing.' To think I almost saw him again!"

"So, if there's a school nearby, we can maybe go and explore," Andy said enthusiastically.

"Yes, but we have to be careful, Andy. This place is very different," she said.

"Well, we can walk around, can't we? And what's that smell? There's a wonderful scent here." She inhaled deeply.

"Okay, we can walk around, but let's be careful. Remember the little thing called Gemin I told you about? Well, it came out of nowhere with its horse. And I want to be sure to find this tree again. It's our only way back."

The last time she had been here, she had left her red elastic but had forgotten to take it back. She realized Zeke had followed her trail all the way from her own schoolyard. She looked around suspiciously but saw no one else. She took her elastic off again, this time a yellow one, and left it on a little branch. Leanne then walked further than where she had last ventured but always remained on the well-kept path. Barely a minute into their walk, something caught her attention.

"Did you just see that?" she asked.

"See what?"

"Something flew above us."

"Like a bird?" Andy asked. "Leanne, you're more nervous than I thought. Just relax."

They walked a little further, past where Virgil had once stood, and arrived at the crossroads when Leanne jumped again. "Okay, I saw it again, and it's not a bird!"

"Where? What are you seeing?" Andy asked, annoyed. All she wanted was to continue to stroll and soak up all the novelty around her. Her friend's interruptions were sucking the pleasure out of it.

"There's something flying from one tree to the next. Look up!" Andy looked up and kept her head tilted as they walked. A minute of silence passed, and every little cracking sound and swoosh of leaves alarmed them both. The walk soon became nerve-racking.

"I don't see anything, Leanne. You're freaking out for nothing."

Leanne began to wonder if she was imagining things. They continued down the path.

"What a pretty flower," Andy said, bending over to smell an orange flower that was in full bloom. She inhaled deeply.

"Mmmmm! This is it! This is what was smelling so nice all this ..." She had barely finished her sentence when a clearly visible dark mass suddenly came out of a tree close by. It jumped across to another tree and vanished. This time, both Leanne and Andy saw it.

"What. Was. That?" Andy said and looked up like a fawn disturbed by a sudden noise. She slowly huddled closer to Leanne.

"That's the thing with this place, it's not what we're used to back home," Leanne said, frowning. She momentarily thought of turning back. Nervous, the two girls, who kept looking up, noticed another dark shadow jump out of a tree in the distance. It seemed to be moving closer to them, and they could make out a crouched body of some sort.

"Do you think it's some sort of animal, like a monkey, you know, from their world here?" Andy tried to downplay the panic that was overwhelming them. Their exploration was no longer pleasant.

"I think we should leave now," Leanne said. Her heart was beating faster, and she could hear the drum in her ear pounding away.

"Good idea," agreed Andy.

"There's no need to leave Leanne," came a voice from behind. The girls spun around. Leanne gasped. She recognized the voice. He continued, "You're exactly where you need to be. You came looking for me, and here I am."

The shadows they saw jumping from tree to tree finally emerged. There were now three of them, just as there had been in the restaurant when she first saw them. They were wearing the same outfits—dark tunics with belts bearing odd triangular symbols that she recognized from before.

"Who is this?" whispered Andy, the hair on the back of her neck rising.

"It's that boy, Zeke," Leanne managed to whisper faintly.

"You mean that freak who set the shop on fire?" Andy asked.

Leanne gave a faint nod, unable to take her eyes off Zeke. His gaze was riveting, almost hypnotizing. In a flash, she recalled her last encounter with him, how she ended up fainting, and how he gave her mouth to mouth. Her senses became momentarily confused when she looked at him. His features were too much like Ezekiola's. She never dared to ask, but now, for the first time, she wondered if it wasn't Ezekiola standing there in front of her, playing a different role. That would explain why they were so frighteningly alike. What if this was a farce all along and that she had been played all this time, being lured into a trap, into another world, for a purpose she could not identify? Zeke began to stroll leisurely around the two girls, never letting his eyes off Leanne.

"You've doubted all along, Leanne. But it's time you know the truth. It's been me all along," he said as if answering the doubt in her mind.

"What? What are you saying?" Leanne said, her mind suddenly clouded.

"You think it's by chance that we first met at your school, that you discovered my world, and you're here now, with me?" he asked, further stretching her thoughts into unchartered territories.

Leanne had no answer to his questions but was stunned as he pieced together this strange puzzle for her. She watched him turn around her in circles. With so many thoughts suddenly running through her mind, a dense fog settled in her head. Despite that, she continued listening.

"I've been meaning to tell you something since we first met in your classroom. You've ignited a very special fire Leanne, one that can do wonders. And there's so much more we can do together, but you'll have to come with me." Zeke stopped walking and stretched his hand out to Leanne, fully expecting her to take it.

"No, we're leaving. This should never have happened," Leanne said and instinctively reached for her friend Andy's hand instead. Grabbing it tightly, she headed towards their exit tree. As Zeke took his time walking, his partners suddenly disappeared, only to jump out and land in front of the tree through which the girls planned to escape. Andy and Leanne were now stuck between Zeke and his accomplices, all of which were closing in on them.

"I'm afraid there's no turning back, Leanne. You'll have to come with me now. As for your friend, you can let her go back." Leanne's hand began to shake at hearing the determination in his voice.

"No, we're leaving this place, both of us together," Leanne said forcefully.

"Oh, I'm sure you'll do as I say, won't you, Leanne? Remember what I told you last time about not being given a chance to put out the fire?" Zeke asked malevolently.

He picked random branches up and swung them in the air like makeshift swords, as if he was testing them. He finally settled on a branch that seemed best suited for his needs. It was long enough to whip someone from a fair distance. Watching his calm demeanor and certain it was hiding some cruel intentions, Leanne began to fear for her life.

Quickly, she glanced at her elastic dangling from a branch a short distance away and judged that they weren't too far from their exit tree, so they could make a run for it.

Zeke suddenly whipped the branch in the air, and fire spat out of its tip, burning a few leaves on the ground. The girls jumped back.

"We just want to head back. Leave us alone," Leanne blurted out.

Zeke's two consorts moved closer, tightening the circle from behind.

"Why must you always resist doing what's best for you?" he continued, repeatedly whipping the branch in the air. Then, with brute force, he struck a tree, leaving a deep burn mark on its trunk. Leanne sensed he was practicing for something much more dangerous.

"What are you doing?" Leanne yelled, aghast at the horror spectacle.

"Watch and learn this time," he replied, exuding a disturbing sense of calm that made his every move scarier.

As eager as she had initially been to return to this place, now she couldn't wait to escape it. As it was, she saw that the whole adventure of meeting Ezekiola had been a setup, and her exciting escapade turned into a nightmare. She scolded herself for having been so naïve and not vigilant enough from the start.

Zeke began to deliver repeated sharp blows with his whip at a massive tree. Remembering what he had done to Madame Camille's shop, Leanne stood motionless. A most gruesome sound suddenly erupted from the trunk. In a few moments, a beautiful, healthy tree with a trunk measuring several meters in circumference came crashing down in front of her.

"What have you done?!" Leanne asked, her hands clasping her face.

"I'm warming up. Ready to let go of your friend and come with me, or shall I practice this on her?"

He whipped another tree, and several synchronized complaints were heard from the surrounding trees. Then Zeke struck another, and another, until the fire he had started danced effortlessly, spreading throughout the forest. Andy started screaming for her life, hugging Leanne closer to her.

"There is movement up ahead. Someone is coming," one of Zeke's men suddenly warned.

Zeke stopped his whipping and looked in the direction where his cohort was pointing.

"Stay with the girls, don't let them get away. And burn that tree where they came from," he ordered.

Zeke and one of his men turned their backs to Leanne and Andy for the first time while the other cohort stayed close to them. Leanne eyed her yellow elastic from the corner of her eye. She was desperate to reach it before something terrible took place. All she and Andy needed was a moment of distraction to make a run for it. They had to wait.

With his whip in his hand, Zeke ripped a few branches off the fallen trees and stared at them for a moment as if he was communicating with them. He then spoke a few words. The broken branches suddenly lifted in the air and, like shooting arrows, violently sped off in the direction of their visitors, hitting their mark. Keenan was first to fall as a thick branch came crashing into him. Borghis barely managed to avoid the objects flying at him and used his staff to deflect the branches. Unfortunately, the staff he was carrying was too weak, and he still felt the impact of one of the branches that hit him.

"Borghis! I'm stuck!" yelled Keenan, trying to yank his leg out from underneath a branch that was nearly twice the size of a regular tree trunk.

"Stay still," said Borghis. He continued to scramble with his staff while more branches assailed him. Suddenly, the wind picked up speed and violently spun everything around. There in front of him, Borghis saw a tornado building up and heading in his direction. He immediately gripped the staff in his hands harder and planted its stem deep into the ground. With a commanding voice, he uttered the words: "Let the wind drown their voices and disrupt their speech."

The leaves and branches forming the tornado swirl all scattered, dispersing far away from him and Keenan.

He crouched down and focused on Keenan's leg. He took his staff in both hands and uttered a different incantation:

"By the powers of Circa, I command you to remove yourself."

The branch lifted slightly, allowing Keenan to pull himself a little out from under.

"I can't!" Keenan shouted.

"Hold on," Borghis said, and he attempted to use his staff

again. Weakened by its battle, the recycled staff broke in half. Borghis looked at it in astonishment and tossed it aside. Using only his might, he succeeded in pulling his friend out. Keenan growled in pain. Borghis looked up and saw there were three men dressed in black tunics with black belts approaching, each of them tall and mighty looking. He had never seen their kind in the Black Forest before. Their proximity made his heart beat faster. When Borghis locked eyes with the man in the middle, he was shocked by what he saw. From the corner of his eyes, he saw two girls in distress. He barely had time to make sense of what he was seeing that the next batch of branches was being hurled his way. Borghis shut his eyes, bracing himself for a hit. To his surprise, something else fended off the incoming danger. He turned around to see Ezekiola brandishing a mighty rod in the air in front of them. It was blazing with some type of fire-light, the likes of which he had heard of but never seen. It was so bright even Ezekiola had to look away.

"How did you...?" Borghis was stunned. "Come help us!" he told Gordi. Ezekiola continued walking ahead. He placed himself in front of Borghis and Keenan, serving as a protective shield. He and his rod were one, and it was doing what Ezekiola willed it to do, diverting all the incoming objects away.

When everything had fallen to the ground, and the winds had stilled, there was a moment of silence. Ezekiola adjusted his eyes to the light and stood still in the middle of the path opposite Zeke. The similarities were startling. With the exception that Zeke looked slightly older and taller, they looked identical. Without fully digesting the scene before him, Ezekiola saw Leanne further in the background. His heart leaped. So, it was all true. Amid the chaotic scene, he saw Leanne being tugged at the sleeve by another girl. The girls had not wasted a moment and instinctively made a run towards their tree when all their assailants were distracted. Leanne, though, turned around just in time to get a glimpse of what she had come to see: Ezekiola. There he was, with his unmistakable ocean blue eyes, standing in the middle of the Black Forest across from Zeke. They locked gazes momentarily. She didn't just dream it all. Zeke's attempt to make her believe otherwise had gloriously failed. Her heart filled with gladness but also despair, and before having any further thought, her friend pulled at her arm, and both suddenly disappeared through a burning tree.

Ezekiola was riveted by what he witnessed. After seeing Leanne appear and disappear in a flash, his eyes rested on the man who stood before him. Ezekiola quickly tuned into his adversary's mind and sensed he had abilities that matched his own. *Who are you?* He asked silently. Zeke looked him straight in the eyes. *A Son of the Night Sky*, he answered.

Ah! He was a mind reader as well. With experience on his side, Zeke knew he could not outweigh his opponent. He could sense the Fountain of Fire being wielded right before him and felt a longing to possess it instead. None of the warriors he knew of had such powers. He had to find a way to isolate Ezekiola from this power and bring him outside his world. *We shall meet again*, he said cunningly before spinning around and jumping into a nearby tree. Like a shadow, Zeke and the two other men disappeared right in front of Ezekiola's eyes as his last words echoed in Ezekiola's mind.

Borghis and Gordi lifted Keenan up and carried him further off the main road. They set him on the side to avoid any chance of him getting knocked out again.

When the intruders had disappeared, Borghis and Gordi immediately took out their horns, a set of tools they carried with them at all times. Keenan was too weak to use his. These horns were specially conceived to resonate certain sounds to subdue forest fires. As they sounded them, the fires receded one at a time until they were all out, and only smoke now filled the air. Borghis' initial rush of excitement at having witnessed something great was overwhelmed by dread when he looked around him. The forest looked like a battleground. Considering the magnitude of the horrific damage done to the trees, Borghis would be required to give explanations to his superiors and to the Forest Stewards. Especially since they were the crew specifically assigned to search for his missing brother and friends. And with the crossovers he had just witnessed of strangers freely entering and exiting their veiled planet Circa, he was certain the Blue Robes and Emerald warriors would get involved in the inquiry.

For once, the Brown Robes were left as confused as the White Tunics. There would be much explaining to be done. While Borghis tried to make sense of what had just happened and Keenan tended to his injury, it was Gordi, with a deranged look in his eyes, found the timing just right to score points with the younger ones: "See, I was right! Virgil wasn't lying! There was a girl! Not one, but two! You three shall be reprimanded!"

<h1 style="text-align:center">Chapter 20</h1>

<h2 style="text-align:center">Silence</h2>

"No one is to speak about what just happened to the Forest Stewards except me! Understood?"

Borghis' message was clear. He stood in the middle of the Black Forest, wondering what he was going to say to the Forest Stewardship Council when they got back. With the three White Tunics gone missing for an entire night, Keenan's fractured leg, his broken staff, utter chaos and destruction in the forest, not to mention these three unknown assailants, and the girls, he had to thoroughly think his story through. The Forest Stewardship Council was comprised of a dozen older Brown Robe leaders who ardently applied themselves to the task of serving nature. They not only took care of the Black Forest and the wildlife within it, but minutely supervised and monitored every mature tree's growth. They also meticulously enforced the Forest Governance Rules and were never ones to hesitate when it came to imposing sanctions. For them, a tree simply dying of old age was considered a major event in the life of the forest. So, several mature trees being violently butchered all at once would surely call for a forest lockdown, among other things. And a thorough investigation would quickly be underway.

Borghis was pacing back and forth, his breath shortening with every stride. He knew he was in trouble. He had broken one fundamental rule when he had ventured out into the restricted part of the Black Forest in search of his brother and his friends: he had not taken his personal staff with him. In fact, he was the one telling his friends that morning there was no need to take their staffs. It was mandatory for Brown Robes to carry their staffs into the restricted zone since there were far more hidden dangers in that part of the forest than anywhere else. It would have given him greater protection. He knew that, and had he taken his powerful staff, he would have probably saved more than a few trees from dying. He could also have saved his friend from a bad injury. Now he was wondering just how much of the truth he should reveal to his interrogators to avoid being severely reprimanded. He ran possible explanations in his head, none of which would divert the question that would inevitably be asked: Did you attempt to remedy the situation with your staff? But he, of course, had not brought it. Neither did his friends. This was just one of Borghis' many worries. The others being who these intruders were, not to mention those girls, and whether the Blue or Emerald Robes would get involved in this mess.

But until he figured out his storyline, Borghis had to have everyone collaborate with him by staying silent. That was key. Keeping quiet wasn't too hard for him and his kind. The challenge lay with the younger fellows, who had to keep bottled up a story they'd be aching to tell.

He looked at Nohlan, Atlas, and Ezekiola and said, "Listen, I want you three to head back to school, wash up quickly, and go to your classes, which will be starting soon. Do NOT say a word about what just happened. To anyone. I'm asking you to keep quiet about this, and in exchange, we won't report any of your actions to the School Council. Despite what Gordi said, there will be no reprimands, but only if we have your word. Is that clear?" he waited a moment to see if this prompted any reaction. But Atlas, Nohlan, and Ezekiola stood with blank looks on their faces, perhaps because it was rare to see Borghis this nervous.

Borghis continued explaining his plan: "We'll merely say that you got lost, that we found you sleeping in the forest, and that's the end of the story," he concluded.

Atlas smiled. That's exactly what he had suggested from the start. How a story could change direction, come full circle and return to its original version was astonishing to him, especially as it was coming from Borghis. In fact, it was almost a miracle. To think that he had barely had to lift a finger for it to happen.

"But these things must be reported immediately to the Forest Stewards! And we must reprimand them!" Gordi asserted forcefully. "I knew we should have taken our staffs with us before leaving our lodge this morning! I can't believe you told us otherwise. Had you listened to me, none of this would have happened! And what will we say about Keenan's leg?" he then asked.

"No, Gordi. No one is saying anything. Keenan simply fell into a ditch, and as for the fallen trees, we didn't see anything. If we say otherwise, we'll all be in trouble," he concluded.

There were no more protests, and the boys made a run back to the school. Ezekiola's mind was swarming with everything that had just transpired. He had just seen Leanne again and had come face to face with a Son of the Night Sky. Most intriguing of all, that vicious character had looked just like him. And not just a little. How could he possibly ignore such a thing and remain silent about it? He wondered what kind of powers the Sons of the Night Sky had. Could it be that they were able to produce doubles in order to confuse their adversaries? Without any further thought, Ezekiola decided he was going to see Nomi after class to tell him everything. His life had never been endangered before, and he was sure his belt had something to do with it. He needed guidance on what was the best course of action for him to take. His mind sifted through all the happenings of the previous day, when they had gone through a Sporadic Door, met a special master and an oracle, and most intriguing of all, how his Emerald Belt had literally come alive. Ezekiola still felt the fire in his hands as if it was now part of him.

While he was letting his thoughts run wild, Borghis caught his arm and took him aside.

"I don't know who those men were, but their leader sure gave me the sense he knew you. He looked a lot like you, Ezekiola. And I don't know what you did with your belt, but we need to speak some more. Meet me after lunch in our lodge. And don't tell anyone about our meeting."

Ezekiola took note of the enthusiasm for the hunt in Borghis' tone as if the falcon inside him had remained shackled for too long and had now finally been set free. It made him ever more wary.

The White Tunics got back to their dorms, washed up, and changed to look orderly for their Platitudes class. Ezekiola couldn't believe he was heading to a morning class after what had just happened. On their way back, he had been able to exchange only a few words with Atlas about what had occurred. He also asked him about the oracle, but Atlas had no recollection of the events in the cave. Ezekiola seemed to be the only one to recall everything that had occurred. He was impatient to ask Nohlan what he remembered, but that would have to wait until after class. Their encounter with Borghis had deprived him of the time he needed to go over the events. Despite everything, they made it to class on time. To their surprise, instead of Nomi, they found Almonte Versutus there, their teacher who taught Latin and other languages.

"Everyone, take your seats. Master Nomi will be absent today as he has some important business to attend to. I will be the replacement for this class."

For a moment, Ezekiola worried that the headmaster might be looking into the very thing they were trying to keep quiet. Why else would he be absent? Suddenly, he couldn't wait to finish his class so he could run off to see Nomi and get everything off his chest. He thought of Borghis' request to meet him after class. From the way this whole story had been unraveling from the start, he could only foresee calamity coming his way. He wrote a note to pass to Atlas: "Borghis asked me to meet him at his lodge after class. You better come along. He's up to something."

All worrisome thoughts evaporated when their substitute teacher announced the theme of the day's lesson.

"I have a surprise for you today. I thought it would be opportune to introduce to you a special trio." The students suddenly stopped squirming in their seats and actually paid close attention, intrigued by this announcement.

"Let's welcome today some fellow students who are quite special in many ways. They are the servants of Circa, better known as the Silence Keepers, for they have taken a three-year vow of silence. They have just finished year one and have two more to go."

The students watched in amazement as three students walked into their classroom wearing grey tunics with no belt. Despite wearing such bland attire, they stood out from the others quite remarkably because of their demeanors, as they displayed the calmest of expressions.

"The Silence Keepers' task is a very hard one, as you can see. It requires a tremendous amount of willpower to remain completely silent. Some of you, I'm certain, would not last a day, and I could even name a few who couldn't last an hour!" the professor said. As timing would have it, Nohlan was the first to raise his hand.

"Professor?" he asked.

"Yes?" Almonte answered.

"Why would someone take a vow of silence?"

"They take the vow in order to purify at a greater level the quality of their thoughts. Being silent, they live in their minds. It makes them acutely mindful of what they are willing to say and of the power their words carry. This transformational period consequently impacts their speech once they start speaking again. And today's lesson is about keeping silent, which will lead us also to examine the principle behind the well-known adage: *There is a time to talk and a time to remain silent*."

Ezekiola stole a look at Atlas and Nohlan. The coincidence of having Silence Keepers visiting them on the very day Borghis had asked them to stay silent was startling. Could it be that Borghis was right? Ezekiola's initial plan of running to see Nomi after class became suddenly shrouded in doubt. Maybe something greater was at work. He gave it further thought and realized that should he tell everything that had transpired, he would surely be investigated as well by the Forest Stewardship Council. He would also put everyone else in trouble too, including his friends. And who knows, once they had the whole story down, they might even decide to remove his belt as a precautionary measure. He would then be completely vulnerable to future attacks, especially if that Son of the Night Sky shows up again. His belt, after all, was what had saved him and his friends in the first place. Ezekiola finally decided it was best to stay quiet and keep everything to himself, at least for the time being.

While he tried to focus on what his teacher was saying, Nohlan grew bored and started needing a venue to entertain himself. His question having been somewhat answered, he stared out of the window, seeking a distraction. Remarkably, he got his wish. It was bird migration season, and a disoriented bird suddenly came crashing into the very window he was staring out of. Nohlan erupted with a guffaw. Everyone turned around to see Nohlan laughing heartily, as did his teacher, who was right in the midst of saying how difficult a task it was to stay silent and how much sacrifice it took. With shaky hands, Professor Almonte took his glasses off, putting them down carefully on his desk.

"You find taking a vow of silence funny, Nohlan?" he asked. His face began to twitch, catching Nohlan off-guard.

"Um, no. I was merely looking outside and..." Nohlan couldn't possibly say he had seen a bird crashing into the window. Nobody would believe him, especially since no one else had witnessed it. And it would most definitely sound like a pathetic excuse. Rather, he opted for a safer route. "And I had a funny thought," he said.

"Really? And what was that *funny* thought of yours, if you don't mind sharing it with us?" the professor asked.

"It was the sheer impossibility of me keeping silent," Nohlan said, chuckling. A few students giggled at the irony of the whole thing: big mouth Nohlan incapable of remaining silent in a class about silence during a visit from the Silence Keepers.

The professor stared back at him incredulously, a faintly crazed look appearing in his eyes. However, Mr. Almonte couldn't possibly lose his cool while teaching a class under-lining the importance of controlling your thoughts. The best he managed to say to keep it short and sweet was: "Get out, Nohlan! There are only so many dumb answers I can handle from you today."

"But what did I do wrong?" Nohlan answered back. He wasn't Mr. Almonte's favorite, either.

"Not another word. Let's keep to the principle of the day, stay silent, and step out of the classroom now. You are dismissed, and I will count this as an absence."

Disappointed by this turn of events, Nohlan shuffled his way out of class, looking at his friends with a truly puzzled look.

Ezekiola watched as his friend exited the classroom, and he himself felt confused. *What just happened here?* He hadn't been following class at all. As he waited for his note to pass hands, he took a look at their visitors, who were still standing silently in the front of the class. Ezekiola picked up on their thoughts and was struck when he heard the thoughts of one of the Silent Keepers, the third to the far right.

"What lame beginners." Ezekiola did a double take and, for a moment, questioned what he was hearing. Was this Silence Keeper mocking them? He continued focusing on him, and indeed, the boy's thoughts continued along those lines:

"They'll never get as far as we have. They couldn't even if they tried. What a waste of our time trying to recruit followers this way."

Ezekiola was growing furious. He had 'heard' right. Yet, their teacher continued to praise the Silent Keepers.

"Bunch of worthless amateurs. Let's just leave already!"

That last insulting thought was too much for Ezekiola to bear. He couldn't stand to listen to the third Silence Keeper's thoughts any longer.

"Professor!" he interrupted his teacher.

"Yes?"

"Is it possible for them to fail in their vow of silence?" he asked, a little more forcefully than was necessary.

"Well, if they speak, yes, they fail," the professor answered promptly, hoping to return to his reverence.

"No, I mean, even if they don't speak. Is it possible for their minds to be full of, umm—say, filthy thoughts?" Saying this, he looked right at the third Silence Keeper, who was now standing with his mouth agape.

"That's a little absurd of a statement, Ezekiola. Where did you even come up with that?"

"It's just a simple question. I'd like to know if honoring their vow of silence successfully also requires them to have no bad thoughts at all."

"Well, to reason with you on this, it is not because they do not speak that their thoughts are necessarily pure. I mean, the purpose of their silence is to govern their thoughts towards purity."

"So, then it is possible that one of our three visitors here today might be thinking things that are quite shameful, like feeling superior to others, for instance."

"First Nohlan, now you! What is the matter with you White Tunics today?" The professor questioned. He could no longer hide his anger.

"But Professor, I'm merely pointing out the possibility that they might not be as innocent as you've been portraying them to be. That any of them might actually be a bit of a hypocrite. A fake!"

"How dare you accuse these Silence Keepers, knowing well their inability to defend themselves with their words right now? It's inconceivable to say such a thing to those who have conse-crated a whole year of their lives to a most strenuous task!" he retorted and went back to shaking again. "Given you have not shown any respect for our visitors, why don't you also step out and join your colleague? You are no longer welcome in their presence either!"

Ezekiola stood up, dumbfounded at his professor's reaction. He exited the classroom and made sure to cast a spiteful, knowing look at the third Silence Keeper, who looked back at him. He thought he saw a slight smile form on the edge of his mouth. At least he had attempted to get his point across, he told himself, even if it had been badly received at the other end.

Atlas now felt left out. The trio was bound together so much that he could not accept being the one left out on this rare occasion, so he, too, piped up.

"Professor, we're only voicing opinions here. Surely you wouldn't forbid us from doing that?" he intervened in the hopes of starting a conversation that would turn into a dispute, an unmistakable trademark of his.

"I will not hear of this, Atlas. Keep your opinions to yourself. And that goes for all of you!" he said, addressing the whole class in case anyone else was about to venture in the same direction.

"Why would you be offended by what we think of your special keepers?" Atlas pressed further, with not a hint of deference in his tone.

"Enough!" the professor yelled. Mr. Almonte, however, did not kick Atlas out, as he thought it would look bad for a teacher whose only way to handle his students was to throw them out one by one. Disappointed, Atlas sat back in his chair.

Outside in the meantime, Nohlan and Ezekiola were playing catch up.

"Your brother asked to meet me in his lodge after class."

"And what did you say?" asked Nohlan.

"I didn't say anything. He made it sound like an order," Ezekiola said.

"Well, I'm coming too. There's nothing he can tell you that he can't tell me."

"Atlas needs to be with us to keep Borghis in check. I thought he would have gotten himself thrown out of class by now. I heard him speak after I left. We need to talk about what happened, especially if..." Ezekiola stopped talking. To his astonishment, two Blue Robes were heading down the hallway in their direction. He was alarmed by their presence. They never lingered in this division of the school. Their pavilion was located much further away, as their classes took place inside mountains. It was a virtual labyrinth if one didn't know the way. One student had once gotten lost for a full day when he was asked to bring a parcel to their reception hall, despite having a three-page map with him, which had not helped at all.

"Don't turn around," Ezekiola warned Nohlan.

"Why?" Nohlan was about to turn around.

"Pretend to talk. There are Blue Robes coming our way. They're picking up on our thoughts."

"Blue Robes?!" Nohlan's eyes widened. "You think they're investigating what happened with Borghis in the Black Forest?" he asked, this time whispering.

"Quit talking about it, Nohlan!" Ezekiola said.

"But I'm whispering! They can't hear us from there," Nohlan reassured his friend.

"Talk or whisper. It's the same," Ezekiola told his friend. He couldn't trust him any longer, for Nohlan was overexcited, and his mind was all over the place.

Ezekiola took charge and changed topics immediately. "Have you seen Nomi's garden lately? He grew a mature lemon tree in less than three weeks."

"Really?" Nohlan said, surprised. "That sounds impossible!

How did he do that?" Nohlan started running through types of master mix in his mind that might have been used to generate such speedy growth. The Blue Robes passed them by, gazing at the two with inquiring eyes. Ezekiola continued: "Yes, I heard it was Ariad who planted her special seeds and timed her planting during Circa's full moons."

Nohlan looked perplexed. "I don't think that's possible."

As soon as they left, Ezekiola sighed with relief, eyeing his friend incredulously. "Nohlan, you really have to work on controlling your thoughts. It won't take much effort to figure you out."

They followed the Blue Robes, now exiting the hallway, speculating on the reason for their presence.

"Maybe there's a special event taking place, or they're visiting classrooms just like the Silence Keepers. Tell me more about the lemon tree!" Nohlan suggested without much thought.

"Forget about the lemon tree, Nohlan! I made that up." Nohlan gave him an 'I knew it!' smile. "And that's very unlikely! I've never heard of Blue Robes visiting students. They know what happened!" said Ezekiola, suspicion nibbling at his mind.

"I have to ask you this, Nohlan. Do you remember what happened when we met the oracle?" Ezekiola finally thought to ask. Atlas had already said he didn't remember anything.

"Oracle? What oracle?" Nohlan asked, surprised by this new change of topic.

"The little girl we met in the abandoned village."

"She was an oracle?!"

"Yes, what do you remember before waking up in the Black Forest?"

It was the first time Nohlan was made to think about their

exit out of the domains of Master Sohan and his other half since they had returned.

"Well, now that you ask, I don't quite remember. How *did* we get back?" he asked.

"I don't know exactly, but I think she brought us back," Ezekiola said, trying to retrieve information from his own mind but without much success. It seemed they had been struck with amnesia of some kind, just like during their simulation class. It's exactly what Professor Balthazar would mention before they underwent their simulation trials.

"Let me ask you another question," Ezekiola said after a moment of pause. "Did you see those girls in the Black Forest?"

"Yes, two of them." Suddenly, the obvious dawned on Nohlan. "Was one of them Leanne?" he asked, eyes wide open.

Ezekiola nodded.

"So Virgil was right when he said he saw her! What do you think happened to her?" Nohlan asked.

"I don't know, but I hope she's alright," Ezekiola recalled what the Oracle had said about the Fountain of Fire, and Leanne's life being in danger. She had been right.

"This means the Brown Robes saw them too, and Borghis might ask us about it later."

"Well, we can't tell anyone about Leanne. If your brother or his friends find out we tried to enter her world yesterday through a Sporadic Door, they'll find a way to blame us for Leanne and the other men crossing over to Circa. We'll speak to Atlas about this, too, before we go see Borghis."

They waited for Atlas to finish and then had lunch, where they discussed at length what their plan was before heading towards the Brown Robe's lodge. They found Borghis there alone, pacing back and forth like a caged wildcat. He turned around as soon as he heard them walk in.

"What's this?" he asked, surprised to see the trio. "I asked only for you to meet me here, not these other latchers," he told Ezekiola.

"Watch it, Borghis! We're not latchers! We support one another just like you do with your own kind," Nohlan retorted, offended by his brother's comments. Borghis cast him a disappointed look but quickly came around to acknowledging that they were inseparable. Ezekiola would undoubtedly share whatever they spoke about with the other two anyway.

"Did you tell them anything?" he asked nervously, addressing Ezekiola.

"Tell who what?" asked Ezekiola.

"The Blue Robes! They're all over the school. They called me in already and questioned Keenan and Gordi too."

Ezekiola's doubts were justified. Those Blue Robes he saw were probably scouring the hallways, appraising everyone.

"What's their business with you?" Atlas meddled in.

"They obviously discovered the mayhem in the forest with the dead trees and all and wanted to hear my account of the story."

"But you had your story so well-rehearsed," Ezekiola said.

"That's right, so what's the big deal then?" Atlas asked.

"I had my story well-rehearsed for the Forest Stewardship Council that's made of Brown Robes, not Blue Robes! The big deal is that we're on their watch list, and they questioned Gordi and Keenan *first* before coming to me," Borghis said, a sincere look of worry on his face. It was rare to see him this flustered.

"Maybe you're a little paranoid and convincing yourself of things. There's nothing strange about questioning others before *you*," Nohlan said comfortingly while looking around the lodge at the neatly placed staffs.

"You don't think? Do you know anything about the Blue Robes, Nohlan, besides them wearing blue?" he asked his brother. Nohlan stood with his mouth agape, seemingly searching his thoughts for an answer. It took too long.

"I thought so," Borghis snapped. "None of you know much about them. Well, know this: everything they do is calculated and has been thoroughly thought through. We Brown Robes may safeguard ourselves by keeping the boasting down, but Blue Robes have ways of finding things out by using simple tactics. First off, they're mind readers, just like you, Ezekiola. That you should know. Now imagine how easy it is for them to catch a lie. And next on their list of tactics is finding contradictions in different versions of the same story. Even if we guard our thoughts well, it takes only one diverging word from Gordi, Keenan, or myself to find the flaws in our so well-rehearsed story," he said, looking at them intently.

"What did Keenan and Gordi say then?" asked Ezekiola.

"I haven't seen them yet. They're in class," he said anxiously. "Did a Blue Robe interrogate any of you?"

"We saw them in the hallway. None of them approached us, though," Ezekiola answered.

"Good. It means they're still hunting for answers. They're probably working in unison with the Forest Stewards. We best be on our guard."

"So, is that it?" asked Atlas, wishing to leave. "You wanted to warn us to stay on our guards?"

"No, that's not all. I intended to only speak to Ezekiola, but since you two leeches have nothing better to do with your time than to latch onto him, it gives me no choice but to discuss this openly. First, Ezekiola, I want to know what you know about those dark-dressed men we encountered in the Black Forest, especially the one who looked like the leader of the pack. And those two girls we saw along with them."

"We don't know anything about these men, or the girls, who they were, or why they were there. And we certainly know nothing of their leader," Ezekiola answered first. He was concerned that the obvious might be said out loud.

"This is not the time to lie. He looks a lot like you, Ezekiola, and I saw with my own eyes the powers you used on him. You performed air slicing with your belt that somehow was transformed into a rod of fire. You mind explaining how that happened?"

"I don't know. My belt was hot on my waist, and I felt the need to remove it. And that's when it all happened."

"Your answer sounds too simple, Ezekiola. Don't you have a more plausible lie?" Borghis said.

"But he's telling the truth!" burst out Nohlan. "I remember him wanting to remove his belt way before we came to help you and Keenan. He was fidgeting the whole time we walked. It must be one of the abilities that come from wearing the Emerald Belt!"

"It can't be an ability from the belt. It's just a belt! He's far from being an Emerald Robe. You did something else you're not telling us. Everyone thinks you've been using forbidden words to gain power. Do you realize that if I report this kind of thing, chances are they'll strip you of your Emerald Belt?" he threatened.

Ezekiola didn't trust Borghis and wondered if this was another tactic to compel him to say more. He surely could not be stripped of his level simply based on hypothetical guesses.

"What forbidden words? I don't even know any! And what about you, Borghis? You saw those intruders first. Where did they come from?" he asked pointedly.

"I saw them exactly as you did."

"Well, I'll be saving you a trip then. I'll volunteer to speak to Nomi after school today and put an end to all of this," Ezekiola said.

Borghis panicked. The last thing he needed was for a White Tunic to report the incident in the forest and have him condemned for his poor handling of the situation, exposing his own wrongdoings and his lies.

"No, you won't..." Borghis cut in. "If you chose to recount everything that happened as it did, you, Ezekiola, will also be investigated. Not just me. And if they find out what you did with your belt, they might find fault in your actions as well."

"Fine. We'll keep it simple then, on the condition that you stop questioning us from now on," Ezekiola said.

"I can agree with that. In fact, I think we should work together on this. I have a proposition I'd like to make. The only way we can find out more about these men is through..." he took a pause, unsure about how to continue, which had the effect of drawing his audience closer, "...a tool safeguarded in the domain of the Cypress Ladies."

They looked back at him with a blank stare.

"A tool?" asked Ezekiola. He already felt queasy about this proposal.

"Yes, a tool. Now our sister Orgali is too young to help, but Atlas," he said, shifting his attention to him, "since you're here with your friends, I thought I'd propose this to you. Perhaps you didn't come here for nothing after all. You'd do us a great favor if you could organize a meeting with your sister."

Atlas was taken aback. "My sister Helva? What does she have to do with this?" he blurted out.

"We need her presence to help us get access to the Lake of Maji."

Atlas, Ezekiola, and Nohlan stood gaping wide-eyed at Borghis. His proposition was as crazy as suggesting they fly off a cliff. The thought of using the Lake of Maji had never crossed anyone's mind. Rightfully so. Not only was it located outside of the boy's division, but it was also accessible only to the High Council of Circa and some of the Cypress Ladies for teaching purposes. It enabled the privileged few to foresee probable events. The lake was also famously called the Eye of the Past, as it revealed earlier events exactly as they had happened. Myth suggested that the sacred lake was guarded at all times by nymphs.

"How can you, Borghis Eridanus, consider such a trespassing offense when you're the first to be appalled by us simply crossing into the restricted part of the Black Forest? My sister Helva would never consent to such a thing," Atlas stated. Then, in the deep recess of his mind, the thought occurred to him that perhaps Borghis was too shy to ask Helva, considering he had a weak spot for her.

"Think about it! This is our only chance to know more. We can access the Eye of the Past and see who those intruders were, where they came from, and if they intend to come back," Borghis continued, determined to change their minds. "Then we'll be better prepared!" He grappled with an overpowering urge to hunt those men down with his staff and make up for his weak performance during their first encounter.

"Forget it, Borghis. This is going too far. I'd rather you report us than get us involved in such a thing. We would get stripped of our belts if they found us near that lake. It's out of our league," Ezekiola tried to cut their conversation short, longing to leave.

"But what if we tried?" Nohlan suddenly asked, much to Ezekiola's dismay. Nohlan was always one to believe they could accomplish anything when it came to incredible ideas.

"No, I think Ezekiola's right. This truly is out of our league," Atlas cut in. "Borghis, we have our share of problems to deal with now that we have the Blue Robes roaming the school. To trespass again, and this time into the Ladies' domain, will just add more fuel to the fire. And we still haven't been interrogated. That, too, will surely come," he posed, finally taking some responsibility for his actions.

"And we also have another class to get to, Borghis. Let's go," said Ezekiola. Without wasting another moment, he led his crew out the door. He was actually glad that such a wild proposition would come out of Borghis' mouth, for he now had something to hold against him should the elder boy want to report anything about his past actions. Borghis was left with a pensive look on his face, however, one that did not indicate any intention of giving up.

The three friends stepped out and walked fast to move away from the lodge's vicinity. Nohlan broke their focused pace when he started thinking out loud: "It did sound like a good idea for a moment."

"I agree," Ezekiola said. "But your brother didn't think this through. To think he was going to ask Helva for her help," he shook his head. He looked back at Atlas, who was trailing behind, walking slower than the rest.

"Maybe he hoped we would listen to him and follow his lead," Nohlan observed.

"He was thinking of Helva to help us out," Ezekiola spoke aloud but more to himself, shaking his head. He was trying to wrap his mind around Borghis' request. "He must be desperate. And even then, I just don't know how we could accomplish this."

They continued walking when Atlas broke his silence. "I know how this could be accomplished," he said, surprising everyone with his claim.

Ezekiola turned around, a quizzical look on his face. "You can't be serious?"

"And not only do I have an idea how we can do it," Atlas

said cunningly, "but we're going to take Borghis' idea and move it up a notch higher," he said, catching up to Nohlan and Ezekiola and putting his arms around their shoulders.

"Borghis just did us a favor, and I think I might have just the right tool to get what we want. All we have to do is to be patient and wait for the excitement to die down. My friends, when all eyes are turned elsewhere, we will forge ahead."

In no time, Atlas had everyone eager to take another walk on the wild side.

Chapter 21

The Little Black Book

Helva had just finished her class on Cycles when her friend Daria hopped towards her like an excited rabbit. Like Helva, her best friend, Daria, was a Brown Belt. Helva wondered what was behind her friend's eagerness; her cheeks were scarlet red.

"Your brother sent me a message!" she said, her mouth stretching from ear to ear.

"Oh, really?" Helva said.

"He asked me to do him a favor."

"What can he be up to now, I wonder?"

Helva was as cunning as her younger brother, Atlas, and had learned over time that there was always something more behind every one of his requests for a favor.

"He asked us to meet him at the Night and Day Inn this afternoon."

"This afternoon? What is he thinking? Students aren't even allowed in that inn anymore."

"I told him that, but he simply said to change clothes."

The inn was the only one located at a crossroads between

the male and female divisions of Cypress School. Seeking an outlet for entertainment, students had flocked to the inn when it first opened, populating its restaurant and occupying tables for hours at a time. The owner had had enough when his inn started looking like a student union center. He eventually put up a sign refusing entry to school kids. That hadn't proven as efficient as he had intended and, in fact, had had the opposite effect. Students had simply started changing out of their uniforms into regular clothes to pass as random travelers, making it even more exciting for them to get in and harder for the owner to differentiate students from other patrons. The owner had finally opted for other more creative means of repelling students and hired fauns to provide music.

"I can't stand their pipe playing in there. I could swear those fauns alter their sounds to make them even more annoying when they sense us coming in," Helva said. "Did Atlas say why he wants to meet us?" she asked.

"No. He was very abrupt. He told me he was running late for something else and had to go."

"Running late..." Helva rolled her eyes. She had heard that excuse too many times to count them and had heard numerous rumors about how Atlas was always tardy.

"Why couldn't he meet us here instead?" Helva asked.

"I don't know. I just promised him that I would deliver this message to you. That's all."

"Fine. We'll meet him then. Anyway, it's been a while since I've seen him. It'll give us some time to catch up."

When the girls arrived at the Night and Day Inn, Helva was shocked to see Atlas there already. He had chosen a seat next to a window at the far end of the restaurant, probably so they could remain discreet, and he was not sitting there alone.

"This is a first, Atlas! It's so rare not to be the one waiting for you," Helva said.

"Happy to see you both," he said, inviting the girls to sit down. Daria turned crimson.

"How have you been, Zek?" asked Helva when she noticed her brother's friend sitting quietly in his chair.

"Good, thanks. You look happy. I guess you're being treated well in your division," he said playfully.

"We always are. You both have me curious now. I don't remember ever meeting you two at Night and Day," Helva smiled at them, but there was a hint of suspicion in her eyes.

"Why do they even call it that?" Atlas remarked. "Shouldn't it read 'day and Night' instead?" he said in a feeble attempt at small talk.

"What makes you so sure that day comes before night?" she asked.

"Well, night comes naturally after the day," he argued.

"Maybe not. Perhaps night gave birth to day. So night may come first, you see," she challenged again. Before Atlas could answer, something came slamming into their table.

"Your drinks!" A raucous voice said. It was their waiter. He had excess saliva drooping down slowly off his goat-like mouth as he dropped his tray. Some of it actually dripped from his lips onto the tray, not too far from Atlas' drink. Atlas stared at the faun serving them with a modicum of disgust which quickly turned to anger when he saw that his glass was only two-thirds filled.

"No, I ordered a pint!" he said.

"So you refuse this?" the waiter asked, pointing to the glass with his hairy hands.

"No, I want it, but I want the quantity I asked for."

"A pint is what you asked for!" the faun aggressively pushed the drink further out with his finger to show the cup size, spilling more of it in the process and adding to the already drenched table. The spillage was slowly making its way toward Atlas' elbows.

"Except you spilled so much of it, there's only a half-pint left!" Atlas retorted.

"Stop arguing with them!" Helva whispered. "You know how they get!"

"There a problem here?" asked a taller faun, probably the boss of this crew, as he set his eyes on the table. His nose had very wide nostrils, which largely contributed to his menacing look.

"No, we're fine, thank you," Daria quipped. The boss snickered at them and left, followed by his waiter, who let his tray drop loudly on another table.

"What's wrong with them?" Atlas said as he looked around the inn. He was suddenly noticing how messy it looked. A pronounced stench hovered in the air, and the floor was almost flowing with spillage. "They're sloppy as ever, and they serve like they're drunk. This is half the size I asked for." He looked at his drink again just as an orchestra of fauns began playing an ear-piercing melody with their pipes.

"Great! Now look what you made them do!" Helva clamped her hands over her ears.

"Let's remember what we're here for," Ezekiola cut in before things went from bad to worse.

"Right," Atlas came around, then took his first sip. "Ladies," he addressed them both but gave Daria a little smile, "there's something we need to tell you, or rather confide in you," he said. The girls leaned in closer, all ears.

The boys had discussed their strategy before the meeting and come up with different ways of broaching the subject, primarily with Helva. Since she was the harder one to convince, the plan was to first have Daria agree to come along. Knowing she had a crush on Atlas, they figured she would be the one most eager to render him a favor and thus influence her best friend to do the same. Atlas hoped that the story he was about to tell would warm them up properly until he ultimately formulated their request.

Atlas spoke first, taking his time. Ezekiola then took over the rest of the story, recounting everything that happened to them, from his first meeting with Leanne through a Sporadic Door, then entering Master Sohan's domain, and their encounter with the men in black outfits and seeing Leanne again in the restricted part of the Black Forest. However, he left out his meeting with Mirhas the Oracle. Helva listened intently without interrupting. Ezekiola had been trying to read her mind to see what she was thinking all along, but he found only silence when he tried to tune in. When he finished speaking, Helva tilted her head and looked back at her brother with a smile.

"Atlas, if I came to see you with such a story, do you think it would stop right there?"

"What do you mean?" her brother asked, knowing well what she meant. He had already run an array of potential questions in his mind.

"What do you want?" She asked straight out. "You can't just be coming to see us to tell us fantastic stories."

Atlas smiled and slowly began his second introduction. "Indeed. There is something we want. We put much thought into this, and it's not exactly an easy thing to ask for. We thought of other alternatives at first, but we rested our decision on this one. It was the only one that made sense, really. Zek was at first reticent, but I was the one who convinced him that this was surely a great avenue since it involved you and Daria. Considering you both have extensive knowledge on such matters as..."

"We need to see the Eye of the Past," Ezekiola suddenly

interrupted. Atlas' speech was taking too long, and something told him to be blunt and quit playing with words.

"The Eye of the Past?!" Helva jerked in her seat. She had not seen that one coming. "Are you mad to ask us such a thing? Do you know what the implications are?" She had thought that her brother had come to ask them to do some sort of presentation for one of their classes.

"Yes, we know what we're risking, and that's why we're here to ask for your help," Atlas said.

"This is some crazy request I never thought I'd hear! All this because you want to see where those intruders and the girls came from and where they went. This sounds more like a confrontation that happened by chance and won't happen again."

"Apparently, it will," Ezekiola stated matter-of-factly.

"How do you know?"

"The Oracle I met told me so," Ezekiola finally broke his silence on this hidden chapter of his story.

"The Oracle you met?" Both girls lit up at hearing that name.

"Which Oracle?" Daria chimed in.

"Mirhas, the Oracle," he answered, unaware that there were many.

Helva and Daria gasped. It was such a rarity to hear of someone meeting Mirhas, the Oracle. The Cypress Ladies were lucky if they ever got a chance to meet even one oracle. To think that a boy younger than them had gotten to meet Mirhas, one of the greats, and lived to tell his tale, was sacred to their ears.

"How did you meet her?" They both asked. Ezekiola did his best to act surprised by their sudden interest.

"Well, your brother can also testify to this. It was a strange encounter because the Oracle first appeared as a little girl," he told them and paused.

"That's right, you would think she was abandoned by her parents in a garden dump," Atlas said. Ezekiola cast him a warning look not to add too much to the story. With the way Atlas could twist words, the last thing he wanted was to add a negative aura to the oracle story the girls were so eager to hear.

"But I had my doubts," Ezekiola continued. "It was odd to see such a little girl in the middle of nowhere picking flowers. She then brought us into an abandoned hut where the doors suddenly slammed shut behind us, trapping us in. Just then, water started pouring through every enclosure, big or small, filling the hut rapidly. We thought we were going to drown, so I called the Oracle's name and asked for her help. All I remember after that is standing in a cave, with Atlas and Nohlan unconscious on the ground and the little girl transforming into a woman. She looked at me, and I was shocked when I saw her face. She only had eyes and nothing else."

"How can we know you're not making this up?" Helva asked suspiciously, reminding herself of her brother's ulterior motives.

Daria answered in his place: "Oh, but he's telling the truth! I read it in our books somewhere that many of them have few facial features and sometimes transform themselves to test their subjects first." At the very least, the girls were intrigued, and Helva was taking the boys more seriously.

"Did she speak to you?" Helva asked.

"Yes. Without me ever pronouncing a single word, she seemed to know much about me. She said my powers have come alive because I've created a link and tapped into the Fountain of Fire. She said Leanne and I are both in danger, and that I must face the one who will seek to crush me and dominate him. She then blessed my belt and told me it will be of help in my coming battle."

Helva gasped. "But that can't be! Only Emerald Robes can do that. You're just a beginner in your field."

"That's what I thought. But that's not what the Oracle said. She was sure about the link."

Helva shifted her eyes thoughtfully towards the window. She reasoned that he couldn't be making all of this up and that Atlas wanted to help his friend. Ultimately, this was a favor for Ezekiola and not for Atlas, which made her more receptive to the cause. Ezekiola picked up on her thoughts and continued in the right direction.

"I also asked her about being exiled into that wilderness where she lived," he told them, adding some extra spice to the tale.

"You asked her about herself?" Helva was shocked.

"Yes, I wanted to know."

"But Oracles never give answers about themselves," Daria said, looking at her friend for confirmation. "I thought it was forbidden to ask them such questions."

"What?" Atlas interfered. "Who makes up these rules?"

"It's an unwritten rule, really, but our Oracles and Origins book gives instructions on what's best to ask and not to ask during an encounter with them," she answered.

"Well, Ezekiola doesn't abide by unwritten rules. And guess what? The Oracle still answered. See, it's important to always ask away, and chances are you'll get an answer," Atlas advised.

"Thank you for the reminder, little brother," Helva said with a sidelong glance at him, then prompted Ezekiola to continue.

"What did she answer?"

"She said that her era of exile is coming to an end and

something about her nature soon becoming acknowledged and understood."

"Unbelievable!" Helva and Daria both looked as excited as Ezekiola had hoped.

"We should perhaps report this to our Oracles teacher and see what she makes of it," Daria suggested.

"No, we can't," Helva cautioned. "If we say such a thing, they'll enquire further, and then everyone will be exposed. This story can never reach their ears."

There was a moment of silence as the girls grew pensive, the boys almost forgetting to breathe as they waited for a reaction. Ezekiola tried to delve into Helva's mind again, but she had so many thoughts running through her head that he was unable to follow a thread.

"So, she told you that you'll be facing the one who seeks to crush you?" she asked.

"Apparently, yes. I believe this is the same person I encountered in the Black Forest. He told me who he was when we confronted each other. Somehow my belt turned into a rod of fire and pushed him back."

"He told you what? I didn't hear him speak!" Atlas was surprised.

"He didn't speak out loud, Atlas. He's a mind reader, like me. We never voiced anything, yet he answered my question when I asked him who he was. He didn't say much except that he was a Son of the Night Sky and that we'll meet again."

"What did he look like?" asked Helva. Ezekiola hesitated a moment before answering.

"Now, this is where it gets intriguing," Atlas told his sister before catching his friend's eye.

"Right," Ezekiola said, preparing himself. "Somehow, this boy who claims he's a Son of the Night Sky happens to also look, well... he looks like me."

"Don't downplay it, Zek," Atlas chimed in. "This boy didn't just *look like* him, Helva. He was his exact double. The resemblance is actually quite scary."

Helva and Daria listened intently, wondering what to make of these puzzling pieces of information. Helva finally spoke her thoughts: "Wait, the Oracle said you created a link. But the girl you linked with is a human from Planet Blue, you said. How can you possibly be linking with someone from another world at your level? Not only is it forbidden, it's impossible!"

"I don't know what to make of all that's happened. All I know for sure is that we linked, and I'm no smarter as to how we did it," Ezekiola answered.

"If you've been tapping into the Fountain of Fire, it might explain your overnight powers. Probabilities are that a link has definitely been created," Helva continued, speaking as if she was an expert on the topic of linking.

Listening to her talk, Ezekiola momentarily grew nervous. "Then what am I supposed to do?" he asked, wondering what was to be expected of those who linked.

"The Oracle told me that Leanne's in danger. I get a sense he's after her too. I also got the feeling he wasn't lying when he said we'd meet again. I've been having nightmares about it," he confessed.

Atlas was intrigued. His friend had never been one to open himself up so easily, especially about having nightmares. He thought perhaps it was the girls who were naturally able to draw so much out of him. Then again, Helva and Daria were expert dream readers. Helva had even won a prize for being the best in her class. The girls were watching Ezekiola like two wide-eyed kittens.

"What are your nightmares about?" asked Daria.

"I'm in a tunnel, and I'm being chased by him. I know I

need to turn around and face him, but I don't and keep running away," he said, a hint of sweat glistening on his brow.

"The Oracle was right then," Helva pondered, "you will face him again."

"You see why we need to use the Eye of the Past, Helva?" Atlas brought everyone back to the purpose of the meeting.

"Atlas, as much as I'd like to help, I can't possibly bring you there. We're not allowed to use the Lake for such purposes," Helva answered, putting aside all her feelings for Ezekiola's story.

Atlas looked at her with a rueful smile.

"What?" Helva asked, wondering why he was smiling instead of being disappointed. She was expecting Atlas to plead with her. Yet she forgot how her brother was as good as she was. Instead, Atlas pulled a small ornamented black book out of nowhere, landing it with a thump on the table.

"What's this?" Helva asked.

"Why don't you open it and see for yourself? I'll let you read only one page," he said, intentionally teasing her.

Ezekiola looked at Atlas, shocked at this last-minute trick his friend was pulling. At the rate they were going, he chose to ignore how much deeper in trouble they had just gotten themselves. Best to close an eye on this, he told himself.

Helva took the little black book and opened the first page. First, there was a look of shock, and then delight crept across her face.

"How did you get this?" she whispered, aching to turn the page.

"How I got it is my business, not yours," Atlas said as he shut the book, took it from her hands, and slipped it into his pouch. "My intention is to give it to you for your mere pleasure of reading and finding out other things. You evidently didn't land on the page I thought you would," he said, smirking, then added, "it's yours on one condition: that you help us. What do you say, Helva? Daria? You think you two can help a good friend in distress, help him stop these nightmares, and save some lives? All he really needs is more information."

Daria would have screamed 'yes' if it wasn't for Helva nudging her to stay quiet. She looked back at the pouch containing the book. This time, however, there was something wild in her eyes, the likes of which could make one leap from a mountaintop. It took her a moment to answer, but she finally did.

"It's a deal. Ezekiola, meet me at the entrance gate of the Ladies' Forest before nightfall at the next crescent moon since they never use the Lake during that lunar phase. Nonetheless, there are always ladies lurking around, so be sure to wear something dark so you don't stick out."

"I can't thank you enough," Ezekiola said, relieved that he would soon have access to something so precious and finally get answers to the questions that had been haunting him.

"I can't say I enjoy breaking rules. But like they say, there's a time for everything, even that—once in a while. Now hand that over!" Helva ordered her young brother.

Atlas took out the precious little book and handed it to her.

They exited the inn and parted ways. Helva was as excited as a pony who had been given wings. To think, she now had access to the most intimate thoughts of the one to whom she had long been attracted, as Borghis' journal was now in her possession.

Chapter 22

The Lake of Maji

Nohlan had grown frantically worried when he found out about Ezekiola's plan to journey to the Lake of Maji. He insisted on tagging along as an escort for his friends, considering the catastrophes that had befallen them in the Black Forest. However, halfway through their hike in the woods, Ezekiola and Atlas began wondering if they shouldn't have left Nohlan behind. Like a forest bard, Nohlan kept telling strange tales about the Lake, including some about lost souls who had never made it back alive. Without realizing it, Nohlan would even whisper when walking through the dimmer parts of the forest, scaring his own wits away.

"You know, Nohlan, you should steer away from those bizarre novels of yours," Atlas commented at one point during their walk. "I saw the last one you read, 'The Crossover Storm.' That author Dunkin Vessel completely exaggerates everything in his stories and always makes everyone disappear."

"You read it, too?" Nohlan asked, surprised.

"No, I just had a peek. Those stories have a bad influence on your imagination!" Atlas would never tell his friends that he had devoured all the novels. Being a dedicated bookworm, he would never admit to his maddening urge to learn how every one of those stories turned out.

"Well, I'm just warning you about the Lake and the things I've heard," Nohlan said.

"Relax, Nohlan," Ezekiola cut in, "it's not like I'm going into the lake for a swim. Don't worry about me. I'll come back alive," Ezekiola said.

While the three friends moved along at a moderate pace, Helva and Daria were patiently waiting for Ezekiola to appear at the outskirts of the school's gates. The day had been windy, and the sun was already setting; it danced through the trees, giving off what was left of the waning daylight. Helva was enjoying the view until she spied three bodies instead of one approaching, each wearing a dark gray cloak, an unpleasant surprise, to say the least. She waved her hands in the air, then ran her fingers through her hair just like her brother did when he grew agitated.

"What are you two doing here?" she asked, looking at her brother and Nohlan.

"He needed guidance in the woods," replied Atlas, the smirk on his face assuring his sister that he was blatantly lying.

"Actually, he needed guidance on which day the crescent moon fell," Nohlan corrected him, focusing on his expertise. He had taken a Moon Cycles class last semester to further explore themes that increased his knowledge of growing plants and had become familiar with the elements concerning the phases of Circa's moons and their effects.

"Sorry Helva, we should have sent you a message earlier," Ezekiola said. "We discussed it among ourselves and thought it wiser, just in case something unexpected happened while we crossed through the Black Forest, you know, like the last time...."

Helva wasn't pleased. She had already agreed to something that could get her into serious trouble.

"You seem to think that this is a party. Well, it's not. If you wish to get to your destination, you better listen well. When we get to the bottom of the mountain that leads to the lake, only Ezekiola and I will go up into the hills, no one else. Is that clear? The lake can only be used by one person at a time, and I won't activate it more than once. You'll soon understand why. You two must stay at the foot of the mountain with Daria, and if you refuse, well then, Ezekiola won't go, and no one will see the Eye of the Past. And I'll readily abort this escapade if I get one more surprise from you. Is that also clear?"

Helva had upped her tone a notch, and the three friends nodded obediently.

Ezekiola had read about the power of the Lake of Maji, which was under the guardianship of the Cypress Ladies, and how it had long been used as a study tool to look into former times and review events that had come to pass. Students would observe the effects of decisions that had been made and speculate on other alternatives and probable outcomes.

The night quickly grew darker, with only the glow of a crescent moon. Thankfully, Helva was one of the few Ladies who possessed the mountain staff with a stone tip that naturally lit up when the light was low, and the boys were grateful she had that special tool for their perilous climb. Soon they arrived at a signpost indicating the way to the lake. Helva turned around. "Alright, this is where we part company. Ezekiola, you come with me."

Helva and Ezekiola began climbing until the hill rose at such a sharp angle it grew harder to keep the same, steady pace. Helva stopped a few times to catch her breath while Ezekiola waited patiently; it allowed him some extra time to regroup his thoughts on what he wanted to know.

"Is it true that the lake is guarded by nymphs?" he asked, breaking their long silence.

"Now, where did you hear that?" Helva chuckled.

"I read it somewhere, I guess," he answered. In fact, there was so much myth and mystery concerning the lake that most students at Cypress could not tell what was true anymore.

"The lake needs no guard. I can assure you of that," she said in a no-nonsense tone. "This way," she motioned and led him into a tunnel completely overgrown with vines. Helva was forced to push them aside to enter.

"You really have to know your way up here. I would definitely have gotten lost," Ezekiola said as Helva's staff lit the way into a cave.

"Actually, we'll be entering the lake from behind, which is a safer entry for us, in case someone else is at the main entrance, although I doubt it. I checked. Nobody had the Lake of Maji on their schedule."

When they reached the back, they paused. Helva pointed her staff at the cast iron gates to illuminate the gargoyle-like figures adorning them. They were massive eagles with grotesque heads, mouths open as if they were screaming. Their wings were spread wide as if they were turning in midair, and they held snakes in each of their talons. The expression on the face of the snakes was of pure suffering.

"This doesn't look very welcoming," Ezekiola said.

"It's not meant to be welcoming. But don't be afraid, they don't harm visitors. They only guard the exit gates," she teased. She made Ezekiola chuckle for the first time.

She pointed her staff at the ironclad doors that immediately responded to it, opening slowly to reveal a charcoal-colored statue of a little girl holding a chalice high up in the air at the center of a very small lake. With such imposing avian protectors guarding the entrance, Ezekiola was surprised. He was expecting something much more majestic. Then again, he reminded himself not to judge anything by its appearance, for the very things that look powerless exude the kind of power that can move mountains. He had learned that from the Oracle.

"Wait here while I wake the lake. You can hold on to this tree. It serves as a safety bar," she said, pointing to some midsize tree not too far from the water's edge. Ezekiola didn't understand why she was suggesting such a thing. He was fine, just standing up. A few leaves brushed past her as she walked towards the lake. She readied her staff and whispered something into its tip, then dunked it into the water. As if on cue, the wind started to pick up, and several voices were heard as Helva continued to mutter under her breath. Ezekiola couldn't tell from where the voices were coming. For a moment, it sounded like the trees and wind were the ones voicing the call, as if a life force had been awakened within them.

The winds picked up speed, and leaves rushed in every direction, reminding Ezekiola of his incident in the Black Forest. He began to understand why Helva had advised him to hold on to the tree. In no time, his cloak was ripped away by the velocity of the wind as he clung to the tree to keep from being knocked off his feet. He heard the voices grow louder, and this time, they were speaking in different tongues. The leaves swirled incredibly fast, round and round, they formed a funnel, rising up like a tornado, and then dispersed. He was sure his friends could see what was happening.

Waking up the lake was creating a powerful commotion. That's probably why Helva had cautioned them that she could only activate it once. Helva removed the tip of her staff from the water and signaled Ezekiola to come closer. He walked to the water's edge and stood next to her, looking down into the lake. Everything suddenly grew quiet.

"I shall leave you two alone. You must speak out loud when

you ask your question, not just in your mind. What you see is for you to keep. When you're finished, meet me by the gate. And remember, the Lake of Maji speaks many languages and in images as well. Its answers may surprise you, so remain open-minded." With those instructions, Helva glided away, leaving him alone with the lake.

Ezekiola continued staring down at the lake. It lay motionless in the dark, looking deceptively like any ordinary body of water. For a moment, Ezekiola questioned its efficiency but then realigned his thoughts. Helva knew what she was doing and had pulled several strings to make this happen. He gathered his thoughts.

"Who is that man I saw in the Black Forest, and how do I best confront him?"

After a few moments of silence, the water level rose. Somehow, water began trickling down from the chalice the statue was holding until it flowed in a steady stream. Like a mirror in front of him, it was in the stream that Ezekiola saw what he was not expecting, the likes of his own reflection staring right back at him. Their eyes met. The Son of the Night Sky, his double, seemed slightly taller and, Ezekiola had to admit, more handsome as well. There was one striking difference, however. His eyes. They were like black pearls, as if there was no soul inhabiting his body. Staring into those eyes sent shivers down his spine, but Ezekiola held his gaze. He began to sense a strange feeling coming over him. It was something he had heard of but never before experienced. A merging of the minds. He felt his body convulse as he became one with the image. He knew, saw, felt, and heard everything he wanted to know. He entered a dark space, surrounded by shining objects that came and went. His focus shifted to two distinct lights, one brighter than the other, their intensity in constant motion as if they were dancing. Sometimes the dimmer one would gain some light only to lose it again. The imagery began fading, and he came back to his senses.

A voice arose from all around: "You must not kill, but you must dominate." He recognized the voice. It was Mirhas, the Oracle. At that moment, he merged with Mirhas' mind. Now endowed with panoramic vision, he knew then what he had to do.

Chapter 23

Guide thy Chase

The end-of-year carnival had more than its share of people crowding into Chester Town. The turnout this year was exceptional thanks to the carnival's much-advertised theme: The Fire Dance. It was popular because it allowed kids and adults alike the chance to play dress up, don costumes that reflected the carnival theme, and enjoy all the rides.

Leanne, too, had decided to attend that night. She hadn't had much fun in a while. She had learned her lesson since her adventures in the Black Forest had ended so abruptly. She and Andy had escaped the wrath of that terrible boy Zeke by a mere hair's breadth, but she couldn't help but wonder what happened to Ezekiola and all the others they had seen in the Black Forest. Did Ezekiola also escape? Did Zeke burn down the entire forest, or did they fight each other? Leanne ran several scenarios in her mind, but her questions remained unanswered. Desperate to find out, she had even attempted to go through the special tree in the Chester schoolyard again.

Unfortunately, the tree had somehow been badly charred and was dying, rotting from the inside out. Shut out and trapped in her own world, it haunted her that there was nothing more she could do. Sometimes, Leanne wondered if she hadn't imagined the whole thing—meeting Ezekiola and finding a secret gateway into his world only to be chased out by Zeke. The one thing that she still had was Ezekiola's name. She held onto it. Like an invisible string tying him to her, she continued to wear his name in her locket. It was Leanne's only means of maintaining their connection, the only place where she could exercise her will and not give up. Thankfully, nothing life-threatening had occurred, and since things were back to normal, making a carnival night most welcome.

The activities of the evening included amusement rides, several shows, and many arts and crafts venues to discover. There were stalls lined up in rows, some serving as entertainment outlets with prizes to be won while others sold local products. The layout was impressive, with a massive bonfire in the center. There were wooden signs signaling the four cardinal directions, and torches lit at every stall. Some even had steel drums with fires burning inside them. Firefighters were at the center of the event, generously displaying their knowledge of both the beneficial effects and the ravages of fire. And with their participation at the carnival, nothing could possibly go wrong.

Leanne had come with Andy. They had prepared a schedule to follow so they could maximize their time at the Fire dance. They would tour the carnival site once, then move on to the adult rides, and finish with the evening shows. The girls had had some trouble coming up with costume ideas and, in the end, had simply opted to wear oversized red scarves they had bought at one of the merchant stalls, which somewhat captured the theme of fire.

"Come take a look!" Andy pointed towards a large sign listing the evening's shows. It started with the folk dance of the traditional Chester Towners, followed by fire eaters and knife throwers, with the final number: spinning fire dancers. This year, all the shows were interesting enough not to want to miss any. The girls decided to go on all the rides first to make it on time for every show.

"Forget the folk dance. They have that every year. Let's make sure we don't miss the fire performances, though," Leanne said, looking at her watch.

"Right! They have all the cute guys there, too," Andy agreed.

"We only have two hours until the good stuff starts, so let's go."

The girls strolled around the kiosks to see if there was anything of interest to them. Each booth had a different theme.

"How cool is this!" Leanne said, looking over a science-themed stall that explained various natural phenomena. For instance, the element of fire was broken down to explain each particle. There were also different types of meteorites. Even the orbital speed and energy of the sun were explained. One stall challenged people to try to start a fire naturally, without the usual tools. Leanne and Andy tried but were unable to create enough friction. Without matches and lighters, most people were just as hopeless.

After an hour of prowling about and going on several rides, they spotted a venue and ordered drinks and some snacks.

As they headed towards the main stage, they were drawn towards a large carousel attracting kids and adults alike.

"I think we're good to do this as our last stop before the show starts," Leanne proposed, eyeing a young couple flirting, one sitting on a unicorn and the other on a dragon. What a match, she thought. She and Andy waited their turn and mounted the carousel. She chose a purple horse, while Andy went for the red dragon. The carousel started spinning, playing a tinny melody. Leanne looked around. There were people already making their way to the main stage. She began to worry that they might not get a good spot when the shows began. As they completed their third circle, a boy in the crowd caught Leanne's attention. With the carousel slowly spinning, she had to wait a full turn each time to see him again. The only thing she noticed was his dark curly hair and a green scarf tied around his neck. She wished the carousel would move faster so she could check him out better. Suddenly, she couldn't wait to get off. When she came back around, however, the boy was gone. Leanne's eyes continued to scan the crowd restlessly in search of the boy with the green scarf. But before growing too discouraged, she had a happy thought: maybe he was one of the fire dancers. With great anticipation, she headed towards the main stage with her friend, arriving right on time as the shows were about to start. Halfway through the performances, though, Leanne became disappointed. The boy in the green scarf wasn't there. She had probably fantasized about the whole thing. Clearly, he was not in the show. Bored and restless, she had managed to put off going to the restroom, but now it was urgent.

"I need to find the bathroom, Andy. I'll be back."

She walked away from the loud music and the assembled crowd and took a dim path that led to the toilet stalls. Heading back, she became momentarily disoriented as to where the main stage was. Opposite from the crowd, there was another stage. In no time, a large group had gathered to watch something there. It seemed somebody was doing a one-man performance with fire. Judging by the sounds that emanated from that direction, the crowd was enthralled by the spectacle. Leanne noticed that more and more people were joining the crowd.

Curious, she headed towards the other stage to observe what was going on. She stopped and looked up and was also struck by the artist's fire performance.

It was extraordinary the height the fire reached as he spit it out of his mouth. It was beyond awesome to see it rise several meters high. This was no firecracker. Moving in closer, she wondered, what could propel that kind of force upwards? She knew the basics of fire, but this? It was unnatural. When the fire swirled right back down into the performer's hands, the crowd burst into applause. Leanne edged closer to the stage. The performer seemed to be juggling fire with his bare hands, and Leanne couldn't discern what kind of object the fire was attached to. For a brief moment, she had the insane thought that there was no object at all but only the element itself, as if the fire was appearing and disappearing at will from the performer's hands. This must be some kind of trick, she reasoned. The enthralled crowd watched closely and, judging by the inquisitive look on most faces, apparently shared her suspicions. Try as she might, Leanne couldn't make out the face of the performer; it was totally obscured by the flames, but she faintly heard his voice.

"I am the heir of the great sun, the commander of the mightiest fire, the dancer of blazing flames!" She did not recall the carnival promoting any such act that night. She drew closer still and suddenly froze in her tracks.

There, standing shirtless on a podium like a demigod, was Zeke. With his fireworks, he was pandering to the adoring crowd, unmistakably in his element.

"How does he do it?!"

"Incredible!"

"Amazing!"

The two men Leanne had seen with Zeke before were also present, standing next to him like warrior statues. The crowd was watching, mouths agape and mesmerized by his every move. He was manipulating fire in a way that left the crowd mystified.

With barely any time to sort her thoughts, Leanne heard him speak.

> *"Behold! I come again this starry night,*
> *Wrestle you, I will and steal your might,*
> *Thousand clashes between us have come*
> *Eclipsed far too long under your sun.*
> *A victor once, I now indulge anew*
> *Call to your senses, you have but few."*

Suddenly, he propelled the fire up in the air, where it took the shape of a three-headed dragon. Knowing him all too well, Leanne grew concerned that Zeke was manipulating his sacred element dangerously close to the crowd. Some people let out nervous laughter when the fire almost touched them. Yet they remained standing, probably comforting themselves that the fire juggler was an expert who knew his limits.

His next move, however, was aimed at a boy standing in the middle of the crowd, who was wearing a delicate green scarf tied around his neck. Leanne's heart skipped a beat when she saw him. There he was, the boy she had spotted a while ago when she was on the carousel, but she still couldn't make out his face with his back turned to her. Miraculously, the boy in the green scarf caught the fire with his right hand, convincing everyone he was part of the show. The crowd cheered, wowed by the trick.

Leanne blinked, then blinked again. Standing there was Ezekiola, the fire subsiding in his hand, staring hard at his opponent, who had just thrown the blazing projectile at him.

"What the hell is he doing?" asked Atlas. He was standing

behind Ezekiola and next to Nohlan. The three were dressed as commoners, in dark trousers and shirts, just as Helva had instructed them to do so they would blend in. Ezekiola had made sure to bring his Emerald Belt, tying it around his neck like a makeshift scarf.

"Your answer's in your question, Atlas," Ezekiola said, not taking his gaze off Zeke, who continued with his speech, looking fiercely at Ezekiola while pacing back and forth like a hungry lion.

"Who among you would like to see us dance with fire?" Zeke suddenly called out to the crowd, seizing the moment. The crowd slowly parted, making way for Ezekiola to join his performance partner, unaware that they were paving the way for something much more dangerous.

Zeke drew a circle of fire around himself, outlining the whole stage, then threw his fire high up in the air again. The crowd burst into cheers again, asking for more. It looked like a perfectly staged show. Ezekiola stared back at him, momentarily hesitant, not knowing what he was being asked to do.

Before gathering his thoughts, his adversary broke his concentration when he addressed him again. "What shall it be? Shall we set these petty fools ablaze, or shall you dance with me?"

Ezekiola tuned into his opponent's mind and understood what he wanted. He had to comply with Zeke's request to join him in the Dance of the Caspol Brothers, or Zeke would burn the whole place down and everyone along with it.

As the crowd parted, Ezekiola turned to Nohlan and asked. "Do you know the rules of the ancient ritual dance of the Caspol Brothers?"

"The rivals' dance, you mean?" Nohlan asked wide-eyed, unsure whether he had heard right.

"Yes, that one," Ezekiola confirmed.

Nohlan nodded. "Yes. But that dance was banned centuries ago since it was used for dark purposes by the Sons of the Night Sky."

"I know its history, Nohlan," Ezekiola snapped. The dance was used in Circa long ago as a way for two people to exchange their powers in a positive way. However, when the Sons of the Night Sky left Circa, they used the dance as a way to kill one another in a deadly spectacle to determine the most powerful among them. When powers were shared, each opponent was able to tap into the life force of the other. It was what enabled a weaker opponent to outperform a stronger one by stealing away his opponent's power to use it against him. This barbaric transformation of a once uplifting ritual had irreversibly tainted its name. Circa had banned the Caspol Dance forever.

"Think for a moment! If you do this, they'll never let you back into Circa again!" Atlas intervened to convince his friend not to make a deadly error in judgment. "You'll be banished for life!"

"I know the consequences, Atlas. But we didn't come this far to do nothing."

"Remember what Helva warned us about. We must not harm anyone on this planet!" Nohlan added, reiterating Helva's warning before leading the three friends through the Sporadic Door she had located. Ezekiola had confided in her the vision he had had at the Lake of Maji, and after considerable contemplation, they mutually agreed on the wild course of action of venturing to Planet Blue to face Zeke. Ezekiola knew that Zeke would eventually hunt down him and Leanne and so decided to meet him head-on.

"Nohlan, he'll do much worse if I don't comply! Since you know the rules of the dance, come up on stage with me and bind our hands?"

Nohlan hesitated for a moment, but as he felt he had no

choice, he nodded. Like a man walking to the gallows, he climbed the stairs onto the stage, his head hunched forward. Ezekiola followed him and slowly removed his shirt. The crowd burst into cheers as the two young men prepared for the dance spectacle.

"And to the victor shall go the spoils!" Zeke suddenly shouted. To Ezekiola's horror, fire swept across the stage and, like a rolling carpet, stopped at Leanne's feet, making her part of the drama. Zeke's two accomplices suddenly appeared next to Leanne, leaving everyone to wonder how they had even got there. Leanne was dumbfounded. To her dismay, her large red scarf made her look like an actor and a part of the show. She stood immobile for a moment, panic-stricken, shaking her head, not knowing what to say or do.

"Come, Lady Leanne, make us suffer not a moment longer. Come claim the one who shall be worthy of you so you may share the sacred Fountain of Fire with the winner!" Zeke exclaimed.

Ezekiola grew inflamed. "What are you doing? You can't make her part of the ritual!" Ezekiola spat out through clenched teeth.

"These are new rules. Now she will be. And she can watch closely as your body is decimated by my flames. After you're gone, she'll be bound to me."

Fire crept up Leanne's feet from behind, making her take a step forward. She tried to step away from it, but the flames grew tall when she tried to go in any other direction. The crowd parted as the fire kept pushing her, forcing her to advance until she reached the stage. Unable to move in any direction other than the ones the flames directed, she mounted the stage and was struck by the vision before her. Ezekiola and Zeke were looking at her, and it hit her like a bolt: they were twins. They had almost the same height, the same facial features, the same build, except that Zeke looked more muscular and trained. But what distinguished the two were their eyes—Zeke's were a fathomless black and Ezekiola's, a blazing blue. When Leanne looked at Ezekiola, she felt the same connection she had sensed when they had first met. It filled her with an odd sense of joy but also dread. How had they gotten to this point? She sensed that she was somehow the cause of this scene between the two. What she had done, she couldn't tell. Ezekiola's eyes held a note of hope when he saw her, making Leanne wonder if he knew what he was getting into. One of Zeke's men grabbed Leanne's arm and took her to the side of the stage. Zeke then turned around and whipped his black belt in her direction. A circle of flames, like prison walls, shot up around Leanne, and she screamed.

"She better come out of this alive, else you will pay with your life," Ezekiola warned.

"Well, that depends on how well your dance performance goes and if you can entertain the crowd," Zeke responded with a malevolent smile. Ezekiola was sickened by the thought of Leanne's life being dangled in front of a crowd for entertainment purposes. All of a sudden, he was looking forward to this deadly dance.

Onstage, Nohlan placed himself strategically between Zeke and Ezekiola and took hold of their right arms. Having a hard time believing that their excursion outside of Circa had brought them to this moment, Nohlan had his first understanding of why there was so much cautioning about venturing into the unknown. Like storms at sea, the best-laid plans always end up forcing you to change course unexpectedly. Their initial plan was for Ezekiola to find Zeke and confront him privately in a forest, then look for Leanne, but the carnival lights had drawn them in. They had innocently decided to explore it a bit. Now he was wondering how much damage they were about to cause.

"We use my belt to bind us, and his stays outside of the circle," Zeke said, gesturing at the Emerald Belt.

"But you're both supposed to use your belts," Nohlan insisted.

"Once again, the rules have changed," Zeke responded, "and they're not open to discussion." Nohlan looked wide-eyed at Ezekiola. What sort of unfair dance was this going to be? To his shock, Ezekiola nodded his consent. Nohlan was instantly crestfallen.

Ezekiola took off his makeshift disguised Emerald Belt from around his neck—and threw it outside the circle of fire. Nohlan took Zeke's black belt bearing the odd triangular symbol. Reluctantly, he tied it first around Zeke's right wrist and then around Ezekiola's, binding the two together. The belt then burst into flames, dazzling the audience once more. Within seconds, Ezekiola bonded with his opponent's mind and immediately fell to his knees. The merging was too extreme to bear. Becoming one with Zeke took a toll on his vitality, and he felt like he was falling into a deep pit with nothing to hang onto; he was in a complete state of helplessness.

As in his experience at the Lake of Maji, Ezekiola entered a dark, hollow space devoid of life. Disoriented, unable to retain any of his own thoughts, he absorbed Zeke's violent, wicked mind, which was warped by cruelty, pain, and anguish. Just when he felt he couldn't endure the agony any longer, he was brought deeper still into the thoughts of his opponent. Ezekiola could see Zeke's intentions, all of them dark, twisted, and malevolent.

Ezekiola knew what he had to do, yet he also knew it would require a Herculean effort to lift his opponent out of this state into a higher one. Zeke saw right through his plans and immediately resisted. The two fighter's attempts at resistance would cause much friction until one of them gave way. The Caspol Dance was as much a battle of the minds as it was a physical and emotional one. Having merged with his opponent for mere seconds before the dance began, Ezekiola now knew he had to confront his other half.

"Brothers, take your position," Nohlan began. The two opponents locked hands while Nohlan kept his own on each of their wrists.

"Remember to respect the rules of the dance and stay within the circle. Right hands must remain bound and left ones unbound to engage your opponent."

He handed each a loose branch that Zeke's men had handed to him. As soon as Zeke and Ezekiola held them, the branches, too, lit up with fire.

"May the powers of each flow into the other." Nohlan looked one last time at Zeke before stepping outside of the circle of fire. He was struck again by Zeke's resemblance to Ezekiola. He couldn't explain why, but he had the urge to make one last statement.

"Guide thy chase till Pollux dominates."

Ezekiola was perplexed. That last sentence seemed out of place as if it wasn't part of the ritual's commencing statement. It wasn't the first time he had heard the name. Just as an intuitive impression trickled into his mind about Pollux, known as the brightest star in the constellation of Gemini, Zeke made his first pull on the belt, forcing his attention away from his reflection. Zeke looked satisfied, already exuding the look of one who had conquered.

"Now, brother, we share the same power," Zeke stated smugly. It was the age-old maxim known in the world of the Caspol Brothers.

"Yes, we do," Ezekiola replied, staring at him hard, "but you don't have my intensity, and you never will," he added. Zeke remained unconvinced.

With their right hands bound together, the two began moving in circles, pulling one another, and slashing the other with the fire whip held in their left hands.

As the first blood was drawn, the cheerful faces of the watching crowd turned grim, and the crowd grew quiet. Despite that, no one dared to leave, for they were mesmerized and wanted to see the show to the end.

Ezekiola and Zeke whipped each other out with their branches, trying to exhaust the life force from one another. Zeke's whipping skills were more advanced, for sometimes, three whips came out of his branch instead of the single one Nohlan had given him. But after a little while, Ezekiola grew familiar with Zeke's creative powers and his skills. He realized how easily he could kill him, yet he refrained, remembering the Oracle's warning not to kill but to dominate. He knew what he had to do but just had to figure out *how* to do it. Nohlan's words echoed once more in his mind, "Guide thy chase till Pollux dominates." Somehow, he knew this was a key.

Slowly but surely, both fighters' bodies grew bloodied, but Ezekiola's was bloodier. His best defense lay in his agility, for he was able to sense where Zeke planned to strike next. Using his opponent's powers, he swung himself out of the way by rising into midair and flipping high up each time to avoid the whip. Zeke would then have to engage his right hand to bring him down. They continued pouncing on each other until fatigue began to set in. There came a moment, however, where Zeke seized an opportunity and fiercely slashed Ezekiola's back, cutting him right to the bone. Ezekiola let out an agonizing scream and fell, making the black belt binding the two come undone. Zeke now held it in his hands, regaining possession of what was his, whipping it victoriously in the air.

"You can't beat me!" he exclaimed, looking down at Ezekiola.

Ezekiola tried to speak but couldn't. His breath was like fire in his mouth.

Zeke laughed. "Don't die just yet, there's something I want you to watch before your life ends." He turned around and whipped his belt in the air, sending off lightning bolts into the surrounding trees. They caught fire, one at a time. Burning branches started falling on the people who had cheered him on in the beginning. Just like he had done in the Black Forest, Zeke continued to lash out like a madman, building a storm from hell, sending branches and pieces of wood violently into the air.

Ezekiola was left on the ground panting, unable to rise. All he could do was watch the pandemonium around him while his friends witnessed the carnage. Atlas and Nohlan were terror-ized, their faces white from watching their friend being beaten. Atlas kept running his hands through his hair while Nohlan chewed away at his nails, making a few fingers bleed from biting through to his skin. All the while, they patiently stood off stage, allowing Ezekiola to fight Zeke. It's what he had come here to do. Nohlan, however, had secretly readied to throw himself on stage to save his friend's life if it came to that. And he was about to do just that when Ezekiola locked eyes with him, motioning with a weak hand towards a young boy in the crowd standing next to his father. Nohlan caught his friend's message and ran toward the boy as the crowd dispersed in panic. The boy was carrying an ornamental horn, probably bought in one of the woodcarving shops. He snatched it away, ignoring the little one's pleas.

Ezekiola lay helpless, unable to dominate Zeke. Every chance he had to kill Zeke, he had recalled the Oracle's warn-ing. He opened his eyes once again and saw an intense gaze staring back at him. Leanne's eyes had swelled up from all the smoke around her. She was crouching down, coughing frantically. His eyes fell on her neck and the locket that swung from it. He realized for the first time that his name rested in it. He recalled again what the Oracle had said: *"The Fountain of Fire has come alive in you, for you have created a link."* He then realized it was Leanne who had created it. She wore his name, and she believed in something more than a simple chance meeting. All at once, his understanding of the significance of her wearing his name opened the floodgates in his mind, bringing him instantly to a higher level of consciousness where he saw things as never before.

In flashes before his eyes, images started pouring in, shedding intuitive light on his dilemma. The images came fast, like in a dream. First, he saw a flash of the nine-headed beast Hydra that lurked in the mud and how he had conquered it by lifting it in the air. He then saw the image of his favorite carving of a hero adorning the library halls of his school, brandishing a severed dragon head victoriously in the air. Then came a flash of Master Sohan turning into a dove and soaring up into the sky, followed by the eagle gargoyles guarding the Lake of Maji with snakes caught in their talons—also in midair. There it was! The answer. How could he have missed such an obvious thing from the start? He realized now how, during their duel, he had been the one lifting up into the air, while Zeke never had. In fact, Zeke's foot had never left the ground. In Ezekiola's presence, Zeke could not rise. There was something about Ezekiola that limited his opponent's powers, something akin to being like the brightest star Pollux, naturally outshining him. He suddenly knew what he had to do.

In that precious moment, Ezekiola's palms became filled with the sensation of fire vibrating from within. Yet, his hands bore no sign of injury. The fire was emanating from inside him as if it wanted to come out. It was the same sensation he had felt when he had first confronted Zeke in the Black Forest, as if his waist was on fire. Ezekiola stared at his palms, and his attention suddenly shifted to a beaming light coming from outside of the circle of fire in which he was caught. Like a glittering jewel in the night, his Emerald Belt was emitting a dim but perceptible light, calling him almost. Ezekiola's hands yearned to hold the belt, and as quickly as that thought crossed his mind, it flew right into his right palm.

Surprising Zeke, Ezekiola instantly whipped his Emerald Belt from floor level and wrapped it around Zeke's ankle. Gathering all his strength, he rose and spun his opponent around continuously. With speed and velocity on Ezekiola's side, Zeke slowly but surely soared into the air, bound only by his ankle. A blazing fire suddenly took over the whole stage, as if explosives had gone off. The scene looked like the finale of a show gone wrong; smoke was rising from every corner. The few curious lurkers who wanted to see the end of the show were unable to. They never saw Zeke land. It almost looked as if he had disintegrated, vanishing into thin air. Atlas and Nohlan could not see Zeke either, and to their surprise, nor could they see Ezekiola. Despite the clouds of smoke, they ran towards the stage in a desperate attempt to rescue their friend, hoping to find Ezekiola's bloody body nearby.

When the fire around Leanne subsided, she seized the moment to make a run into the nearby woods. She ran as fast and as far as she could, but having inhaled so much smoke on stage, her lungs were failing her. Suddenly, waves of darkness filled her vision. She struggled to maintain her breath and sight, but they seemed to simultaneously shut down. Her body wavered, and she inevitably started to fall. She could barely make out flashes of hands reaching out from beneath brown garments to catch her. Then everything went black.

Meanwhile, Nohlan wasted no time with the horn he had snatched from the child. In the middle of the chaotic scene, he sat down and played a tune with it. The sound emanating from the horn was aggressively high-pitched. Astonishingly, the fires rose higher as if responding to that sound.

"What are you doing?" asked Atlas, bewildered, terrified by the rising flames.

"I thought I had the right note, but this thing is jammed! I don't even think it's built right!" he said, pushing the air out of the horn.

"Bring down the fires on stage, fast! We have to find Ezekiola and get out of here now!"

Nohlan started playing again, and this time the sound was much lower in vibration. A few flames began subsiding. Sirens were heard not too far from the site. They were coming from fire trucks making their way towards the stage. Nohlan had seen the fireman in their stalls and was curious as to why they used water to douse fire. He couldn't understand why opposing elements were used to cancel each other out so violently when all they had to do was to make use of sound. He continued again, trying to manipulate the instrument so it could emit lower notes. He then heard other sounds very different and refined than his, lower still in vibration, coming from the other side of the stage. He stopped and looked up. The flames on stage died out one by one, enabling him to witness an impossible sight on the other side. For there was Borghis and his crew, standing with their distinctive horns in their hands, extinguishing the flames up on the stage. The face of Nohlan's brother was creased with anger.

"Is that Borghis?!" Atlas asked in disbelief. He wasn't sure if he was relieved or not. And Borghis was not alone but had several Brown Robes with him, Gordi and Keenan among them. Borghis rushed over.

"Where is he?" he asked, completely distraught. This was the second time he had witnessed such a maddening scene. Oddly, this was the type of situation he had hoped to find himself in, one that would require him to use the powers of his staff. Only now did it dawn on him how much havoc needed to be sorted out each time.

"Who?" asked Nohlan.

"What do you mean who, Nohlan? This is not the time to act dumb! Your missing friend, that's who! To think you were going to do this on your own. You're truly mad, all of you!"

"How did you find us?" Atlas asked. He was confused by how Borghis had miraculously appeared when their getaway into Planet Blue was supposed to have been a secret.

"How did I find you?" Borghis repeated. "How did my journal end up in your sister's hands? How about you answer that?!"

Atlas's jaw dropped. He would later be told that Helva, having learned that Borghis was madly in love with her from reading the stolen diary Atlas had gifted her, had been unable to contain herself when Borghis had come over to ask about his brother's whereabouts. She had spilled the beans about everything to him, including about having just guided Atlas, Ezekiola, and Nohlan towards the Sporadic Doors that had brought them straight into Planet Blue. Borghis was both happy and furious; happy because his feelings for her were reciprocated, and furious because he now had to head into a danger zone to bring the boys back to Circa. Time being of the essence, he hadn't been able to muster a group of Emeralds to bring the boys back. He had decided to take a chance and do it himself, along with a few other Brown Robes. He had split his team in two, one to reach the main stage and the other to stand guard in the forest to locate their portal door.

"Where's Ezekiola?!" Borghis asked again, the urgency making him fierce.

"I think that's him!" Atlas asked, noticing a motionless body on the stage.

"Where?" asked Nohlan. The clouds of smoke made everything look like a mirage.

"There, look!" Atlas pointed to a small gap of air that the smoke had not yet invaded.

They ran towards the stage. Very few people were left after the crowd had dispersed. Smoke filled the air, and their eyes teared up. Uncertain whether he was dead or alive, they rushed to grab hold of their friend, who was lying face down.

"Wait! Don't!" Atlas was first to notice it wasn't Ezekiola on the ground. They approached the body, and Nohlan turned him around. It was Zeke, unconscious. If it wasn't for the rising of his chest, he would have passed for a dead man.

"He's still alive," Nohlan said.

"But where's Ezekiola?" asked Atlas. He looked around. No one else was onstage.

"Find him! Quick!" Borghis commanded. His crew looked frantically for Ezekiola's body.

The firemen were jumping off their trucks, and the sound of sirens increased as more firetrucks made their way toward them.

"There's no more time. The door will soon close," Keenan warned.

"But we can't leave him here!" Nohlan pleaded.

"We have to leave now! The door won't stay open, and we don't have time to find another one," Keenan reiterated.

"Wait just a moment, for goodness' sake!" Atlas yelled, his mind racing wildly. How could they have come to this? He did one last round within the vicinity of the stage and could not find his friend. "He should have listened to me! Why couldn't he have just listened to me? I told Ezekiola not to confront that vile..."

"Enough! Move! Now!" Borghis ordered, grabbing hold of his brother and Atlas and pointing to Zeke. "Gordi, take him too. The Emeralds will detain him, and he'll have to answer to them. He'll tell us what he did to Ezekiola, and the Emeralds will go look for him. Right now, we can't do more than this."

Gordi grabbed Zeke and flipped his body onto his shoulders. Nohlan thought he saw the same scar that had struck Ezekiola's back, but he was unable to look more closely and was rushed forward by his brother.

Borghis was readying himself to confront a storm of chaos upon returning to Circa. With Ezekiola still missing, he would have no choice but to tell his superiors everything. He, too, was in trouble for handling a situation that virtually called for the presence of the Emeralds. Not only that, he hadn't seen his second team of crew members who were supposed to stand guard in the forest. Where had they gone? *Maybe they've already headed back to Circa.* Borghis hoped for no more surprises from them.

"This way, follow me," Keenan said, leading the pack through the wooded area behind the stage.

"This had got to be the worst case of trespassing in the history of Cypress School, if not of Circa!" Borghis muttered under his breath. Atlas heard him well.

"Trespassing?! But Ezekiola said he had to do this!"

"Stop arguing, Atlas! We're all about to get expelled for your stupid actions!"

Keenan led them through the Sporadic Door. Without saying another word, they walked back into Circa, one at a time, leaving all the madness behind.

Atlas remained quiet the rest of the way. He desperately wished it had all been a dream. Yet somewhere in the back of his mind lurked a deep-embedded desire to prove Borghis wrong.

If only there was a way.

Chapter 24

We Rise by Kneeling

"Where am I?" Nomi was looking out of his glasshouse when Ezekiola finally sat up and spoke. To both their surprise, his voice was an octave deeper than it had been.

"You're back on Circa, in your headmaster's glasshouse at Cypress School, and you've been asleep for a little over three days," Nomi answered, careful not to disclose too much at once.

"Asleep for three days? What happened to me?" Ezekiola asked. He sat searching his memory until the image of Zeke and a brilliant burst of fire suddenly flooded his mind.

"What happened is you created a link with Planet Blue and tapped into the Fountain of Fire," Nomi answered, a gentle smile playing across his face. Yet even Nomi would have to get used to what he was seeing. After three days of lying unconscious in the therapeutic ward with no results, they moved Ezekiola into Nomi's glasshouse, where plants used for medicinal properties were grown. The Gemins had been all over themselves with excitement bringing in their favorite curing plants to help out. Some saw this as an opportunity to test out their newly concocted herbal drops, generously sprinkling them on the boy in the hopes of waking him up. Bopen's new concoction had been the only successful one.

Ezekiola sat on the cot, shirtless, slowly gathering his senses. His body felt heavier. He glanced at his arms and chest curiously. They seemed to be bulkier than what he was used to. Nomi allowed himself to continue: "And when that happens, well, hmm... interesting things can happen."

Ezekiola was only partially listening, too busy examining the rest of his body. A strange thought suddenly crossed his mind. He noticed a mirror placed nearby in which he could see the reflection of the plants and trees growing around him. He slowly rose and headed towards it. He had to see for himself. Noticing where he was headed, Nomi gave him a gentle warning.

"Life takes many forms, Ezekiola. Do not be afraid."

Ezekiola stopped in front of the mirror and stared at his reflection. A look of mystification appeared on his face. His mind couldn't seem to come to grips with the reflection looking back at him.

"How is this..." he stopped short. He had been through something similar before while standing in front of the Lake of Maji. Now it was real. The reflection before him was of the one he had last confronted: Zeke. Only this time, it was his own blue eyes gazing back, not those of his foe, black and soulless beads. Just like Zeke, he looked slightly older and taller, as if he had matured drastically in just a few short days.

"What's happened to me?" he said, barely above a whisper.

"What happened is you confronted your twin, and by wielding the power of the fountain, you merged with him. Successfully, I might add." Nomi came up behind him.

"Merged?! With my twin?" Ezekiola asked, shocked. The

longer he stared at himself, the more he hoped to wake up from this disconcerting dream.

"You see, the Emerald Belt you wore presented you with an opportunity that even we masters could not foresee."

"I thought the Emerald Belt just gave freedom of movement," Ezekiola moaned plaintively. He looked closer still at his features and touched his face.

"True, it did give you freedom of movement."

"I don't understand," Ezekiola said. None of Nomi's explanations made sense to him. He stared at the reflection—at his arms, legs, shoulders, face, and hair—feeling like he was stuck in someone else's body.

"Come now, let's give the mirror a break. Staring at oneself for too long has never been a good thing. Here, have a seat," Nomi said, motioning him towards a chair.

"There is something I must confess to you, and I have waited a long time for this moment. Some time ago, a meeting took place with the members of the High Council of Circa. You were naturally unaware of it, as most students are of these things. At the suggestion of a member, it was decided to bestow you with the Emerald Belt to allow you to fulfill a task. Without you knowing it, they agreed to assign to you, Ezekiola, the task of linking with Planet Blue. The High Council took a chance the likes of which they had never before attempted, and they succeeded, all because you did the job."

"But why me? I was never interested in the warrior's path."

"That's one reason why. You were outside the norm, without expectations, and without any fear of encountering enemies. The Emeralds needed to change their ways, as their methods were no longer working. When a member proposed to try to link in an unconventional manner, it was construed as a wild idea but one that eventually sat well with the High Council. The day after your ceremony, I was half expecting you to come to see me and to return the Emerald Belt you had received. I knew you were expecting the Blue Belt, which is more in line with mind readers like yourself. But then, something interesting happened to you after your ceremony that made you go back on your decision. Isn't that correct?"

Ezekiola nodded numbly, still in a daze. He quickly brought himself back to that day. Standing in the hallway, that Sporadic Door almost calling him...

"The Emerald Belt allowed you to shift from one world to another. And you happened to meet Leanne from Planet Blue. You read her mind and felt a connection, although you didn't quite understand it at the time. That's when you decided to keep your belt and do a little exploring," Nomi said.

He seemed to know everything, Ezekiola thought, and then wondered if Nomi had known all along.

"Leanne," Ezekiola whispered. Then it dawned on him. As if he had just been dunked in cold water, he snapped out of his trance. The last thing he remembered was a wildfire blazing all around her.

"What happened to her? Where is she?" he asked. He replayed the scene of his confrontation but could not recall what had happened at the end of his duel. Everything had gone blank.

"Yes, Leanne. She was found by the Brown Robes, and she is fine. That's all I can say for now."

"Will I see her again?"

"Perhaps. I cannot say more," Nomi said, keeping his answer vague. Ezekiola sensed that this wasn't the end of his story with Leanne. With what they had just been through, there had to be more. He decided not to press his headmaster further for the moment.

"How is it that I never knew I had a twin?" Ezekiola asked.

"Your parents kept this family tragedy from you. In their

recruitment frenzy, the Sons of the Night Sky invaded many homes, demanding that the family's first-born child be given to them, or else another member of the family would die. Your mother had birthed twins, born in the very constellation of Gemini. That's where your name came from. Your parents had no choice but to give one of you away. Your brother, Zeke. He was brought up as a warrior amongst selfish men. So, when you linked with Leanne, you naturally drew the attention of the SONS. The SONS knew that if they sent your twin after you, it would necessarily result in a sure death, for a twin coming from the constellation of Gemini killed by the hand of its other half fatally wounds itself. Had you killed your brother, you would have died as well. What the SONS ignored, however, was that by wielding the power of the fountain, these same twins also had the ability to merge with one another instead of leading separate lives. You brought the two poles of your being under one roof, so to speak. You're now unified."

He then fell silent to allow Ezekiola to absorb the explanation, but instead, he saw him shake his head.

Nomi looked apologetic. "I'm sorry all this is revealed to you in such a coarse manner."

"I can't believe it. I just can't believe that Zeke is... was...." Ezekiola stood up, unable to finish his sentence, and started pacing back and forth like a caged animal. "I'm in my twin's body. Where's *my* body? How is this even possible?" he asked.

"You wielded the power of the Fountain of Fire, Ezekiola. The two of you are one. You now dominate your twin, including his body, and this is for the better. For all the magnificent power Zeke possessed, your twin was never steered in the right direction, instead serving the Sons of the Night Sky. Lacking proper guidance, he was leading a life of desolation. He would never have seen the light if you didn't dominate."

"Pollux dominates," Ezekiola suddenly said, recalling Nohlan's words. "Is that what Nohlan meant?"

"Oh, yes. This is one of the many metaphorical sayings I've taught in one of my classes: Guide thy chase till Pollux dominates. As you know, Pollux is a star in the constellation of Gemini, along with Castor. And those two stars chase after one another. Over time, Pollux increases in brightness while Castor wanes. The lesser is integrated into the greater, as has become of you and Zeke, turning you into a tremendously potent being. The feats you will be able to accomplish from this point on will be far greater than you could ever have imagined. He's integrated within you, and you now have him under your control. His strength, knowledge, and power are now yours."

"No, I can't be like this. You masters have powers, please undo this!" Ezekiola pleaded.

"I'm sorry, but this is not something we can undo. It's beyond us."

Ezekiola looked back into the mirror. His jaws clenched, seeing his reflection. He sensed a wave of aggression he never felt before and felt like punching the mirror.

"So that's it? I just live another person's life?" he asked incredulously.

"No. You live your life but with more powers than the ones the Emerald warriors use, and you need to train with them to learn how to wield them."

"And what if I don't want to live a warrior's life?" Ezekiola asked defiantly.

"The choice is always yours. But know this: we're in a battle, Ezekiola. The SONS are about to unleash something terrible upon us, and if you abandon these powers now, you forsake everything. Do you think it makes sense to have come this far only to let go?"

· · ·

Ezekiola sunk back down on a chair and dropped his head in his hands. A knock on the door interrupted their conversation. A Gemin appeared with a note in his hand. Nomi opened it and read its content. Ezekiola saw only four words, thanks to the sunlight in the room, but felt too weak to tune into his mentor's mind to decipher the rest. Nomi seemed to be wearing a hint of a smile. He looked like he was about to share the information.

"You are to be on strict bed rest for another week or so until your body and spirits have regained their strength. There will be no class for you until then, and maybe even longer. Take all the time you need."

Ezekiola nodded. Somehow, he sensed it wasn't exactly what the message contained.

"Has anyone seen me yet? I mean like this?" he asked, once again surveying himself in the mirror. Each time he caught sight of his image, it frightened him.

"Why yes! Your friends have. Even some of the Brown Robes came to check up on you. Borghis especially was worried sick. He's been driving us mad, asking for news about you almost on an hourly basis! But don't worry. Your friends have gotten over their initial shock. So, this will not be the first time they see you. More than anything, they will be happy to see you alive and conscious," he said gently.

Once again, Ezekiola looked at himself in the mirror, still unsure how he was to simply go about his days at school in his newly altered body. Nomi sensed his hesitation.

"Just so you know, your friends have been briefed and have pledged not to disclose anything to anyone. We will be holding a meeting soon to discuss your reintegration in school so that your peers can understand what has happened to you," he said, looking out the window. "I know this is hard to believe, but you are still you. You really don't look that much different on the outside. After all, you were twins. But I can see how different you might feel on the inside." Something caught Nomi's attention. Ezekiola noticed the curious frown on his face.

"I believe some of your friends have found a new location to enact their exercise routine."

Atlas and Nohlan happened to be strolling back and forth, unusually close to Nomi's quarters. "They have been doing this every time they have a break in the hope of seeing you come out," said Nomi with a hint of a smile. "You may go and see them if you wish. We would, however, like to keep you here for the week until our meeting with the School Council."

Ezekiola nodded in agreement.

"Oh, and one more thing. Come meet me in the Northern Wing of my garden tomorrow morning after your first breakfast. Someone wishes to have a word with you."

When Ezekiola finally stepped out, it was he, not his two friends, in a state of shock. He was so mindful of being inside the body of a well-trained warrior that it stressed him to think about how everyone would react to his new appearance. His only consolation was that he was the twin image of his old self.

When Atlas and Nohlan saw him, they broke into nervous smiles.

"Haven't changed a bit, I see," Atlas said sarcastically, clapping his friend in the back.

"Watch his scars," Nohlan scolded him. He shuddered at the memory of them. "How do you feel?"

"Not quite like me," he said, looking for his friends' reactions. Clearly, they were simply relieved to see him again.

"I imagine Nomi told you that we've seen you already?" Nohlan asked.

Ezekiola nodded.

"Well, we got used to you. It's not so bad," Atlas said, then added: "But what's going to be bad is all the attention you'll attract. And I'm not only talking about jealous Brown Robes but the attention of the ladies as well."

Ezekiola shook his head, embarrassed.

"Oh, and forgive me for the nonsense I told you at the carnival about you being banished. I was only trying to scare you out of your decision to fight." Atlas had been ruminating over the carnival incident for days.

"Don't worry, Atlas. I, too, had to take back a few things I said and did to myself, as well as my other half," Ezekiola responded, which made Atlas laugh at the irony of it all. They walked for a while, talking about everything that had happened. They reached the peak of a hill and took a pause when they saw lanterns lit up below, a stage surrounded by Gemins galore. There seemed to be a party of some sort. Bopen was the center of attention, beaming amongst his peers.

"What's this?" Atlas asked, curious about the gathering.

"I think it's best we leave them alone," Ezekiola said, spying Bopen.

"No, wait, I want to see what that scoundrel is up to," Nohlan said, also spotting Bopen.

"Would you look at that..." Nohlan stood at the highest peak, observing the happy gathering below. He then saw the unthinkable. Bopen, on stage, with Nohlan's stolen plant in one hand and a vial in the other.

"Is that MY plant?!" he asked in disbelief.

They all saw it, but his friends did not dare confirm.

"I guess that's how your brother felt when he saw his staff in your hand," Atlas remarked, cringing at Bopen's fate.

"This is where the madness ends." Nohlan suddenly forgot that his friend had just come out of a coma and strode with uncontrollable rage towards what he figured was some party the Gemins were holding for Bopen.

"Wait! Nohlan!" Ezekiola ran after him. "What he has in his vial is what worked on me. It's what woke me up!"

Nohlan was not sure if he was glad to hear that or not. It was ultimately his work that had helped his friend, yet the plants had been surreptitiously taken from him and were still not in his possession.

"He stole those from me!" he burst out like a child.

Atlas and Ezekiola ran downhill after Nohlan to prevent a furious confrontation.

"Nohlan, wait!" Ezekiola yelled, "I know they were stolen, but look, they worked!"

"It's not worth it, Nohlan!" Atlas tried this time. "Those Gemins have nothing better to do than give each other empty praises. Let's not get ourselves into trouble again! Just let it go!"

But Nohlan ran faster than his friends and crashed the Gemins' party, shoving the decorative flowers off the stage.

"Hand that over, Bopen!" he yelled wildly.

To his dismay, Bopen beamed even broader and shouted out to his adoring crowd: "And here comes Nohlan!" The Gemins madly applauded when they saw Nohlan step on stage. There was a word carved underneath the blue plant that could only be read from up close. Gemins always initiated a plant and dubbed it a name once it became useful. The name on this one read 'NOHLAN.'

Nohlan froze at the sight. How could he consider it stolen if it carried his name? He stood dumbstruck on stage, hesitating a moment deciding whether or not he should remain angry while everyone was applauding him heartily. Then he began to laugh.

Ezekiola and Atlas finally made it on stage as the applause continued.

"See, Nohlan, sometimes the fruit of your efforts has an odd way of coming back to you," Ezekiola said, catching his breath. They ended up spending the whole afternoon partying with the Gemins and watching Nohlan being lavished with praise.

The next day, Ezekiola made his way to Nomi's garden. He couldn't stop thinking of Leanne and what might have happened to her. He wanted answers. Nomi had said she was fine and that perhaps he may see her again. He hadn't said more. What was he hiding? Ezekiola wondered. He thought of Nomi's invitation. He had been invited to the Northern Wing to keep their conversation private, probably. Perhaps Nomi intended to surprise him with Leanne. He was almost sure of it. In great anticipation, he reached the Northern Wing but saw no one except for a lone gardener hunched forward, weeding the flowerbeds. He decided to wait around, and it wasn't until a few minutes into his waiting that the gardener noticed him.

"Are you here to meet Master Nomi?" he asked, taking a break from his chores.

"Yes."

"Ah, well, he said to tell you he was sorry. Something came up. He had to absent himself," the gardener explained.

"Oh." Ezekiola was disappointed. He had built such high hopes that coming down from them proved to be a strenuous effort. The gardener went back to his task, and Ezekiola was left wondering if he should wait or leave.

"Well, did he tell you when he'd be coming back?" he asked.

"Not really," the gardener answered, pulling one weed that seemed most stubborn. Ezekiola noticed it was the viper weed. Those were hard to manage. He waited a few minutes in case Nomi showed up and observed the gardener in the meantime, noting how he was applying the wrong techniques. It was unlike Nomi to have an unskilled gardener doing such chores. Usually, Ariad managed this section. Ezekiola had helped her many times with this type of weed and had the urge to offer his help to the gardener instead of watching him toil haplessly. Perhaps Nomi would show up if he would wait just a little longer.

"Would you mind if I showed you something here?" Ezekiola asked politely, crouching down next to the gardener. He began to forcibly bend the leaves of the viper weeds, stamping and covering them with wood chips and grass clippings.

"These ones are strong-willed," Ezekiola said. "I usually do this with Ariad, and we've tried every possible way to prevent their growth. The best way we found is to bend their leaves as much as we can and cover them with garden mulch. They eventually give out and stay down, starved of sunlight," he said with a smile, hoping his intrusion was not going to be taken personally.

"Ah! A good trick, bending the stubborn leaves as you would the bending of one's will?" he remarked with a laugh.

"Right!" Ezekiola agreed, also laughing at the odd analogy and looking at the gardener a little more closely for the first time. Something about the man's face struck him. He had seen it before but couldn't picture where. Yet he was certain it was the first time he had seen him in Nomi's garden. They worked alongside each other silently for a while. When the task was done, Ezekiola bid him farewell and left. On his way out, Master Nomi arrived.

"You're here already?" he asked.

"I was here an hour ago after my first breakfast, as you asked."

"But I had said after your second breakfast," Nomi

corrected him. Ezekiola was sure he had said his first breakfast but dared not challenge him on such a lame point.

"The gardener there told me you were delayed and might be absent. So, I waited a little while longer."

"Well, I'm here now. Come along this way then." Nomi turned on his heels and bid Ezekiola to follow him to his library. When they arrived, there was already someone with a book in his hand standing by the windowsill.

"You're here already too! My, my, I have to rearrange my clock," Nomi said, looking scattered, motioning Ezekiola to take a seat.

Ezekiola sat down and looked up. He recognized the gardener. "Hello again," he said, surprised. He must have run exceptionally fast to make it to the library before them. The gardener returned Ezekiola's greeting.

"Oh, you've met?" Nomi asked, looking pleased.

"Yes, we did, just outside in your garden," Ezekiola answered.

"Oh, good then. Because ever since you have linked, he has asked about you every single day and has overseen your progression as an Emerald Belt."

Ezekiola was confused. Perhaps Headmaster Nomi was also confused, yet he continued: "Of course, you should know that all Emeralds and Blue Robes are under his stewardship, and as such, he oversees...."

"Professor," Ezekiola interrupted, "I'm not quite sure I understand. Your gardener knows about me, about what we spoke of yesterday?"

"Gardener? Who told you that?" He looked at his visitor, who was wearing a suspicious smile.

"I just assumed since he was weeding your plants," Ezekiola sensed, for the first time, that something was afoot.

"Oh, this is no gardener," Nomi said with a lighthearted

laugh. "I believe proper introductions are in order, even if you say you've met. Ezekiola, it is my honor to introduce you to Meredus of Loggia, the Crown Head of Circa's Privy Council and the Chief of the Grand Triangle of the Order of the Southern Star. He is best known as the Count within the High Council of Circa, and he was the one who wanted to have a word with you."

Hearing the Count's full name had almost managed to blow Ezekiola's head right off. As much myth as man, the illustrious Count Meredus was standing right in front of him, posing as a gardener and, quite frankly, looking like the most ordinary fellow anyone could imagine. It struck him then where he had seen that face. It had been at the library, in the book entitled 'The Meridians Belts.' He and his friend had been poking fun at the image, with Atlas going as far as saying he was a myth.

"I thought he was your gardener?" was all Ezekiola could manage to say.

"It is an honor to meet you, Ezekiola," Count Meredus began. "Thank you for helping me in your headmaster's garden. It is a great quality to render service to someone when no one is looking. It is what we look for from the bearers of such belts," he said with a smile.

Ezekiola remained stunned for a while, then snapped out of his daze when he realized he had been tested. Count Meredus suddenly seemed altogether another man. He recalled Blue Robes had the ability to appear in two places at once. That explained his sudden presence in Nomi's library. He realized that Count Meredus was a Blue Robe as well as an Emerald.

"It is an honor to meet you as well," Ezekiola finally replied.

"Young warrior, you have done something of great importance for us all here on Circa, leaving us elated with joy," he said and took a seat next to Ezekiola. "What you have done is revive a hope we thought lost. You created a link between—in effect, re-linked—with Planet Blue and tapped into the Fountain of Fire, something we had achieved but lost some time ago. Your initial decision to keep the Emerald Belt allowed you to not only rise ahead but to elevate everyone along the way."

Ezekiola listened intently to Count Meredus, who was putting the missing pieces together for him. Everything had happened so fast that he barely had time to analyze the recent events in his life.

"As you'll soon learn, the only way we can tap into that powerful jewel we call the Fountain of Fire is through the magnetic bonding of twelve planets. This was a chance discovery Circa made ages ago, and the final world needed for this scheme to work is Planet Blue. Our Emeralds have currently linked with all the other planets but have been unsuccessful in this last task. To link with Planet Blue, we need a correspondent in that world to link with you, like a magnet. One emanates a negative and the other a positive charge, and when properly linked and bound together, the combination opens the floodgates to that great element, the Fountain of Fire, a force that can be wielded to any desired end.

"When you met Leanne, she hoped to see you again, and despite being worlds apart, she firmly held onto that belief. It sounds simple, but by so doing, she created a link using the unseen elements of nature, which, if you recall, you yourself made use of in the presence of Mirhas, the Oracle: believing that which you cannot see. You invoked the Oracle's presence, and she saved your life. Your link with Leanne allowed us to complete the bonding of twelve planets, allowing you to tap into the Fountain of Fire once again.

"The task of the Emeralds is one of fusion, linking every living thing with the Fountain of Fire, restoring once more the fellowship of the twelve planets. The power that flows through you is to be taught to Leanne and to be spread like wildfire. We have much work ahead of us." Count Meredus paused, waiting to see any signs of confusion on Ezekiola's face. But his message had clearly sunk in.

"But before any further teaching, it is of utmost importance that we seal your link with Leanne. We now have the full attention of the Sons of the Night Sky, who will do everything in their power to break your link. Thus, the High Council has decided to authorize a sacred ceremony known only to Emeralds for the purposes of sealing your link so it can be protected from destruction. I'm aware Nomi had this conversation with you, so if you choose to continue down this path, we will hold the ceremony tomorrow, for time is of the essence. Afterward, we will teach you about the forces of the Sons of the Night Sky, and like me, you will undergo a twofold training, as a Blue Robe and as an Emerald. Your mind reading skill is an asset that cannot be ignored, and it is crucial you further develop it."

Ezekiola nodded quietly. He was humbled by the proposition and the Count's attention, yet something was still bothering him.

"Where's Leanne? What happened to her?"

"Your headmaster did not tell you?"

Ezekiola shook his head.

"I thought I would wait until you spoke to him first," Nomi interjected.

"Then I will leave your headmaster the task of informing you when he's ready to do so. All I can say is this: meeting Leanne was no coincidence. There is something more about her and her family than meets the eye. More will be revealed to you, but not yet. Be well and good, Ezekiola of the Emerald Belt." With that, he exited towards the garden, leaving Ezekiola wondering if Meredus was going to disappear instantly, as Blue

Robes could easily do. His last words about Leanne reverberated, leaving Ezekiola with a burning desire to see her again.

That night, he told Atlas of his encounter with Count Meredus of Loggia.

"He was doing *what?*" asked Atlas, incredulous. "Pulling weeds? Who pulls weeds if they're the royal head of everything!"

"Had I decided to leave earlier instead of helping him, he might have forsaken me right then and there!" Ezekiola said.

"Unbelievable. They're crafty, those Blue Robes, showing up unannounced, setting up a trap you could have easily fallen into."

"There's news from Helva!" Nohlan came dashing through their dorm, crashing the conversation.

"The rumors abound amongst the Ladies. Look, fast!" He pointed to an article in the Ladies' daily journal called *The Eclipse.*

They all butted heads, going for the journal at the same time.

"Ouch! Watch it, you two!" Nohlan yelled.

"Where's the passage?" Ezekiola asked. He sensed there was something of import, judging from Nohlan's nervous demeanor.

"Here, under the segment, *Rumors Abound.*"

Atlas and Ezekiola began reading when Nohlan decided to read the item out loud at a dramatically slower pace:

"An unusual amount of closed-door meetings has taken place in the school's West Wing in the past week. It has come to the attention of the Ladies that there may be several reasons behind this. Some say there are

*newcomers beginning next term that the school is unpre-
pared for, while others hear of the possibility of Blue
Robes arriving on campus to teach. One beloved lady of
ours swears she saw a renowned Count strolling happily
in the hallways. Myth or truth? Time will tell. Signed
your rumor expert, Lady."*

"Hell! This is news!" Nohlan said, gleaming with joy. "Oh! And Helva asked me to give this to you. She told me it's for your eyes only." Nohlan handed him Helva's note. Ezekiola took it and read it. A hint of awe was perceptible on his face as if he had momentarily glimpsed the heavens.

"What does it say?" Nohlan asked, more jittery than his two friends.

"But you just said it's for my eyes only," Ezekiola protested with a mischievous smile.

"No, that's what Helva asked him to tell you. Which he did," Atlas corrected. "Now that you saw it with your eyes only, you can share the information. This part, Helva doesn't decide," he said, eager to know more. It was out of the question to leave this room without finding out what the note said.

"If you really insist." Ezekiola turned over the note to them. They silently stared at the four single words: *'She begins next fall.'* They were the very four words Ezekiola had spotted on the message delivered to Nomi.

To their knowledge, nothing like this had ever happened. It would only be a matter of time until everyone in his division raved about it. This would raise all sorts of notice. If Ezekiola thought the Emerald Belt brought on hard attention to manage, it was just about to get ratcheted up to another level. The Brown Robes would probably have a field day.

"Whoa! This is some news! But I mean, it's good, isn't it?!" said Nohlan, his eyes full of excitement.

"Good news, you say? This is unbelievable!" Atlas accentuated his words and grabbed the note again to stare at it closely. "How is this possible? I mean, she can't just leave her world behind!" Atlas remarked.

"I don't know Atlas. The Count said meeting Leanne was no coincidence, and there's something more about her and her family than meets the eye." Ezekiola had never stopped ruminating over those words. More than anything, he was looking forward to uncovering the enigma behind the Count's message. He never thought he would admit it, but he was glad to have gone off the beaten path and stuck with the Emerald Belt. It brought him much more than he could imagine.

"Well then, this is GREAT news! To think you two will become the power couple, making all the Brown Robes jealous. Just imagine the fun we're going to have with them next fall," Atlas said. His thoughts were like horses running wild in his head.

"For once, I have to say, I can't wait to begin anew again," Ezekiola said.

The ceremony to seal Leanne's and Ezekiola's link took place on Circa's Night Bridge, right across from the waterfalls. Over a dozen Blue Robes and Emeralds were present, including Count Meredus of Loggia. To Leanne's greatest surprise, her parents were also there. After Leanne had fainted and was found in the forest by the Brown Robes, she was taken under the protective custody of the Blue Robes. In the presence of the Count, her parents then revealed to her a long-held secret about her ancestry, something they had kept from her until now. Her parents were one of the few handfuls of people who knew about the existence of Circa and the Fountain of Fire all along.

When Ezekiola came out of his coma, he didn't have much time to get to know Leanne. To remedy that, the Blue Robes helped them both do a merging of the minds to quicken the process, as time was of the essence. They became immediately acquainted with each other and were getting along as if they were child-hood friends. The ceremony, as was customary, took place at dawn within the Limestone Mountains of Circa.

As the masters of ceremonial order, the Purple Robes, all shining in their robes, were also present to conduct the cere-mony. Ezekiola had never witnessed a scene as colorful as this one. As part of the pageantry, he was dressed in his usual white tunic, except for the addition of an emerald cape that he now wore for the ceremony. Leanne was dressed in a white tunic as well, but more elegantly defined than Ezekiola's, as it was orna-mented with pearls, silver beads, and ribbons. Resplendent in his Blue Robe, Count Meredus stood in the center of the bridge. In his hands, he held a massive rod that was as tall as he was. Its tip was gold, adorned with triangular shapes of every angle, symbolizing the link with the everlasting Fountain of Fire. Ezekiola and Leanne walked to the middle of the bridge, and the Count spoke a few words to them. The couple then turned around to face the waterfalls and kneeled. The Count gripped his rod firmly with both hands and made a sacred invo-cation. Suddenly, a thunderous sound reverberated in the air, shaking the bridge and all living things around it. The water-falls stopped, and silence descended. From beneath the pool of water emerged a hidden volcano. It rose effortlessly until its tip was at eye level, revealing a barely perceptible cave from which two Emerald Robes emerged, bidding the young couple to enter. Count Meredus led both Leanne and Ezekiola into the cave, and what happened next is the greatest secret guarded by the Emeralds, about which naught can be said. A while later, after Ezekiola and Leanne sealed their link, the celebrations began.

The Count was enjoying the festive scene from afar, a slight smile on his lips. His eyes followed the hundreds of lanterns floating above the sea as music filled the air. Suddenly, an Emerald warrior was by his side, handing the Count a note with shaking hands. The Count started reading the letter but stopped after the first sentence.

"Who else knows about this?" the Count asked, his face clouded with tension.

"Only the leader of the Emeralds knows. This just happened, I..." the warrior's voice cracked. "I saw it with my own eyes."

As one event is celebrated in a world with joy, thought the Count, tragedy befalls another. Mad with rage, the Sons of the Night Sky had done the unthinkable.

The Count gazed deep into the eyes of the Emerald warrior before him. He read his mind and saw something that no combination of forces could ever remedy. He then looked at Ezekiola from afar.

"Don't tell a soul. He must never find out about this."

The end

Acknowledgments

Many thanks to my wonderful editors Gina Roitman and Marc Lapointe for helping me carve this book out of its block of marble. I'd like to thank my family who encouraged and cheered me on to the final page. I am most grateful to my dear friends for providing me with their unwavering support. A special thank you to Eric, the love of my life, whose patience I could not repay in a million years, and to our children, Diana and Jesse, who make life's journey worthwhile. And to my readers: Thank you! You're each a shining star, unique and beautiful, and remember that collectively, you illuminate the universe.

About the Author

Through an obsession with pirates, Lucy Kyan first began creating fantasy worlds and characters in her early teens. She spent endless hours writing poems, drawing maps, memorizing flags and imagining sword fights. Later on in life, she took up fencing, and nourished her fantasy world by dream journaling for many years. In her quest to explore more worlds, she studied mythology, history and political science, and graduated from law school. She then entered the world of corporate law where she practiced as an attorney for over a decade. She lives in Canada with her family and their adorable doodle named Louis.

You can find out more about Lucy at www.lucykyan.com.

Also by Lucy Kyan

The Fountain of Fire Series
1. Ezekiola and the Emerald Belt
2. Ezekiola and the Rising Sons

www.ingramcontent.com/pod-product-compliance
Lightning Source LLC
Chambersburg PA
CBHW030151310726
48970CB00005B/1695